white lilies

SAMANTHA CHRISTY

Books Publishing Group

Saint Augustine, FL 32259

For my son, Dylan.
Don't mess with fate.
Always have faith.
Never stop believing in family.

white
lilies

part one

skylar

prologue

"Oh, God. Not again," I mumble, tasting my horrid morning mouth. I look around the dim unfamiliar room hoping to gain some clue as to how I got here and who the guy lying next to me might be.

I lift the covers to investigate. My eyebrows shoot up in appreciation of what I find underneath. I'm vaguely amused at myself for not having beer goggles on last night.

The scorching-hot, totally naked man snoring at my side is the epitome of every girl's panty-soaking fantasy. My mouth waters at the sight of him, reminding me of my rancid breath. I spy my purse on the floor next to the bed, along with two condom wrappers. *Two!* I reach in the pocket for a breath mint before resuming my perusal of Adonis.

He must be tall. His feet are practically hanging off the bed. He has large, toned thighs like that of a cyclist—points for that. It looks like you could bounce off his tight abs and I wonder momentarily if I did. His face is hard and rugged, even in sleep. I'll have to give him a pass on the hair because of how delectable the rest of him is. It's short. Buzz-cut short. And it might be red. I lift the sheets again. Yup—red.

While my gaze is focused on Ginger's nether region, the south starts to rise again. And what a generous lift-off. My eyes widen and flicker to his only to find him, um… appreciating my body in return. Our glances meet in an awkward recognition. Recognition that neither of us recognizes the other.

He snickers and motions to his erection. "You want to do something about that?" he asks, his voice dripping with a Boston accent that to my discerning ears is like fingernails on a blackboard. I bring my finger to his lips to stop him from talking anymore lest he strip the horny right out of me.

I stare at him for a moment and contemplate leaving. But given that we've already screwed twice, I rationalize I should at least have the decency to be able to remember what it feels like. So, what the hell?

"First things first," I say, reaching over to grab a few provisions from my bag. I hold out a breath mint for him in case his mouth tastes anything like mine did.

"Thanks." He takes it and pops it in his mouth.

I rip the condom open and roll it onto his impressive length right before I straddle his body and bring myself down on him. It stings because I'm not fully ready.

"You don't waste any time, do you, honey?"

Honey? God, that's even worse than his biting blue-collar accent. I look at the clock. "I have to be at work in an hour," I say.

"Oh. Where do you work?" he asks nonchalantly, like we're having afternoon tea instead of his long length stroking my sweet spot.

"Can we just move this along… honey?" I ask.

He laughs, thrusting deeper into me while tightly gripping my hips. "No problem."

Ten minutes and a not-so-satisfying orgasm later, I'm cleaning up in his bathroom. It's filled with a shitload of girl products. I peek in the cabinet under the sink. Tampons.

I quickly finish getting dressed and stomp back into the bedroom to retrieve my purse. "You have a girlfriend, you asshole?" I ask, watching him light a cigarette, hoping the ash will fall and burn his cheating cock.

He answers me with a shrug and a wrinkle of his nose.

Douchebag.

I shake my disapproving head at him, step into my heels and walk out of the bedroom without speaking. I think I hear him mumble a word of thanks as I slam the bedroom door.

Doing a solitary walk of shame through his apartment, I notice a few toys strewn about the floor. I stop to look around.

Son of a bitch!

There's a playpen in the corner. A highchair at the table. A pack of diapers by the closet. And a large portrait depicting the perfect-fucking-family hanging over the fireplace.

I am such a slut.

chapter one

"Well, what do you expect, Skylar?" Baylor, reprimands me. "If you're going to hang out at meat markets and drink like a sailor, you're going to wake up in strange places. You can't let the guy take all the blame."

"Ugh!" I pout. I take a long sip of the strawberry margarita Baylor poured me as part of girls' night. She may not be able to drink because she's knocked up, but she can still make a good one. "He's married with a goddamn kid. What right does he have to pick someone up in a bar?"

"Maybe," she says, re-filling Jenna's and Mindy's glasses. "But if it wasn't him, it would have been some other random guy, so does it really matter?"

She's right. She's absolutely fucking right. The past several years flash through my mind and my illustrious reputation of sluttiness almost makes me choke on my drink. I rarely even bother to stay with a man long enough to like him. And if a guy has feelings for me? Forget it. Feelings lead to love. Love leads to broken hearts. Broken hearts lead to shitty lives. I've seen it firsthand. Okay, so maybe it all turned out great in the end for my big sister, Baylor, who was crushed by the man she loved when she was eighteen. But I vowed back then, being two years younger than her, that I would never let it happen to me.

So, here I sit, twenty-four years old and a bed post with enough notches on it to rival a cat's scratching pole. I hang my head in shame while my sister and our friends try to sympathize.

I sigh. "I'm a terrible person," I say.

"No you aren't," Jenna tells me. "You just don't make the best choices, sweetie."

Visions of the shameful choices I've made over the years trample through my head. "No—I'm a terrible person," I repeat.

"Come on," Mindy says. "It's not that bad."

I shake my head at my roommate. Mindy is my closest friend, next to my sisters, Baylor and Piper. She's also the best waitress at Mitchell's NYC, my parents' restaurant. We have a walk-up apartment only a few blocks from the restaurant that I manage. We also have—okay *I* have—a signal for said apartment to alert the other one of us that we should get lost for a while. When we have a guy over, in our tiny apartment with thin walls, we leave the light on in the hallway out front. And in this very moment, it occurs to me, that not once has Mindy ever turned it on. Not that she doesn't have anyone over. She does. But I guess she plans it when I'm working. Or they go elsewhere. She's a considerate slut. I'm a selfish one.

"Not that bad?" I say. "It's worse. I'm a self-centered slut and inconsiderate lush. I don't even buy Girl Scout cookies. I hang up the phone on charity callers. I sleep with men who have families for Christ's sake. Face it, I'm going to hell."

Jenna fails at trying to sound like she's not scolding me when she says, "Skylar, you do this every time. You get drunk, wake up in some random stranger's bed and then tell us what a bad person you are. If you're so tired of this happening—and I think I speak for the rest of us when I say *we're* tired of this happening—then do something about it."

I look from face to face as they stare at me to see what my reaction will be. They are all so damn perfect. Jenna, who is Baylor's best friend and agent, is engaged to a batting coach for the Yankees. She volunteers her time working for a charity set up by the team that raises money to vaccinate kids in Africa. Mindy comes from a life of money, but refuses to live on her father's dime so she became a waitress and is putting herself through college to become a physical therapist. And of course, Baylor is a successful author. She is finally with the love of her life and they are expecting their second child. Even my little sister, Piper, is off living her dream life backpacking the world with her best friend.

Everyone has something going for them. What the hell do I have?

Man... don't want one.

Kids... hate them.

Happiness... overrated.

Dignity... absent.

Self-worth... on vacation with dignity.

The only thing I really have going for me is my job. I love managing Mitchell's NYC. In fact, my parents have entrusted me with it almost completely. Yes, they still keep tabs and show up at least once a week to make sure I'm not royally screwing up their empire, but they've moved on to location number three in Long Island. My job is my life. My life is my job. And that's pretty much the way I like it. Or I did until my epiphany ten minutes ago. But that was then and this is now. And now is when I tell myself to shape the hell up. Turn over a new leaf. Toe the line. Do something with my life. Become meaningful.

Oh, God. I've swallowed an existential pill and it's regurgitating itself all over my fourth margarita.

"Okay, so let's say I wanted to change," I muse. "How would I go about that?"

They all share a look. I know what they're thinking. I want to tell them to piss off, but they know me too well. They think this will all blow over. I'm sure I say ten times a week that I want to change something about myself. But they know as well as I do that I never mean it. Until now, that is.

"Well, what exactly is it that you want to change?" Mindy asks. "I mean there's just so much to work with." The other girls laugh, but I sulk in the face of the truth. She places an apologetic hand on my arm. "Skylar, you know I love you. You have my full support and I'll help you any way I can."

I look down into my alluring margarita. "I need to stop drinking." They all nod their heads in agreement. "I need to stop fucking." More emphatic nods. "I need to do something deeply meaningful with my life."

It's the last one that has them drawing their eyebrows together.

While they think it over, I take a drink. Baylor eyes me skeptically, watching me drain my glass. "I didn't mean this second," I spit at her. "Tomorrow. I'll start tomorrow."

"The floor is open for suggestions," I tell them.

Jenna turns to me with a playful grin. "You could become a nun. It covers all the bases. No sex, no drinking." Her brows draw together in thought. "Wait, nuns can't drink, can they? And you can't get any more meaningful than serving The Big Guy, can you?"

"A *nun?*" Baylor offers. "This is my sister we're talking about here. Let's try to be a little realistic."

I stick my tongue out at her like a petulant five-year-old.

"Oh, you could join the Peace Corps," Mindy says. "You'd be helping people all over the world, and you'd have to go to really remote places that probably don't have hot men and alcohol."

I shake my head at them. "No. I love my job. I won't leave Mitchell's. It'll have to be something else."

"You could get fat," Jenna says. "You know, to keep the men away."

I roll my eyes at her. "First of all, there are guys out there who love fat chicks. And second and third, how does that solve my drinking problem and my do-gooder problem?"

"Yeah, I guess there's that." Jenna studies me, waiting for inspiration.

Baylor rubs her hand in a circle on her growing belly. "You could get knocked up," she teases. "That would easily solve your first two problems. Men are fundamentally turned off by pregnant women unless they happen to be your own super-hot husband." She sighs and I can tell she's fantasizing about her man.

"Ewww. Please don't make me picture you and Gavin having dirty pregnant sex." I shiver with disgust. "And, me, pregnant? God, no. I hate kids."

"You love Maddox." She looks at me with soft eyes.

"Of course I do. I can give him back," I explain. "It'd almost be a good idea if it didn't mean I'd end up with a snotty-nosed brat and some unemployed loser for a baby daddy."

Mindy sits up straight. "You could have a kid for someone else."

"As in give one up for adoption?" I ask, my forehead creasing into a dubious frown.

"No, like you could be a surrogate," she says excitedly, as if coming up with the most brilliant idea to trump all brilliant ideas. "You know, get knocked up in some lab and carry someone else's baby and then hand it over when the thing pops out. It's the perfect solution." She holds her hand up and counts off on her fingers, saying, "You can't drink. No man in his right mind would want to have sex with a knocked-up stranger. And to top it all, you'd be doing something totally awesome for someone."

"And you could still run the restaurant," Jenna adds.

"I could?" I look back and forth from Jenna to Mindy who are both nodding encouragingly. I think about what they've said. "Yes. I could."

"What?" Baylor shrieks, her face arranged in a scowl. "I was kidding, Skylar. You can't get pregnant."

I shoot her a venomous look. "It's not like you've cornered the market, big sister. I have a perfectly good uterus that'll grow cobwebs if I don't use it."

Mindy ignores Baylor's disapproving stare. "There's a big demand for surrogates. A lot of women can't have their own kids. They'll pay you a goddamn arm and leg if you can give them a baby. My mom was recently telling me about this couple she knows who can't have a kid because the woman had cancer."

I shake my head. "I don't want to do it for the money, Min. That'd kind of be against the whole do-something-meaningful premise."

"There's a slight problem, guys," Jenna says, tapping away on her phone. "Skylar can't be a surrogate."

"What? Why?" I ask, disappointed that the idea would get debunked so quickly.

"It says here in order to qualify as a surrogate, you have to already have your own kid," she says. "I guess they want to make sure you won't change your mind and run off with it."

"Makes sense," Mindy says.

"Crap." My shoulders slump towards the table. "It was a perfect solution."

"Perfect solution?" My sister looks at me through incredulous eyes. "Skylar Mitchell, you mean to say you'd have actually considered it? That's ludicrous."

"Hell yes! Why not?"

"Why not?" she spits back at me. "Because your body wouldn't be your own for nine months. Because you'd throw up and get hormonal and get stretch marks. Because you'd have some strange woman watching everything you do to make sure you didn't mess up her kid. Because you'd fall in love with the little baby the instant it was born. Need I go on?"

"Those first things you said about the throwing up and stretch marks—that's what'll keep the men away. The second thing you said about the woman watching me—that will keep me from drinking and doing stupid shit. And fall in love with the baby—are you crazy? Do you remember how I gave little Maddox back to you every time he so much as looked at me the wrong way?"

I frown at them. "It might have been perfect. But if I can't even qualify to do it, there's no use harping on it."

"Hold on," Mindy says, not yet ready to concede defeat. "Who's to say you have to go through an official agency? Why not just find someone who needs a surrogate and have their kid. It happens all the time."

"What, like run an ad in the newspaper?" I giggle at the absurdity. "'Womb for hire'?"

We laugh. Everyone but Baylor, that is. Baylor looks pissed. "Would you guys shut up!" she shouts. "Quit encouraging her. This is seriously not a good idea."

Jenna snaps her head to Baylor. "Not a good idea? What kind of world would we live in if people like Skylar didn't step up and do selfless things for others?"

Baylor rolls her eyes. "The exact same world we lived in two seconds ago," she pouts. "She's *not* doing it!"

"What if you and Gavin couldn't have kids?" Mindy asks. "What if you wanted them so much you thought you would die from want. What if you didn't have a sister to loan you her uterus, so some random woman stepped up and said she'd have a baby for you. Are you seriously going to sit here and deny that to someone?"

Baylor puts her hand on my arm. "Promise me you'll think about it long and hard, and without margaritas flowing through your veins, before you jump into anything, Skylar."

"So," I ignore my sister and turn to Mindy. "A newspaper ad?"

"I guess you could," she says. "But if you're serious about it, I could probably hook you up with this couple my mom knows."

"They aren't going through an agency?" I ask.

"No." She shakes her head sadly. "The woman, Erin, I think her name is, she had cancer so no agency will touch her. I think there's also a family history of medical problems, too. I guess they don't want to risk giving a kid to a sick woman when there are so many healthy ones who want kids, too."

"That's sad," I say. "So I could give a baby to a woman who used to be sick and really wants a kid but nobody will give her one?"

"Yup." She holds her drink out to me in a toast. "It'd probably pave your way straight to the pearly gates."

I can feel the smile creeping up my face. It's a feeling I haven't felt in… well, ever. I want to do this. I want to give someone what nobody else can give them. I look at Mindy. "Let's do this. Make the call."

Mindy smiles and pats my hand. "You are an amazing person, Skylar," she says. "But, if it's all the same to you, I'll let you sleep on it."

"Wait, you can't be serious," Baylor says.

"As a fucking heart attack, big sister."

chapter two

I'm nervous. What if they don't like me? What if they are like Stepford people and want to control every morsel of food that goes into my mouth and make me do yoga and shit every day? What if they demand I give up coffee? I've already given up alcohol, what else do I have left? What if they don't want their kid to grow in my slutty womb?

I have vowed to be as honest as I can with them about my past, even at the risk of them rejecting me. It's all part of my resolve to become a better person.

Two weeks. Baylor made me consider it for two entire weeks, thinking I'd chicken out. When I not only didn't flake out, but did substantial research on surrogacy and how it benefits both parties, she finally came around and is now on Team Skylar. As opposed to Team What-The-Fuck-Are-You-Doing?

I keep checking my watch. It's almost four o'clock. That's when they're supposed to show up. We had to meet on a Saturday because of their jobs. I'm not even sure what they do. I don't know anything about them except their names. *Griffin and Erin Pearce.*

And according to Mindy, they don't know anything about me, either. Her mom said it would be better if we got to know each other in person rather than have someone else relay our information.

I look around the restaurant and try to guess what these people might look like. I see a couple having a late lunch. Or an early dinner. They are about mid-thirties. He's burly like a cop or a fireman maybe. She's petite and looks like she could be a nurse. Yeah, a fireman and a nurse. They'd make good parents, right? The woman looks over at me and I freeze. *Oh, God, is that them?* Then Mindy walks out from behind me, taking them their check. "Breathe, Skylar," she says on her way by.

I've been anxious all day and my staff has definitely noticed, although Mindy is the only one who knows what's going on.

I walk into the bar area seeking water to quench my bone-dry anxiety-ridden mouth. As my bartender, Trent, serves me a glass, I see several groups of men enjoying our happy hour. Some of them stop talking and look over at me appreciatively while I survey the area. *Keep looking, boys. These legs are closed for business.* There's a woman sitting alone at the end of the bar. She's eyeing all the guys in the room, probably looking for a date for the evening. *Slut.*

Hmmfp. Hypocrite, I chide myself.

My eyes fall on a man sitting at a high-top by himself. He's reading a magazine, oblivious to the woman at the bar trying to get his attention. He's stunning. *Can a man be stunning?* He's got exceptionally dark hair, almost inky black. It falls to his collar, curling up at the ends. He reaches up to push a piece of it out of his eyes as he reads. He's wearing jeans and a blue button-down that is open to a slate-gray t-shirt underneath. The sleeves are rolled up to the elbow, revealing a small tattoo on the underside of his forearm that I can't quite make out.

He looks up and catches me staring. I can't pull my eyes away, because his eyes—they're incredible. Gray eyes, that are the exact color of his t-shirt, hypnotize me as the edges of his mouth curve up to reveal a smile that only adds to the smoldering appeal of his roguish face. Stubble, as dark as the sculpted shag on his head, dots his strong jaw and I wonder if he's gone without shaving for a few days, or if this is simply his usual testosterone-laden five-o'clock-shadow.

As quickly as he looked up, he resumes reading his magazine after briefly eyeing the restaurant entrance. I sit at the bar, mourning the loss of the brief moment we shared. It almost makes me want to scrap this whole surrogacy idea and mount myself on his smoking-hot lap.

Get it together, Skylar. I make my way to the bathroom to splash water on my face. I lean against the sink and take a few calming breaths. Then I smooth out my dress, running my hand over my flat stomach, wondering if in a few months, it will be a distant memory.

I reach up and tighten my dark-blonde ponytail, wondering if I should let my hair down. Wearing my long, wavy hair up makes me look severe, like a bookish librarian. But when I work in the kitchen, it's easier to put it in a hairnet or tuck it under a cap. In the end, I keep it tied up. If they don't like me the way I am, screw them. I'll just find someone else's spawn to grow. My green eyes stare back at me in a silent pep talk before I walk out into the restaurant.

Mindy grabs me and pulls me aside. "They're here," she says. My heart races and my eyes dart around quickly assessing the couples seated in the main room. "In the bar. He's totally hot. She looks like she just stepped off a fashion runway. She's nice. She came up to me asking where she could find the most amazing woman who ever walked the face of the earth."

I take a deep breath and blow it out. "Here goes nothing."

"Okay. Break a leg," she says. "Wait, is there an appropriate encouragement for someone in your situation?"

"How about 'get knocked up'?" I laugh awkwardly, walking towards the bar.

I spot the woman immediately when I get to the hostess stand. She's at the same table where gorgeous-testosterone-man was sitting. She's standing up and leaning over the table. Her goddamn legs go on for miles. Her long blonde curls hang in loose spirals down her back. She has the perfect hourglass figure that has a tiny waist flaring out to shapely hips underneath her designer pencil skirt.

I look down at my nothing-special dress that houses my not-so-prominent curves and suddenly I'm jealous of her. I'm jealous of the woman who is barren because cancer took away her ability to have children.

I shake my head at my callousness and attempt to rub the tension from the back of my neck.

She stands up from the greeting she was dolling out to her husband and takes a seat, leaving me stunned, as the recipient of her affection was indeed Mr. Gorgeous-testosterone-man.

Holy shit—that's *the would-be baby daddy?*

My shaky legs carry me over to the table and I introduce myself. "Uh, hi. I'm Skylar Mitchell," I say, leaving any shred of confidence back at the hostess stand.

"Oh, Skylar." She stands up, pulling me into a crushing hug, her generous boobs suffocating my meager ones. "We are so very glad to meet you. I'm Erin and this is Griffin." I reluctantly give her a pat with hands that hang by my side. I'm not big on displays of affection. I look around the bar uncomfortably as she continues to stifle me.

"Uh, I'm glad to meet you, too," I say when she finally releases me. "Can I get you anything to drink?"

She shakes her head. "Trent is already getting us some water. Thanks." She motions to the stool next to hers. "Here, sit."

I watch her take a seat, crossing her statuesque legs. I go to sit and miss the top of the stool, sliding off to the side only to be caught by Griffin before I'm completely sprawled out on the floor.

"Oh my God," I say, smoothing out my dress and extricating myself from strong, toned arms. "I swear I'm not this clumsy. I mean, I won't be like falling down and shit with your kid. Uh, I mean, I'll be careful. And I won't cuss. I don't know if they can hear in there, but I won't—" I stop talking mid-sentence when it occurs to me that I'm rambling and they must think I'm crazy. "Sorry. I'll shut up now."

A throaty, sultry laugh bellows out of Erin. "It's okay, Skylar. We're completely nervous, too."

"Oh, good," I admit. "I thought it was just me."

Griffin offers me his hand. "Thanks so much for agreeing to meet with us." His deep voice is sinfully smooth, like aged whiskey. His rugged spicy scent still lingers around my head, making me think inappropriate thoughts such as how I might offer to extract his sperm with my pulsating orgasm.

I put my small hand into his large one and try to ignore the spark that courses up my arm, through my chest, over my abs and right to my core. I purposely refrain from any eye contact, remembering the moment we had a few minutes ago.

Wait! Wait one goddamn second. We had a moment a few minutes ago. And now he's sitting here expecting me to loan him my uterus to grow a baby for his lying, cheating ass?

Trent brings a tray full of waters to the table.

A squirming Erin takes a long drink of hers before asking, "Skylar, I need to use the bathroom. Can you point the way, please?"

I direct her to the restrooms in the back and watch her gracefully leave the table. Then my eyes snap to his. My lips pucker. My eyebrows shoot up. My arms cross in front of me. I'm ready to chew up and spit out his totally hot, wandering-eyed ass.

Griffin looks behind him and then back at me, confused. "Are you okay?"

"Am I okay?" I ask, pinning him to his seat with my accusing stare. "Five minutes ago you were eye-fucking me and now you want me to loan you my lady parts?"

His jaw drops. "Eye fu… uh… no." His hand comes up to rub across the stubble on his face. A low, grumbly nervous laugh escapes him. "Ms. Mitchell, if I can be candid here; when I acknowledged you earlier, I was simply smiling at a beautiful woman who was looking at me." He holds my gaze with his steely eyes as he draws his brows together in concentration. "Rest assured, I don't intend to 'eye fuck'—as you so eloquently put it— or do any other type of 'fucking' with you or anyone else who is not currently my wife. I never have and I never will."

An unexpected wave of shame, coupled with a dash of disappointment courses through me. I don't normally get embarrassed. In fact, nothing ever makes me blush. Except apparently Griffin Pearce putting me in my place.

He's right. How could I have read so much into a simple smile? Probably because I was being the old Skylar who would hook up with anyone who had the body of an athlete and a condom in his wallet.

"Call me Skylar. Wait, never?" I raise a doubting brow that all but calls him a liar. "As in, she's the only one you've ever been with?"

He nods. "High school sweethearts."

Of course they are. Hell, my sister will probably write a damn book about this. High school sweethearts fall in love, get married, lose the ability to have kids because of cancer, find baby-mama to carry child, live happily-ever-after. I can see it now.

Heels click on the concrete floor behind me. "You aren't scaring her away, are you Griff?"

"No, sweetheart." He stands and helps her back onto the stool. Maybe he thinks they're dangerous now.

Erin sits down and puts her hand on top of Griffin's. "Okay, so I guess we should tell you about ourselves." She flashes me her luminescent smile. "We're both twenty-seven years old. We grew up in Ohio, started dating our senior year in high school and then went to college together at NYU. Griffin is a freelance photographer who shoots anything from still-life photos to glamorous magazine spreads. I teach second grade in lower Manhattan. I got cancer when I was eighteen, shortly after we started dating. Stage two cervical. I did chemo and radiation which were unsuccessful, so they ended up taking my entire uterus in a hysterectomy."

She gives Griffin an endearing look. "He stood by my side back then and has every day since." She turns back to me. "I've always wanted kids, but Griffin wasn't so sure. I mean, he doesn't have any experience with kids. I work with them every day and see how wonderful they can be. I eventually wore him down and now we're ready. Actually, we've been ready for a few years, but we have been unable to find an agency that will allow us to adopt or find us a surrogate."

21

She nervously traces the top of her water glass with a finger. "What questions do you have for us?"

I'm still stuck on *cancer at eighteen*. That must have been awful. "I guess I'm wondering why the agencies won't let you adopt. I mean, you don't have cancer anymore, do you?"

She shakes her head. "No, but they are very thorough, and unfortunately there's a prominent history of cancer and heart disease in my family. Combine that with my medical past and I'm not exactly the ideal candidate for a new mother."

"So they deny you the right to adopt based on your cancer that's now gone, and other shit that might not ever happen in the future?" I ask, belatedly chiding myself for the bad language.

"Yeah, that pretty much sums it up," Erin says. "So, will you tell us about yourself?"

"Well, I'm twenty-four. I manage this restaurant. You probably figured that out by the name. It's my parents' place. We also have one in Maple Creek, Connecticut and a third one is being opened this year over in Long Island. I have two sisters, one older, one younger. I don't do drugs—well if you don't count smoking the occasional cigarette and drinking—which I promise I won't do if I get pregnant. I love to ride my bike around the city. I've always been pretty healthy. I've never been married or pregnant, but, uh… I think my parts are in good working order."

"You sound like a well-rounded person, Skylar," Erin says.

I try to hide the disappointment in myself as I fold my restless hands together on the table. *If she only knew the half of it.*

"There's one more thing you need to know about us," Griffin says, looking sadly at Erin.

She nods her head at him. "Full disclosure," she says.

"Huh?" I ask, unsure of what's passing between them.

"We need to be totally honest with you before we get any further into this process. I don't want to dupe you into anything and then change the rules," she says.

"I thought it was all pretty clear." I juggle my eyes between them.

"I can already tell you I'm very excited and totally interested in having you carry a baby for us." She fidgets with her fingernail, another sign of the anxiety she must be feeling. "When they took my uterus, they left my ovaries in because I was so young, even though they said the radiation and chemo could possibly affect my eggs. But at eighteen, I was devastated at the cancer diagnosis and couldn't imagine going through the fertility treatments required for egg retrieval which would have delayed my cancer treatment. And as fate would have it, I went into early menopause a few years ago. It was always a possibility. We were just hoping it wouldn't happen quite so soon.

"What I'm trying to say is that I don't have any eggs. We would have to use yours." She looks from me to Griffin, who gives her an encouraging smile, nodding at her to continue. "This baby would technically be yours and Griffin's, so you'd have to not only become our surrogate, but you'd have to legally give your own baby up for adoption."

I'm in awe of her total candor. She could have waited until we established a relationship to tell me this. She could have, as she said, duped me into it, pulling a bait-and-switch on me. But, she didn't. She also didn't have to be totally honest with me about her family history. How would I have ever found out about it? She's laying it all out on the table.

I decide to do the same.

"You haven't yet asked me why I want to do this," I say.

She leans her elbows casually on the table. "I was getting to that. What makes you think you can even go through with this, having never had a baby?"

"Full disclosure?" I ask.

"Please," she says, looking nervously at Griffin.

"I'm not exactly what you would call a morally sound person. Until a few weeks ago, I, uh… overindulged in booze. And, um… men." I shamefully glance at Erin, who gives me a sympathetic look, and Griffin, whose jaw is tight and unreadable. "I've never been in love and don't ever intend to be. I don't even like kids that much, well, with the exception of my nephew and Chris's kids— the Maple Creek Mitchell's manager. And I only like those kids because I don't have to deal with them all day. I couldn't do that. I'm not cut out to be a mom.

"I just woke up one day and wanted to change my life. I vowed to quit my destructive patterns and do something that really matters. I hope this qualifies." I look Erin square in the eyes. "I don't want you to worry, though. I promise I won't fall in love with your baby."

She grabs my hand. I watch a tear escape her eye. "Are you for real?" She wipes her tears with her other hand. "Griffin will attest that I'm a firm believer in fate. I believe fate brought us together, Skylar. I believe nobody else would want to have a baby for us. I believe nobody else would want you to have their baby." We both share a laugh.

"You're probably right," I say. "Well, maybe not about the whole fate thing, but about the fact that nobody else would want my slutty womb carrying their kid."

"So you'll still consider it?" Erin asks, hope swimming in her eyes.

Not only would I feel guilty denying this woman a baby, since I appear to be her only option, but I kind of like the fact that her drop-dead-gorgeous husband has only ever been with her. Maybe it's Baylor's romantic side rubbing off on me.

Erin is also the nicest woman I've ever met who could probably get by on her looks, but chooses to use her intellectual qualities instead. She's the complete opposite of me.

"Of course," I say.

Griffin holds up a hand in hesitation. "Hold on. There's still so much to discuss. Skylar has to go over the contracts. And she'll have to get a physical of course, what with her provocative past and all."

"Griff!" Erin scolds.

"No, it's okay," I say. "I'll get checked out. I completely understand that you don't want your kid growing in a cesspool of syphilis and gonorrhea."

Griffin pulls some paperwork out of a camera bag sitting at his feet. "We've had legal papers drawn up. You can take these home and go over them. I would suggest you have a lawyer look at them as well. Then there is the matter of compensation. Obviously, we will pay all of the medical bills, but what do you require on top of that?"

"As in, how much do I charge to rent out my baby oven?"

"Yes," he says, not laughing at my attempt at a joke.

"I don't want anything. That would go against the reasons I have for doing this," I say.

Griffin eyes me skeptically.

"There has to be something," Erin says.

I look at her stylish clothing. Too stylish for a second-grade teacher. Clearly she has a good eye for fashion. "Well, you could outfit me with maternity clothes that don't make me look like I'm wearing a potato sack."

Erin laughs. "Done. What else? There has to be more."

I lift my shoulders in a casual shrug. "If it would make you feel better, you can buy me a tummy tuck after."

She gives me a genuine smile. "From what I can see, I doubt you'll need one. But I'll take you to New York's best plastic surgeon if it comes to that."

We continue to talk for hours. Mindy serves us food as we get to know each other. Erin tells me about her second-grade class. I can tell she adores kids. It's clear to me that she wants to be involved in the pregnancy as much as possible, attending every appointment and Lamaze class.

By the time we're done talking, Erin and I have become fast friends. I can't get a read on Griffin, however. I watched him during dinner. Mostly to see if he was sincere about what he told me before. He's been nice to me. Cordial. Friendly, even. But his attention was undoubtedly on Erin. It's obvious to me that he dotes on her. Maybe he's skeptical about how fast this is all moving. I say what the hell. Go big or go home. Even if it means having to be around Erin's drool-worthy husband for nine months.

I must have said something right during dinner. When we get up to leave, Griffin says, "Okay. Let's do this." I remember the very same words I said at Baylor's house a few short weeks ago.

I look at Erin and we both smile. "Let's do this," I say.

chapter three

Erin is nervous. Her leg is shaking. And she keeps picking at her fingernail. She does that when she's anxious about something. I've learned that about her in the past three months. Erin and I have become practically inseparable. That is when she's not working and when I'm not working, which really only comes down to a few hours each week.

However, she was able to get away from school early today to join me for our first ultrasound. Eight weeks. That's how far along we are. It only took two tries to get us knocked up. I still grimace when I think back to the first insemination. I remember lying on the table, my legs in stirrups, crotch bared to the world, and all I could think about was what Erin's hot-as-sin husband was doing moments before in the next room to provide the sperm that could potentially impregnate me. I imagined those smoldering gray eyes looking into mine as he stroked himself until he stiffened, calling out my name as he came all over me.

Then, Erin interrupted my colossally-inappropriate fantasy, handing me a bundle of cards her second graders made for me. I mentally bitch-slapped myself before opening the cards. I carefully read each one to keep my mind off the doctor shoving a syringe up through my vagina and into my uterus to deposit Griffin's sperm that had been quickly 'washed'—*was it dirty?*—before introducing it to the sole egg that hopefully was making its microscopic way down my fallopian tube. We had decided against fertility treatments for me, for which I was grateful. I couldn't even imagine the possibility of carrying multiples. Thank God, they agreed.

I look over at Erin, who smiles at me nervously as we wait to be called back to see the first picture of her baby. She jumps every time the nurse comes through the door only to call a name that is not mine. See—if this is what wanting a kid does to you, I don't want any part of it.

Erin has been incredible. She's been pampering me with twice-monthly mani/pedis. And shortly after the stick I peed on turned blue, she took me and my very-pregnant sister, Baylor, for a spa day. I kind of get the idea that money isn't an object for them. She's a schoolteacher, so he must be a really good photographer.

Erin wasn't even upset the first go-around when my test was negative. She came to my apartment a few days before my period was due. She brought five pregnancy tests with her along with a bottle of sparkling cider and a bottle of champagne. Of course, I thought the champagne was going to be for her if the test was positive. Not so.

When the test was negative, she simply put the sparkling cider in my kitchen cabinet and gathered up the sticks, depositing them into the trash while she said, "It rarely happens the first time, anyway." There were no tears of sorrow. No pouting around. No cussing—not that she would ever do that anyway.

Then I watched in wonder when she carefully opened the expensive bottle of Brut, pouring us each a glass. "Why are we drinking champagne when there is nothing to celebrate?" I asked.

"First off, you haven't had a drink in what, two months?" She handed me a glass as I nodded. "You deserve this. We *are* celebrating. We're celebrating you and this incredible thing you're doing for us. And also how truly happy I am to have a new friend in my life."

"Okay." I raised my glass to her in a toast. "To new friends."

The smile on her face brightened her intense blue eyes. "To new friends," she repeated, clinking our glasses together.

I savored the taste of the first alcohol I'd had in months, but at the same time I realized that I didn't really miss it all that much. They say it takes twenty-one days to break a habit. And it's true, it was hard those first few weeks. But Erin kept sending me encouraging texts. She would show up at the restaurant after school sometimes, just to say hello. She was entwining herself in my life without being overbearing. I got the idea she didn't have many friends. I couldn't understand why because she's about the nicest person I know. So, it only seemed natural to invite her along when the girls and I got together. Baylor, Mindy, Jenna and I have treated her like our long-lost sister ever since.

The next month, she showed up with five more tests and a new bottle of champagne—one that we never opened. The top on the cider was popped and we toasted her baby right before she called Griffin to tell him the news. She was so excited she nearly fainted. I swear she would have hit the floor if I hadn't caught her and helped her to the couch, fetching a cold compress to put on her head. She was positively over the moon. Me—I sat stunned wondering what the hell I'd gotten myself into and if it was too late to bail.

"I'm not too late, am I?" Griffin says, walking through the door to the doctor's office, pulling me from my thoughts.

I look directly at his crotch. I can't help it. I don't do it intentionally. But ever since I thought about him masturbating in the next room, I can't help but stare at his anatomy every time I see him.

"No, we haven't been called back yet." Erin leans over to kiss him.

"Oh, well, I was just going to sit out here and wait for you guys anyway." He settles into the seat next to Erin.

"What? That's fucking crazy." I wince at my choice of words. "Sorry." Breaking my cursing habit has proven even harder than quitting drinking and men. "This is your kid. Both of you need to be there."

Erin grabs my hand as her eyes mist up.

"Ms. Mitchell?" the nurse calls out. The three of us share a look of excitement, or maybe panic, as we head into the back.

The ultrasound tech has me undress from the waist down and get on a table like I'm having a pelvic exam. She drapes a blanket over my lower half and then invites Erin and Griffin into the room. They take a seat on the opposite side from the tech and the monitor.

The tech picks up a long wand thingy that's not even as thick as my vibrator. It looks like it has a condom on it. She squirts on some lube and I giggle, raising my eyebrow at it. She says, "Relax, this won't hurt a bit."

I glance over at Erin who is nervously bouncing in her chair, and Griffin who looks embarrassed as the tech glides the wand inside me.

"We should be able to determine your exact due date and we may even get to see your baby's heartbeat," the tech says, smiling at me.

"Not my baby. Their baby." I gesture to Erin and Griffin. "I'm just the incubator."

"Awww, you're a surrogate? That's awesome," she says.

"It is awesome," Erin agrees. "Totally and completely awesome." She smiles at me.

The wand moves around inside me as the tech taps on the keyboard. She stops moving. "There." She points at the monitor. "The little thing that looks like a kidney bean, that's your baby," she says, looking over at Erin.

Erin grabs Griffin's hand and my hand at the same time. I see the little pulsating heart on the monitor and I'm genuinely happy. Happy for Erin because she's getting the kid she always wanted. Happy for me because I don't have any innate maternal feelings towards the kidney bean on the screen.

I realize I'm no longer watching the monitor. I'm watching the emotions flow across Erin's face. She takes in a breath. Tears well up in her eyes. She's completely speechless. Her jaw drops as she absorbs the very first picture of her baby.

Her baby... *their* baby. I never once thought of it as mine. I simply see it as making a donation. It may be growing in my body, but that doesn't make it any less theirs. I'm simply keeping it for them for the time being.

I look at Griffin to see him doing the very same thing—looking at Erin. It's obvious to me that he's doing this for her. Not that he doesn't like kids. He's played with Maddox a few times when Baylor had all of us out to her house. I can tell he'll make a great dad. It's just that I can see being a mom is Erin's life dream.

And although it may not be Griffin's, he is not about to deny her that.

The tech tells us all about the baby—size, weight, due date. She prints out a picture and Erin stares at it while the tech cleans me up.

She hands the picture over to Griffin and leans over the table to pull me into a hug. "I love you, Skylar Mitchell," she sobs. "Do you know how much I love you? Do you even understand what an incredible gift you are giving us?"

Tears prickle my eyes. I almost feel selfish. This is what I wanted the entire time. To feel good about doing something meaningful. Yet, I don't feel deserving of all the praise she is laying on me. It seems so simple, this thing I'm doing for them. I would do it again in a heartbeat.

Without another thought, I blurt out, "I'd be happy to help give little Bean a sibling if you ever wanted it to have one."

Erin buries her head in my chest, still crushing me with her overbearing embrace. "You are the most incredible person to ever walk the earth. Do you know that?"

My humbled eyes find Griffin, who is laughing at Erin's smothering hug. He raises an eyebrow at me. "Bean?" he asks.

I simply nod and try to ignore the electricity that shoots through me when he puts a gracious hand on my arm.

"You are my best friend," Erin randomly blurts out at the late lunch she's treating me to. "It's okay, I know you have lots of other friends and I know you think I'm saying it because you're doing this wonderful thing for me. But you'd be wrong. I think you are a fun, kind, generous person who I'm honored to know. Maybe I'm not supposed to come out and say it. Maybe that makes it not as genuine. But I don't have many friends." She gestures to her body. "This tends to intimidate women so I don't make friends easily. But I don't seem to intimidate you at all. And I wanted you to know, that even though I'm not your best friend; you are mine."

I give her a sad smile and look down at my salad. "I've thought about this. A lot, in fact. And Erin, you have to admit it could be really awkward once the baby comes. I would completely understand if you didn't want to hang around me afterwards. I mean, if I were you, I wouldn't want me lurking around, making the little bean wonder who I am and all."

She reaches over to grab my hand. "Are you kidding? You're Auntie Skylar," she says. "I've never for one minute thought I would rip the baby from your arms and never see you again. That's not who I am. It's not who Griffin is. I come from a big family, Skylar. I know more than anyone that it takes a village to raise a child.

"Griffin and I have already discussed this. As soon as the baby is old enough, he or she will know what a wonderful thing you did. I would never keep it a secret. We have nothing to hide and I want you to be a part of our family. I meant it earlier when I said I love you."

"How can you not have friends, Erin? You are quite possibly the nicest, most genuine person I've ever met," I say. "And you *do* intimidate me, by the way. You're gorgeous. Most women would kill for your hair. You have really great boobs. You're super sweet. And your husband is hot as hell. What's not to be jealous of?"

She laughs. "You don't get it, do you? *I'm* the one who's jealous. You lead this carefree life. You've always been healthy. You can have a baby which is something I can never do. And you don't even realize how beautiful you are. Especially now. It's true what they say about pregnant women glowing, you know."

She takes a drink of her iced tea as I study her, trying to see myself from her perspective. Then she asks, "So you think my husband is hot, huh?" She giggles.

"Well, *duh*. I do have eyes," I say. "Does it bother you that women lust after him. Uh, I mean, not me, but other women?" I'm a terrible liar.

She tries to hold in her grin. "No. Not really," she says. "I know what I have. If he didn't stray on me when I was bald and sickly, I'm pretty sure he won't do it now."

"He's a good man to have stuck by you."

"You don't know the half of it," she says. "We weren't even in love when he took it upon himself to take care of me. We had only been dating a month when I got the diagnosis my senior year in high school. I started chemo and radiation right away. I lost my hair. I looked incredibly gaunt. I was sick almost every day for months. Most of my friends were scared away by the 'cancer girl.' But not Griffin. I guess it's because he had been through it all before."

"Before?" I ask in horror. "He had another girlfriend with cancer?"

"No. It was his mom," she says. "She died of breast cancer when he was fifteen. His dad turned to alcohol, leaving Griffin to care for his mom. I was actually kind of surprised when he said he wouldn't leave me, knowing that it could end so badly. But he always seemed to know exactly what I needed, right when I needed it.

"After my surgery, I thought he might leave me because I wouldn't be able to have kids. But that's when he said he loved

34

me—in the hospital right after I woke up from my hysterectomy. He said he loved me and that he'd always take care of me."

"That's awful," I say. "Not about him staying with you, but about his mom."

"Yeah, it was hard for him trying to be the adult of the family when he was so young. His dad eventually went into rehab a few years after his mom died, but it damaged their relationship beyond repair." A grin tugs at her lips. "That's when he became a photographer, you know. When his mom was dying. He wanted to have pictures to remember her by, so he took thousands of her those last few months.

"Oh, hey, that reminds me, Griffin is going to Africa next week for a National Geographic photo shoot. Can you believe it?"

"Holy shit, really?" I say.

She bursts out laughing at my blunder. Then suddenly she grabs her temples, wincing in pain.

"Are you okay?" I put my hand on hers. "What's wrong?"

She doesn't speak. She takes a few long, deep breaths, like a woman in labor. She moans, closing her eyes and I see beads of sweat emerge, dotting her upper lip.

"Erin, are you okay?" I ask again, not entirely sure she's even hearing me.

She finally nods her head slightly, rubbing at her temples. "Yeah, I think I have a migraine coming on. I used to get them when I went through... through... uh—" She stares at me blankly.

"Menopause?" I ask, completing her sentence that she couldn't finish due to the pain.

"Yeah. Menopause," she says.

I wave the waitress over and ask for the check.

"Come on." I quickly leave some money on the table. "I need to get my best friend home."

chapter four

Erin texted me saying I needed to be home at 10:00 a.m. for a delivery. Not a problem. I've been barfing up a goddamn lung every morning for the past few weeks, so I don't leave the apartment until almost noon. And although I haven't seen much of Erin since our lunch together, she sends me sweet care packages of crackers, ginger ale, green apples, and everything else that's supposed to help with morning sickness.

I'm beginning to wonder if she's having second thoughts about our friendship. Maybe she said all those things about best friends and 'Auntie Skylar' when she was still riding the high from the ultrasound. She could have gone home and thought about it and now she's pulling away from me so it won't be so bad when she dumps me like a hot potato the second Bean is born.

The doorbell rings just as I'm finishing up brushing my teeth after my latest vomit session. Good timing, it'll be almost an hour before I throw up again. It's the same every day. Three barfs with an hour in between each. On the bright side, I've only gained one pound in ten weeks.

I look through the peephole in the front door to see a dark head of messy-yet-perfectly-sculpted hair.

Griffin Pearce.

Before I even realize what I'm doing, my hands go up to my hair, pulling it loose from the confines of my ponytail. I look down to see what I'm wearing, making sure it's not spattered with vomit. While giving a million thanks that I just brushed my teeth, I slowly open the door vowing not to look at his crotch.

"Hi, Skylar," he says in that deeply smooth voice of his.

Does he mean for his voice to drip with sex or does it do it all on its own?

"Uh, hey." I peek my head out and look down the hall for Erin.

He's alone. Suddenly I feel very self-conscious. Alone with the man whose crotch I'm trying to avoid looking at is not a particularly good position to be in. I don't know where to look. I try looking at his eyes, but those steel-gray eyes that burned into me the first time I saw him are not going to make my guilt-ridden fantasies of him disappear. I give him a quick smile and then move aside so he can come in.

He walks past me into my apartment, leaving a trail of his scent lingering as I shut the door behind him, struggling not to inhale sharply through my nose.

It occurs to me that this is the first time we've ever been together without Erin. We've socialized on many occasions. We've been out to dinner. We've gone to barbecues at Baylor's. Erin's family had me out to their house in White Plains. They even came to Sunday brunch with my family a couple of times. But Griffin and I have never been alone. Until now.

In my apartment.

With a bed.

My belly churns and I wonder if I'm going to throw up again or if it's nervous flutters.

I recall Erin's declaration that Griffin would never cheat on her. Which is good, because I'd never do that to her. *Never.* I'm well aware that I've probably ruined enough marriages in my lifetime. I'm not about to ruin theirs. And I know he won't put me in that position, but I'm just sayin'—if he did, I wouldn't go there.

No matter how much I'd love to run my fingers through that inky-black hair.

No matter how much that spicy-rugged smell of his permeates through me.

No matter how much I long for that stubble of his to rub between my thighs.

Stop it, Skylar.

"Is it here yet?" he asks, pulling me from my inappropriate thoughts.

"Is what here yet? Erin said there was going to be a delivery, but she didn't say what. I thought it would be another one of her morning-sickness care packages."

He gives me a look of concern. "She told me you were pretty sick. Sorry about that."

"It's not that bad. A few hours every morning and then I'm pretty much good to go for the rest of the day. I usually work at the restaurant from one until ten, so it's not that big a deal."

"Good," he says. "Let me know if there's anything I can do."

"So, the package?" I ask, trying to distract my wayward thoughts from all the things I can think of that he could do to make me feel better. I blame it on my pregnancy hormones.

"Oh, right. We got you a bike," he says. "We know you like to ride, but it can be dangerous around the city with all the traffic, especially when you start to get bigger. So we got you a stationary one that you can ride right here in your apartment."

My eyes snap up and hold his. "You got me a stationary bike? Really?"

"Yes." He smiles and I look away, frazzled like a little schoolgirl. "It should be here any minute," he says.

"So if it's being delivered, why are *you* here?" I belatedly realized that comment might have been a little bitchy. "Uh, not that I didn't want you to come. I mean, not that you shouldn't have come. It's okay that you're here, but why would you come if the delivery man is coming?"

Oh my God. Stop saying come, *Skylar.*

"Ugh!" I cover up my eyes and wallow in embarrassment.

He chuckles.

Does that mean he knows the effect he's having on me? I'll bet all women go batty-eyed over him. I'm sure this is nothing new. He's a hot photographer who probably has gorgeous models falling at his feet.

"You'll have to ignore me. Pregnancy hormones make me stupid," I say, realizing once again, I'm blushing in front of Griffin. What is it about this one guy that makes my face bleed emotion whenever he's around?

"It's fine," he says. "I'm here to put it together. They'll deliver the bike, but they won't assemble it."

"Oh, well, thanks." I try to sound grateful, but I'm not exactly happy that he's going to be here for a while. The quicker he gets out of here, the better. Being around, and lusting over, Erin's husband makes me feel all slutty inside.

I look at my watch, praying for the doorbell to ring and ease the awkward tension I've created.

"Can I get you a drink?" I ask.

"Water would be great," he says.

I walk the short distance from the living room into my galley-style kitchen. I can see him looking around my apartment from where I stand at the refrigerator. He starts moving some things around, I suppose to make room for the bike. He clears an area in the far corner, behind the couch. It's not where I would have put it, but I remain quiet as I'm mesmerized watching his muscles flex as he pushes the bookshelves out of the way.

I emerge from the kitchen and hand him the bottle of water. "I was thinking over by the window would be better. That way I can at least see the outdoors while I ride." And I can watch those muscles move the heavy shelves again.

"You can put it there if you want, but the bike comes with a large monitor that you can program for almost any ride in the world. You can bike through the national parks, or do the Tour de France. Or bike to a volcano in Hawaii. It's pretty cool, actually. I test-drove one in the sporting goods store."

My jaw hangs open. I know how expensive those things are. Plus, I think you have to buy a monthly subscription to use the programmed trails. "Fuck, Griffin. You shouldn't have spent so much."

"Don't worry about it," he says. "And don't say fuck."

"*You* don't say fuck," I tease.

"I only said fuck because you said fuck." He shakes his head. "Why don't we both stop saying fuck."

We share a laugh and sit down on opposite sides of the couch. I check my watch again.

"Is everything okay with Erin?" I ask, trying to pass the time. "It seems like since the ultrasound, she's been avoiding me. She's not having second thoughts about Bean, is she?" I joke. Well, I think it's a joke. I'm half-serious.

41

"I'm not exactly sure what's going on with her." He leans back into the couch, hooks an ankle over one knee and picks tentatively at his shoelace. Then he furrows his brow and gives a small shake of his head as if something has just now occurred to him. He looks over at me. "She's been acting differently since I got back from Africa. Maybe this whole thing is a little overwhelming. She's wanted a baby for so long, and it's finally happening. I think we need to give it some time to sink in."

I'm about to ask him how his trip to Africa went when the doorbell rings.

Griffin hops up from the couch. "I'll get it." He strides over to the door and follows the delivery guy downstairs. A few minutes later, they carry in a large, heavy box that has their muscles bulging.

The delivery guy is extremely good looking. Big. Burly. Blonde. Ripped. And he's totally checking me out. The old Skylar would flirt with him relentlessly. Hell, the old Skylar would probably bed him here and now, giving him one hell of a tip. The new Skylar, however, would rather stare at the unavailable man standing next to him.

"This for you?" the guy asks.

"I guess it is," I say.

He stares at me appraisingly as Griffin watches. "Doesn't look like you need it," hot delivery guy says.

"That's exactly why I do it," I tell him, giving him my best cocky smile.

"Damn." He turns to Griffin. "You're a lucky guy."

"Oh, we're not together," Griffin says.

Even though it's true—and I know being with him isn't even a remote possibility in any life—his saying that still stings my heart momentarily.

Delivery Guy raises an eyebrow. "Then you won't mind if I ask her out."

It wasn't a question.

Griffin's face hardens. "We may not be together, but she is carrying my baby," he says.

All the air gets sucked out of the room, taking what's in my lungs right along with it.

What the fuck?

My jaw is still on the floor when Griffin hands the guy a twenty on his way out the door that he practically sprinted to.

The door shuts.

"What the hell was that?" I spit at him.

"What?" He shrugs an innocent shoulder.

"Don't *what* me," I raise my voice at him. "Why did you have to tell him that? He probably thinks I'm a slut."

"Why do you care what the delivery guy thinks?"

"You've got no fucking right to say things like that!" I yell.

"Quit saying fuck," he says calmly.

"I'll say fuck whenever I want to say fuck. As in, fuck you, Griffin. You had no right to say that shit!"

He laughs which only fuels my anger. "Are you telling me you would have dated the guy?"

"No, I wouldn't have dated the guy," I say. "But you have no place taking the choice away from me."

"I'm only trying to keep you safe. He could have been a psycho killer for all you know," he says. "And if I recall, you said you were done being promiscuous. It was one of the reasons you wanted to do this." He nods to my still-flat belly.

"Well, thanks *Dad*," I say petulantly. "But I think I can handle myself. I'm twenty-four fucking years old, and I've made it this far without your goddamn help."

"Maybe I'd treat you like a twenty-four-year-old if you would stop cussing like a rebellious teenager," he says, irritated.

"Maybe I'd quit cussing if you'd stop cock-blocking me," I retort.

"Oh, so you *do* want to get laid." His arms cross over his chest.

"Ugh!" I kick the huge box with my foot and then wince at the bolt of pain that radiates up my leg. "No! I don't want to get laid," I say. "But, I'll be the one to decide that, not you."

Oh, crap. My stomach heaves and I feel round two coming on. No time to run to my bathroom. I barely make it over to the kitchen trash can where I hurl the rest of the green apple I ate for breakfast.

My hair hangs down into the trash can and before I'm done throwing up, I feel Griffin grab my hair and hold it away from my face. He places a gentle hand on my shoulder.

How is it that I'm retching into a garbage can and all I can think about is the heat he's sending into my body through the thin t-shirt I have on?

I sit on the floor and let my abs recover. Griffin rummages through my cabinets, finding a glass to fill with cold water. He hands it to me along with a wet paper towel to wipe my face.

I'm horrified that I threw up in front of him.

On the other hand, maybe the sheer mortification of him seeing me like this will stop the erotic dreams I keep having about him.

"I'm really sorry." He holds out his hand to help me up. "Did I cause that by getting you upset?"

"No." I glance at my watch. "It was right on schedule."

"You have a vomit schedule?" He laughs.

"Pretty much," I say. "At least it's predictable."

I pull the trash can liner out and tie it off, then take it to the door. He grabs it from me. "Let me take that."

"God, no," I say, pulling it back. "I'll do it myself. There's a trash chute in the hallway."

"I think I can handle it, Sky." He takes the bag from me despite my obvious mortification over it.

"Lar," I say.

"Huh?" he asks, opening the door.

"It's Skylar, not Sky," I say. "Nobody calls me Sky."

I've always hated the nickname. It's too personal. Too much like an endearment. A pet name. A way to get close. I don't do close.

So, why then, does part of me want to kick my ass for telling him not to use it? Then the other part of me wants to kick *that* part's ass for thinking it.

"Oh. It seems like such an obvious nickname," he says.

I leave to go brush my teeth and take a long shower. The less time I spend with him the better. I'm just not sure if it's because he's so freaking hot, or because he's figured out how to infuriate me.

An hour later, when I emerge from my bedroom, the bike is set up and the packaging, along with Griffin Pearce, is missing from my apartment.

chapter five

Mindy watches in fascination as I inhale the greasy cheeseburger and chocolate milkshake she placed in front of me mere seconds ago. Her eyes go wide, presumably in wonderment as to how one small woman can annihilate a meal so large it would give a man pause.

I don't care. I'm freaking starving. Now that my morning sickness has waned, I crave meat. Lots of it. I have it all the time. My arteries are starting to beg for mercy.

Thanks to the stationary bike Erin and Griffin got me, I'm keeping the pounds off despite my newfound obsession with animal flesh, and I've only gained two in twelve weeks.

Twelve weeks is apparently cause for celebration, according to Erin, who has been more like her old self the past few days. She said this is when you can breathe easily and start telling people about the pregnancy. She's on her way to the restaurant to take me shopping for maternity clothes during our Saturday afternoon lull. Not that I need them. In fact, my skinny jeans are only now beginning to feel snug. I mean, there's still not much to the little bean. Erin says it's only two inches long, about the size of a lime. But she has insisted we start shopping now so when the time comes, I'll be stylish and chic. Two words I've never associated with pregnancy, but whatever.

Coming from the bathroom after washing up, I see Erin walking through the restaurant. She's holding two flowers. A red rose and some white flower. It's an orchid or lily, or maybe a tulip. I don't know much about flowers. As soon as any man presents me with them, it's my cue to bail and run like hell. The only flowers I know about are the fake ones we keep on the tables at the restaurant.

She approaches me with her arms outstretched, holding the flowers out to me, one in each hand. A bright smile curls her lips. "Pick one," she says.

"Why?" I ask, skeptically. "Is this a test?"

She smiles in silence.

I try to analyze what she's asking me to do. The rose is the obvious choice. It's the flower of love, the go-to flower for pretty much any occasion. The one most women would probably select. The white one reminds me of Easter. Or maybe funerals. I'm not sure which, but I like it. It brings back memories of the field behind our house growing up. The house that is now Baylor's house. Piper, Baylor and I would run around in that field for hours playing hide-and-seek, and then we'd pick the pretty white flowers to bring to my mom.

She giggles. "Just pick one, Skylar," she says, rolling her eyes at my hesitation.

I reach for the white one. I never did like to conform.

She pulls me in for a hug. "Oh my gosh, we're having a boy!" she cries.

I let her hug me. I've gotten used to her hugs by now. Sometimes I even hug her back, because let's be honest, it's the only real human affection I've had in almost six months.

And dammit, I'm horny. The vomit phase of this pregnancy has morphed into the insatiable phase. As in, I swear blood is being pumped to my lower half, causing my clit to swell at very inopportune times. Yesterday, I actually had an orgasm riding the stationary bike. All the vibrations from pedaling... I didn't even bother to stop riding. I just reached down and pushed myself over the edge, slowing my progress momentarily as I squirmed around on the seat.

Last Sunday at brunch, when Griffin leaned over, brushing Erin's hair behind her ear to whisper something, I almost combusted at the table. I imagined what it would feel like with his hot breath flowing over my neck as he whispered into my ear. I actually had to get up from the table and go relieve myself in the public bathroom.

I've become very proficient at silent orgasms.

"A boy?" I ask, eyeing the flower in my hand.

She pulls me over to an empty table and sits me down. "It's an old wives tale," she explains. "You present a pregnant woman with a white lily and a red rose. If she chooses the rose, she's having a girl. If she chooses the lily, a boy." She gestures to the flower I'm holding. "And white lilies just happen to be my favorite flowers, so that's an added bonus."

"Hmmm," I mumble. "Kind of a girly flower for a boy, don't you think?"

"Actually, Greek mythology holds the lily as a symbol of eroticism and sexuality, the long pistil of the flower suggesting a phallus."

"So you think the bean has a long pistol, huh?" I tease.

"If genetics play a factor, a *very* long pistol."

Oh, hell. The last thing I need to know is how well-endowed Griffin is. My mouth waters as if the aroma of another cheeseburger had been floated under my nose. I can already feel the blood rushing downward.

"Uh, Erin," I say. "I really don't want to hear about your husband's phallus."

She laughs and grabs my hand, pulling me up and leading me out the door. "Okay, no more talk of Griffin's incredible man member or his expertise where it's concerned. Let's go shop."

Oh, God, she did not just say that. I swear it's like she can read my mind and is deliberately making an effort to feed my atrociously inappropriate fantasies. Maybe she's trying to torture me because she knows I lust after him. He's the proverbial forbidden fruit—with a long, talented pistol, apparently. Why is it ingrained in human nature to want what we can't have?

On the way out the door I remind myself that she's only ever been with Griffin, having no comparison on the matter. Therefore I rationalize that he may not, in fact, be the sexual expert she touts him to be.

We walk a few blocks over to an upscale maternity boutique. The whole time, while Erin is talking about how glamorous she's going to make me, I'm thinking about the fact that for several weeks she all but checked out of my life, save a few texts and an e-mail. But she seems fine now. Happy even. Carefree. Whatever it was, I guess she got over it. Maybe Griffin was right and she simply needed time to adjust to her new reality after seeing the ultrasound.

At the store, we're greeted by a sales lady who proceeds to tell us exactly what's in style. She shows me the dressing room which is outfitted with several sized 'baby bumps' that I can strap on to see what the clothing will look like as I grow bigger.

Erin picks out a crapload of outfits for me to try. She gets everything from yoga pants to cocktail dresses. I can't even imagine filling out the front panel in the designer jeans she hands me. Surely these must be for women having twins.

The one thing I notice about most of the clothing she's selecting for me is that they all show a good bit of cleavage, something I have a generous amount of for the first time in my life.

"Erin, is there some reason you think I need to flaunt my boobs to everyone?"

"Hell yes," she says. I laugh because that's as close to cursing as she gets. "You have awesome boobs now. Not to say you didn't before, but you should enjoy your voluptuous curves while you've got them. You know, show them off a little."

I roll my eyes at her. "Why would I want to do that? Men don't even look at me now. And that's fine—it was one of the points of doing this whole thing, in fact."

"Are you crazy, Skylar? You're oblivious. You turn heads all the time, everywhere you go. Including my own husband's."

I stiffen and hope to God she doesn't notice the heat dancing across my face. "I never, uh, Erin, I don't—"

"It's okay," she says, putting a reassuring hand on my arm. "You're gorgeous, Skylar. Men are going to look at you. Griffin is going to look at you. It doesn't bother me."

"You're imagining things," I say. "He doesn't look at me. Not that way. And not when he has you, I mean you are hot. Like, Sports-Illustrated-swimsuit-edition-cover hot. Plus, I think he hates me, actually. Didn't he tell you about our fight the day he set up the bike?"

She laughs. "He did. I think it's adorable how protective he is of you."

"Maybe you think it's adorable. I think it's annoying," I say. "Last week at brunch, when a guy followed me to the bathroom, Griffin jumped up from the table and made a loud comment about pregnant women having to pee all the time. The poor guy wasn't even coming on to me. He was just going to take a piss."

"You're wrong," she says. "After you left the table, we all heard the guy tell his buddies that he was going to come back with your phone number. Men do still want you, like it or not."

"Well, just wait until I'm fat. Then I won't need your cock-blocking husband." I point to my stomach. "Cock-blocking Bean will take over the job."

"Are you saying you *want* to sleep with a man?" she asks, tentatively.

"No, not really." I lower my voice and look around to make sure nobody's listening. "Except I'm really horny. As in—all the time. If there were a word for horny times ten—that would describe me."

"You know there are ways to take care of that yourself, right?" She raises an eyebrow.

"Yeah, I know. I already wore out my damn vibrator," I say, shamelessly, walking into the dressing room and drawing the curtain as her laughter follows me.

I decide to strap on the medium-sized tummy that reads 'six months.' The large, 'nine months' one is humongous. There's no way I will ever get that big. I pull one of the new dresses over my head as Erin talks to me from outside the room.

"I know I don't have the right to ask anything else of you since you are doing this one, larger-than-life favor for me already, but…"

"What is it? Just spit it out," I say through the curtain, already knowing I'll do anything she asks. Erin is one of those people you don't turn down. She gives so much of herself in everything she does. She's compassionate, friendly, and selfless. It still shocks the hell out of me that she doesn't have swarms of friends vying for her attention.

"Griffin can't cook, but I don't want to be burdened with it all the time after the baby comes," she says. "I was hoping you could maybe give him some cooking lessons, you know, being that you work in a restaurant and have access to loads of great recipes and all."

I sigh. "Not that I don't want to"—okay, I sooooo don't want to—"but, why don't you just teach him yourself? You're a good cook." It's true, she's had me over for dinner a few times.

"You know our schedules don't mesh very well. He works a lot of evenings and I know he'd never agree to it on the weekends, especially since he's a little hesitant to do it anyway."

"Hesitant? You mean, he hasn't agreed to it?" I ask, peeking out of the curtain. "And, in case you forgot what you said two seconds ago, he works nights, so he couldn't cook for you anyway."

"Oh, he's agreed to it alright." She winks at me. "I was very convincing."

The way she says it has me picturing him naked and against a wall while Erin gives him a blow job. I hide behind the curtain again, wallowing in my jealousy because she gets to see him naked.

"He's just not exactly thrilled about it," she says. "I was thinking he could help me by cooking during the day. Then I could re-heat it when I come home after work. You know, you could teach him to make casseroles and stuff."

"Not thrilled?" I ask. "About learning to cook, or *me* teaching him?"

She laughs. "Learning to cook, of course." I peek out and raise a brow at her to see if she's telling me the truth. She gives me a pleading look. "Please, Skylar. I'll pay you."

"You'll do no such thing," I say.

"Oh, then you'll do it?" Her face lights up.

Shit.

"He could come by the restaurant during your least-busy times. At say, two or three in the afternoon. Whatever works for you would be good. Or he could come to your apartment if that would be more convenient."

Double shit. "No, no, the restaurant would be fine. We'd have a lot more options there than I have at home."

She pulls me out of the dressing room and into her arms. Did I just agree to this?

"Thank you. I'll owe you big time."

I look down at the price tag on the designer dress I'm wearing. "You don't owe me anything. Buy me this dress and we'll call it even."

She pulls back and holds me at arm's length. Her eyes go straight to my belly with the artificially-augmented baby-bump. Her eyes tear up. She puts her hands on the bump as if it were really an extension of me. "God, I hope I get to feel him move."

I draw my brows at her. "Don't be ridiculous. I'm sure you'll feel it, just not for a while yet, according to that gigantic book you have me reading. But you have my permission to grope me whenever you so desire." I look around after I replay the words in my head. "That sounded wrong." I giggle, but she doesn't find it funny. I wonder if she even heard what I said.

She looks sad, eyeing my false tummy. Maybe she's wishing that Bean was growing in her instead of me.

Of course that's what she's wishing.

She takes a cleansing breath and looks me in the eye. "You are positively glowing in this dress. And your boobs look completely drool-worthy. You should wear this Monday."

"Don't you think it's still a little big for me right now?"

"Nobody will even notice the extra material at your waist. They'll all be too focused on your boobs." She reaches out to pull the dress even lower than it already dips between my more prominent breasts.

"Would you quit it," I whine. "They're spilling out enough as it is."

"I just want you to feel pretty. Desirable," she says. "Because you are. Any man would be lucky to have you. Don't ever forget that." She sighs. "So, Monday, okay?"

"Okay, okay, I'll wear the damn dress on Monday. Geez." Far be it for me to argue with a non-pregnant woman who seems more hormonal than I am. "Can I go try on the other stuff now?"

It takes a while to get through the piles of clothing she picked out for me. In the end we settle on the boob-enhancing dress along with six or seven other uber-stylish outfits.

Erin removes her wallet to pay, dropping it on the floor. She goes to pick it up and drops it again. And again. And another time after that. I finally reach down and pick it up for her.

"Sorry," she huffs in frustration. "I seem to have butterfingers today." She shrugs, getting her credit card out awkwardly with her non-dominant left hand as she fists and releases her right one over and over.

"You okay?" I ask.

"I'm fine, Skylar. My hand just fell asleep." She gives the clerk her card. "I can't wait to see you in these again. You are going to be the hottest pregnant lady in the city."

I decide not to argue the fact that me looking hot is *so* not the point of this whole surrogacy exercise. But if she wants to live vicariously through me, who am I to stop her?

chapter six

Sunday afternoon, my doorbell rings and I look through the peephole to see a man holding a basket. Another care package from Erin, I imagine.

I thank the young guy who doesn't stop grinning at me as he hands over the basket covered with dark-blue cellophane, completely hiding the contents.

I sit down on my couch and carefully remove the covering. My eyes bug out when I see what's inside. It's filled with sex toys. Vibrators of various sizes, a pocket-rocket, some egg-shaped thing, tubes of lubricant, and a few unknowns with names like 'Rampant Rabbit' and 'Vibrating Bullet,' that I'll have to read about to figure out exactly what they are. God, just looking at the stuff makes me horny.

I laugh when I remember the comment I made to Erin about breaking my vibrator. She really does like taking care of me.

Guilt washes over me. If she only knew who I'll most likely fantasize about when using these products, she not only wouldn't have sent them, she would probably cut me out of her life, only sticking around to get the bean.

Maybe I could think about the bike delivery guy. Or the guy who delivered this—he was hot, too. Oh, *duh*, no wonder he had a grin plastered on his face. I'll bet he knew exactly what was in the package.

We have a new waiter at work, Jarod. He's only nineteen. Brown hair, strong dark eyes, a body built for sex. I should dream about *him*. Hell, even Trent, one of my bartenders, could provoke a pretty decent sex fantasy.

As I try to make a list of all the men who should replace Griffin in my fantasies, my phone rings, causing me to startle and drop the G-spot wand I was holding.

"Did you get it?" Erin squeals into the phone.

My lips twitch in amusement. "If you tell anyone about this, I will kill you and hide the body."

She laughs. "Oh, good. You got it, then. I didn't want you to be so... frustrated."

"I don't even know what half this stuff is," I say. *Oh my God, does she?* "Do you?"

"Let's just say yours is not the first basket I've ordered from that particular store."

All of a sudden I'm having thoughts of the prudish schoolteacher coming home to her leather-chaps-wearing husband, who holds a whip while commanding her to perform sexual acts in front of him.

I hear a giggle. "You are totally picturing me and Griffin using that stuff, aren't you?"

"No. Absolutely not," I lie. "Oh, God, Erin. Griffin doesn't know about this, does he?"

"Why, would it embarrass you to know that Griffin might think about you using those things?"

"Erin, shut up," I say. "First off, yes, I'd be mortified. Secondly, he would never do that. I don't know why you keep saying such things. Do you get off on your husband lusting after other women?" I tease. "Oh, shit, you don't want to like, have a three-way, do you?"

"I don't know," she says. "Would you be interested if we did?"

What the hell? I was kidding. She knows that, right?

It's always the most innocent looking people who turn out to be the most perverted. Still, there is no way I've known Erin for over five months without becoming privy to this information.

"I'm kidding, Skylar." She's laughing. Hard. "Oh, how I wish I could see your face right now," she says. "Listen, I'll let you go. I know you have a busy day ahead. Or at least you do now." She giggles. "But, hey, don't forget to wear the dress tomorrow."

"What is it with you and that dress?" I ask.

"I just think you look really pretty in it, Skylar. Pregnant women need to feel pretty, too, you know?"

"Yes, Mom, I'll wear the dress," I say rolling my eyes.

We say our goodbyes and I'm left thinking about how much she's changed over the past few weeks. She's different. She's more open. Forward. Demanding. I've even heard her cuss a few times, something I thought she wasn't even capable of. Whenever we get together, she wants to try new things. Last week, Griffin was working and she invited me to go on a carriage ride through Central Park. She said she had never done it before and wanted to treat me to the experience. Then she wanted to try sushi, something neither of us had ever tried, but that I got out of on account of being pregnant, and thus not allowed to eat raw fish. I figure she's either getting more comfortable in our friendship or she's wanting to cross a few things off her pre-baby bucket list.

Mindy walks out of her bedroom. She stares down at the contents of my gift basket, her eyes going wide as she takes it all in. We spend the next hour giggling while we read through the instructions of some of the more complicated battery-operated products.

Mindy leaves for work a few hours later. "Girlfriend, I don't even have to ask what you plan on doing tonight." She winks. "Just try not to wake the neighbors."

I put the basket in my room and try to forget about it. I catch up on some episodes of 'Top Chef'. I clean the kitchen. I ride part of the Appalachian Trail on my new bike. I do everything I can think of to keep my mind off the toys that keep beckoning me.

I call Baylor.

"What's up, little sister? Miss me already?" she asks, having just seen me this morning at Sunday brunch.

"Uh, so does pregnancy make everyone completely horny, or is it just me?"

"Don't get me started." She laughs. "Gavin actually said he thought I was going to break his penis a few months ago. I'm thirty-five weeks along with a ginormous belly and still, all I can think about is sex."

"Ugh!" I sigh. "So, it doesn't get any better?"

"It's different for everyone," she says. "Some of the women in my Lamaze class claim they don't even want to be touched anymore. Some of them never went through the horny phase at all. Consider yourself lucky, Skylar."

"Lucky?" I spit out. "Baylor, I'm trying to stay away from sex, not think about it more. And I'm having very inappropriate thoughts about very inappropriate people."

"You're not masturbating to Gavin, are you?" She giggles. "Although I suppose it would be a nice compliment."

"God, no! Of course not." The thought of me getting off to her husband makes me vomit a little in my mouth.

"Well, then who is it?" she asks. "Wait. Let me guess. Trent, the bartender."

"I wish," I say.

"John, the liquor distributor."

I didn't think about him. I add him to the list. "God, that tight shirt he always wears," I say, trying, but failing, to get myself hot and bothered over him. "But, no. It's nobody, really. Forget it."

"Hmmm," she mumbles in thought. "Griffin's pretty hot."

I try not to blow out my deep sigh into the phone.

"Oh my God, it's Griffin, isn't it?" she shrieks. "You're fantasizing about the baby daddy, aren't you?"

"Ugh! I have to go."

"Skylar," she says, stopping me from hanging up. "It's okay, you know. It's okay to fantasize about him, or anyone, as long as you don't act on it."

"I would never—"

"I know you wouldn't," she says. "And that's why it's okay."

I hang up the phone and go to bed, never having played with any of my new toys. And even though Baylor thinks it's okay, I try my damnedest not to think about Griffin Pearce.

The doorbell rings. Once. Twice. On the third ring, realizing Mindy isn't going to answer it, I crawl out of bed half asleep and stumble my way across my dark apartment to open the door. I'm too tired to bother looking through the peephole. I open it.

"Did you get the basket?"

My eyes snap up to see those familiar slate-gray eyes that are even darker than I remember. Except now they are lidded with desire.

"She told you?" Embarrassment causes even my fingers to pink up. How is it that this man can get me to blush? After twenty-four years, I thought it wasn't possible. And it isn't. Except with him.

Cold air creeps in through the open door. It makes me realize I'm only wearing my sleep shirt that barely covers my ass cheeks. Griffin notices, too.

His unblinking gaze rakes over my bare legs. I can feel his eyes on my flesh as they wash over me, prickling my skin with heat everywhere he looks. He caresses me with his stare and I'm just sleepy enough to let him. His eyes grow wide when they fall on my chest, my nipples pebbling under the thin material of my shirt.

His reaction, however wrong, makes me hot. My libido—that is set to a constant simmer these days—is instantly taken up to a full-on boil simply by the heat of his stare.

"She didn't tell me anything," he says, his voice dripping with lust and need. "I'm the one who sent it."

I shake my head in confusion. "You?" *Was I dreaming earlier when Erin called me?*

"Yes, me." He comes through the front door, uninvited, and closes it behind him. "I've seen the way you look at me. I've seen the fire in you. I know you're horny. I don't want you with other men. I got you these things so you don't need anyone else."

"Then why are you here?" I ask.

"Because." He grabs my hand, pulling me across the room. "They would deliver it, but they wouldn't set them up." He gently pushes me down on the couch. "I'm here to help you with that."

"Uh…" My mind races. *Is this some kind of joke?* I reach for the blanket to cover myself up, but he grabs it.

"No." He throws it on the floor behind him. "I'm not here to watch you cover up, Sky. It's quite the opposite."

He walks into my bedroom, leaving me in a pool of unanswered questions on the couch. He called me Sky. He's here to help me with the sex toys. I'm trying to wrap my brain around it when he comes back in the room with the basket.

Shirtless.

Oh, God.

He kneels before me, putting the basket beside him. "We'll get to those later. The first one is all mine."

Before I can ask him what first one, he parts my legs and stares at my crotch. He smiles a half smile. A crooked, sexy smile that has my brain shutting down and ignoring all the reasons flying through my head that assure me how wrong this is.

Maybe this was part of the package, I surmise. Maybe Erin sent him to me. She said he looks at me. She said he would think about me using the things in the basket. Wait, no, she didn't send them—*he did.*

Desire blurs my vision as well as my judgment. I can do this. We can do this and not ruin everything. It's just one time. One little act. It doesn't have to mean anything.

My body trembles and I look down to see Griffin touching me there, through my wet panties.

He holds up the lubricant with his other hand. "We won't be needing this," he says. "You're so wet, Sky. You want this."

"No. We can't." My weak words are a direct contradiction of what my body is telling him.

"She wants this, baby. It's okay," he says, moving my soaked panties aside, slipping a long finger inside of me.

She wants this. Who, Erin? Maybe they're not who I thought they were, after all. Maybe they want to pull me into some sort of polygamous relationship.

Griffin adds another finger, crooking them up to find the precise spot that has me throwing my head back, not caring who is doing what to me as long as it results in me coming all over, satiating this carnal need building inside me.

"That's it, Sky, ride my fingers. Just like that." He lowers his head, showing me what he intends to do. "I'm going to taste you now. I'm going to make you come over and over. First with my tongue and then with every single thing in the basket."

Before I can protest, his tongue laves me. *Oh. My. God.* He's only been at this for thirty seconds and all I can think of is that Erin was right. He's got fucking talent.

My thighs tighten. Heat burns through my belly. A wave comes crashing over me. I buck my groin into him, pushing his fingers deeper, drawing out every last quiver of my orgasm.

"Griffin . . . Oh, God. Yes!" I cry out. My eyes fly open and even before the spasms die down, guilt washes over me. I look down at Griffin only to find him gone, replaced by my own fingers that are still caressing my center, heavily coated with my juices.

I quickly look around to see I'm in my bed. And I'm completely alone. My head falls back against my pillow.

Thank God!

A dream. That's all it was. Another fantasy about the man who is forbidden.

An unexpected sob causes tears to spill over the rims of my eyelids, the salty liquid rolling down the sides of my head and into my hair. I'm just not sure if they are guilty tears, or if I'm mourning the loss of a man I can never have.

chapter seven

Erin has incredible fashion sense. I have to admit, the dress looks damn good on me. Even the extra material at the waist looks intentional. My newfound cleavage is the clear purpose of this dress, and like Erin said, why not flaunt it while I've got it.

I do feel pretty, which is welcome considering yesterday— only one day after I was proud that all my jeans still fit—I had trouble buttoning up my favorite pair.

I decide to put my hair in a French twist and add a little more mascara than I usually do. I even have the perfect green wedges to pair with the dress. The whole look has me feeling new and fresh. I'll have to remember to thank Erin again later.

Walking to work, I make a point to notice some heads turning. It makes me feel good even though I won't do anything about it. The new Skylar doesn't do hookups.

I smile to myself when Trent gives me a low whistle as I pass by the bar on the way to the back.

"Whoa!" Mindy stops in her tracks to stare at my boobs. "Where did those babies come from? You look incredible, Skylar. What's the occasion?"

"No occasion," I say. "It's something Erin bought me and she said I should wear it. That's all."

"Can you ask her to outfit me, too?" she jokes. "Because you could seriously get any man you wanted wearing that number."

I roll my eyes at her exaggeration while I inventory the morning deliveries.

"Hey, speaking of Erin," Mindy says, "she called earlier to set up a cooking lesson for Griffin."

I stiffen. I can't look at Mindy. If I do, she'll see my flushed face. The last person I need to think about right now is Griffin Pearce.

I nonchalantly ask, "And?"

"And she asked if you were busy today at three. I checked your schedule and you're free," she says. "So Griffin is coming then." I can feel her eyes bore into the back of my head.

"Today?" I chide myself for speaking two octaves above my normal range. I look at my watch and then up at Mindy. "As in, he's coming in a few hours?"

"Yeah. Why, is that a problem?" A smile creeps up her face, turning into a full-on smirk.

"Problem? Uh, no. But—"

"But what?" She raises a devious brow. "But you were screaming his name in bed last night. Is *that* the problem?"

I'm certain the blood drains from my face.

Thankfully, Jarod, our new waiter, comes in the back to tell Mindy she has a new table. She winks at me and heads out front.

I spend the next few hours thinking of an excuse to call and cancel. I have Griffin's number programmed into my phone for baby emergencies. I could simply text him and tell him we got slammed here, or that a waiter called in sick and I need to cover. Anything to move his lesson to some other day. *Any* other day where I hadn't just orgasmed from dreaming of him.

I vow to send a text when I'm done talking to Trent. Well, I'm talking to Trent—Trent is talking to my boobs. After he tells me what to put on today's liquor order, he nods to a nearby table. "You expecting someone, boss?"

Even before I turn around, I know he's here. There is a crackle in the air. It causes the fine hairs on my neck to stand at attention. The oxygen exits my body and my heart rate goes up.

I turn around to see Griffin sitting at the same high-top where he sat the day we met. And like that day, and every day I've seen him since, he sports the same dark-as-night stubble on his face. A manly sprinkling of coarse hair along his jaw that has me wondering if he ever uses a razor.

I can barely look at him, let alone into his eyes. The man gave me an earth-shattering orgasm last night. Hell, I practically needed a cigarette afterward. I can't ever remember coming that hard before. I'm sure I'm three shades of red when I finally convince my feet to walk the ten steps over to his table.

"I know I'm early," he says. "But I just finished a job nearby. I can wait here until you're ready."

I look out into the main room. There are still quite a few tables occupied. I try to think of a way to get out of this. I could go tell Mindy to fake being sick. But then I'd have a lot of explaining to do later at home. Plus, this seems to be important to Erin so I'll have to do it sooner or later. I might as well start now.

"Trent can get you a drink," I say. "Before we get started, I'll have to make sure most of the orders are ready and we've finished prepping our catering bids for the day." I turn to Trent. "Get him a drink on me. I'll be back in a few."

I go to the kitchen to see it winding down after the lunch rush. How am I going to get through this? I go in my office and, on my laptop, I pull up a few simple recipes I can teach him. I settle on lasagna. I print it out and quickly use the bathroom.

Looking in the mirror, I'm reminded of what I'm wearing. Of what Erin insisted I wear today. Today—the day she sends her husband in for a cooking lesson. Sometimes I wonder if she's got her head screwed on right. Is she testing him? Me? I take a few deep breaths. I can do this. I simply need to focus on the cooking. As long as I don't look at him, it'll be fine.

I grab a few things on my way back to the bar. I put them down on Griffin's table. "First things first," I say. "You can choose between a hat and a hair net." He picks the Mitchell's ball cap I offered. "And you need to wear a chef's coat or an apron." He chooses the 'Eat at Mitchell's' apron.

He follows me back to the kitchen. "How does this thing go on?" he asks, fumbling with the long straps of the apron.

I laugh when I look at him. The man has no idea how to put on an apron. I take it from him. I lean in and slip it over his head. When I do, I realize my mistake. Getting this close to him—smelling him—is not a good idea. It's causing some kind of visceral reaction in my body that I don't seem to have any control over. I reach around his back, crossing the straps, bringing them around to his front. Our faces come close. Too close. I realize I'm practically hugging the man and when I unwittingly look into his steely eyes, my stomach flutters. I momentarily wonder if it's the baby moving, but I remember Erin telling me it would probably be another month before I could feel that.

Griffin is keeping a respectable distance, with his arms held out to the side, giving me room to work. I try not to think about the fact that he is draped in Mitchell. He looks damn good with my name all over him. I close my eyes while I finish tying the apron.

"Are you okay?" he asks. "You're not still sick are you?"

I shake my head. "No. Not for a few weeks now." I take a few steps away from him, over to where I keep my own cooking uniform. My body relaxes a little at the distance between us. I put my apron and hat on, take another deep breath and turn back around.

Now it's his turn to laugh. He's looking at the apron I'm wearing. I wear it so often, I sometimes forget what it says. It has a picture of a cartoon pig and says 'Every Butt Loves a Rub.' I look down at it and feel the heat coming up my face.

Then he eyes my ball cap. "Yankees, huh?"

"Well, I did grow up thirty minutes from here. Plus, my friend, Jenna, is engaged to their batting coach, Jake Hanson."

"I'll let it slide, since I know you have to wear a hat in the kitchen," he says, mocking irritation. "But I'll have you know, if I see you wearing that on the street, all bets are off."

"Not a fan?" I ask.

"I grew up in Ohio," he says. "Indians all the way."

I feel a twinge inside my heart. I wonder if he's as big a baseball fan as I am. Growing up, my dad would take me and my sisters to Yankees games one at a time. It was his way of bonding with us individually. Some of my fondest childhood memories are from those games. It makes me smile thinking that maybe Griffin will do something like that with his kid.

"You know, Jake could probably get you some good seats when they play here, if you want me to ask."

His face lights up. "Really? That would be fantastic." He eyes me skeptically. "Wait, he wouldn't make me wear Yankees crap, would he?"

Laughing, I say, "Well, if Jenna comes, she'll probably spit on you if you aren't."

He contemplates this. "I don't think I could, in good conscience, wear anything but Indians garb."

I nod, understanding loyalty to sports teams. "I could try to get you tickets to a game when Jenna is working."

"Aww, that'd be great!"

The sincere smile on his face makes the skin of his eyes crinkle. He looks almost childlike and for a brief second I wonder if the kid I'm carrying will look like him.

I nod towards the kitchen door. "You ready to get started?" I ask.

"Yeah," he says. "Hey, thanks for doing this. I know Erin strong-armed us both into it."

"It's not a problem," I tell him. "Besides, have you *met* your wife? She's kind of hard to say no to."

He laughs. "You have no idea," he says, shaking his head.

We spend the next half hour gathering supplies, boiling homemade lasagna noodles, browning Italian sausage and hamburger, and putting ingredients into a pot of sauce.

"So, what kind of job did you have earlier?" I ask.

He stirs the sauce exactly like I showed him. "It was for Vogue. Their regular photographer got held up in L.A., so they called me in. I've done stuff for them before."

"Vogue, really?" I try not to sound too impressed, but I totally am. "What did you shoot?"

"It was a Valentine's Day spread," he tells me.

"Isn't it kind of early for that, like six months early?"

"That's how far out they shoot them," he says.

"It must be pretty great for a guy like you to be surrounded by hot models all the time," I say.

"Nah, not really," he says, shrugging it off. "Most of them get Photoshopped anyway. They've got nothing on Erin and you."

I give him my 'have you grown a third arm?' look.

"What?" he says. "It's true. You and Erin could both be models."

"Erin could be a model," I say. "She's gorgeous."

"Don't sell yourself short, Skylar," he says. "You're very beautiful, too. You are much more natural than the models I shoot. They're all anorexic. You are real. And that dress you have on today, it really brings out the green in your eyes. You really look great."

I smirk when he quickly averts his eyes from the cleavage that still shows above my apron. I grab a disposable tasting spoon and reach into the pan to take another bite of sausage.

Griffin eyes me. "You're going to get fat eating that much meat," he jokes. "Isn't that like your millionth taste?"

My jaw drops. "I know you didn't just call out a pregnant woman for eating," I scold him.

"I was teasing," he says, rolling his eyes.

"Do you not read any of the books Erin buys for you?" I spit at him. "I mean, it's Pregnancy 101: don't call a pregnant woman fat."

"I wasn't calling you fat," he says, shaking his head. "I said you would *get* fat if you kept eating. There's a difference. I wasn't sure you were aware of the fact that you'd eaten half the sausage."

"Ugh!" I pout, stomping my foot. He just did it again. "It doesn't matter that you didn't actually say those exact words," I say. "It still makes me feel self-conscious. I mean, imagine you were going to get fatter than you've ever been, but you couldn't do anything to stop it. And then someone points out how much you eat."

He holds up his hands in surrender. "I'm sorry," he says. "It won't happen again. For Christ's sake, Sky, you're thin and healthy. I don't know why you're making such a big deal out of it."

I throw the spoon into the trash with so much force that it bounces back out. "Skylar," I say. "My name is Skylar. Not Sky."

"Geez, *Skylar*," he says, putting emphasis on my name. He walks over and picks the spoon up off the floor, depositing it back into the trash. "Those pregnancy hormones are really doing a number on you."

My lips come together, forming a thin line as my eyes spit fire. What a jackass. I can't believe *this* man made me come in my dreams. "Are you fucking kidding me?" I ask.

"Don't say fuck," he says.

"I'll say fuck if I want to say fuck," I bellow out, causing my kitchen staff to stop and watch our exchange. "First you tell me how hot I am, even though you're married—to my best friend, I might add. Then you say I'm fat, and now I'm hormonal? Griffin, you're batting a fucking thousand today."

He comes close and whispers through gritted teeth into my ear. "Will. You. Please. Stop. Saying. Fuck?" Each word a staccato that has his hot breath flowing over my neck. I almost have to leave the kitchen. Pissed off Griffin is even hotter than regular Griffin.

He pulls away and tries to speak so only I can hear. "Listen, Skylar," he says quietly, holding me in place with his stare. "First of all, Erin told me to compliment you. She said pregnant women feel ugly and I should tell you that you're pretty. I'm trying to make her happy. I'm trying to make *you* happy. Hell, she's as hormonal as you are. She cries at the drop of a hat these days. *You* should feel sorry for *me*. I have two women to handle."

"Handle?" I ask. "This is you handling me? And Erin told you to say that shit?"

"No, that's not what I meant." He throws up his hands in defeat. "Cut me some slack here. I've never done this before. Yes, Erin told me to compliment you, but I meant every word. You *are* beautiful. And I should be able to say that without you thinking I want to have sex with you, Skylar. Not every man wants to bed a gorgeous woman, you know."

Gorgeous. He thinks I'm gorgeous? Or did Erin tell him to say that, too? "Listen, can we just get through this lesson?" I ask. I can't decide if I'm more pissed that Erin told him to compliment me or that he doesn't really see me that way.

He nods. "Yeah."

We only talk food for the next hour while we layer and then bake the lasagna. While it's cooking, I show him how to make garlic bread and throw together a simple salad. When we're wrapping it all up for him to take home, I tell him, "You should take Erin some flowers along with dinner."

He silently nods. I wonder if he's scared that I might bite his head off again. I make a mental note to ask Mindy if pregnancy has turned me into a bitch, or if Griffin Pearce has.

"White lilies," I say. "They're her favorite."

"I know what my wife's favorite flower is, Skylar," he says petulantly.

I ignore his sour mood. "You know she thinks the bean is a boy, right?" I ask.

A small smile flashes across his face and I wonder if he secretly wants it to be a boy. "Yeah, she told me about the flower thing," he says. "What do *you* think?"

I shrug my shoulders. "I think I just prefer white flowers to red roses."

I see another hesitant smile creep up his face at my comment. I gather that, like me, he's not into the whole 'fate' thing like Erin is.

"I've heard some pregnant women get a feeling," he says. "You don't have that?"

I shake my head. "This is your kid, Griffin. I try not to think too much about that kind of stuff."

"Oh, right," he says with a guilty look. "I guess that makes sense. Sorry."

I pack his food in a catering cooler. "You can bring the cooler back when you come for your next lesson."

"So, you'll still teach me?" he asks. "Even though I was an ass today?"

I laugh. "Yes. Even asses need to know how to cook."

We walk out of the kitchen and he hands me the cap and apron. "Thanks, Skylar." He extends his hand to me and I shake it. Charges of electricity run through my body, and I realize I haven't had this feeling since the last time he put his hand on me at the ultrasound more than a month ago.

I walk away disappointed in myself that I'm keeping track of his touches.

chapter eight

Erin is giving Mindy and Jenna a tour of her house. My very pregnant sister and I have already seen it, so we stay in the kitchen making drinks for girls' night.

The house is quite impressive. Erin's fashion sense obviously spills over to home decoration. The brownstone she and Griffin live in is only nine subway stops or a six-dollar cab ride from my apartment. They managed to get their hands on one of the rare properties in the city that has an actual backyard. They are lucky. It's perfect for kids.

I couldn't imagine growing up without a place to run and play. Our house in Maple Creek wasn't flashy and modern like a lot of New York City residences. But it was a place you could feel comfortable putting your feet on the coffee table or leaving a bottle of water on the counter. And the acres of fields surrounding our property made for endless hours of playing tag and hide-and-seek.

Somehow, Erin has accomplished both. Her house is flashy. It's modern-contemporary with all the latest technology. Yet, it feels content and homey. It's a place where I can see kids running around the maze of rooms that span four floors.

Their great room has a paneled wall of glass that slides open, disappearing almost completely into a wall, creating one massive indoor/outdoor space that extends to a large tiled patio complete with a kitchen and hot tub. From where we sit at the gigantic kitchen island, we have a clear view through the open floorplan all the way to the backyard. I wonder how long it will be before Griffin adds a play set. Or maybe a tire swing dangling from the sole oak tree.

Hanging over the kitchen island is a stainless steel chef's rack adorned with what I know is thousands of dollars of high-end pots and pans. It's any cook's dream kitchen. I laugh to myself thinking how Griffin doesn't even know his way around a stove. No wonder Erin wants him to learn to cook. It would be a shame if she were the only one to make use of all this great stuff.

The three of them come back to join us. Mindy and Jenna are raving about Erin's exquisite taste as I set up my laptop so Piper can join us via Skype.

Baylor pours daiquiris for everyone, making the two of ours virgins. On the black marbled granite of the kitchen island, Erin sets out the trays of hors d'oeuvres we all contributed.

"Where's the hot husband?" Mindy asks Erin.

I smile, glad at the fact I'm not the only woman affected by his gorgeous looks.

"Out with *my* hot husband," Baylor says. "Gavin, Griffin and Griffin's friend, Mason, went out to a club."

I realize in this moment just how well Erin and Griffin have fit into my circle of friends. I wonder if they know that once you're in, you're in for life. That means I'm sentenced to a life of lusting after my best friend's husband.

My brother-in-law, Gavin, has lots of connections being he's in the film production business. He got them a VIP invite to the exclusive pre-opening of a new club in SoHo.

"Too bad Jake couldn't join them," I say to Jenna. "But then, I'm sure Jake gets plenty of his own VIP invites coaching with the Yankees and all."

Jenna nods and in mock pretention, says, "Yes, darling, but it does get rather tiring hobnobbing with the rich and famous all the time."

We laugh. Jenna can't pull off being a snob, even though, as a literary agent, she works with plenty of them.

"Jenna, that reminds me," Erin says, "do you think you could get us a few tickets for an Indians game next week? Griffin has been talking about it non-stop ever since Skylar mentioned it to him. He's such a baseball junkie."

"Sure, what day?" Jenna asks. "They play Tuesday through Thursday."

"The only day I can get a sub is Wednesday," Erin says. "Would that be okay?"

"Yeah, of course," Jenna says. "I won't be able to go with you, though. I'm always booked with meetings on Wednesdays. How many do you want?"

Erin winks at me. She knew Jenna couldn't go on Wednesday. She wants Griffin to be able to root freely for his home team. She asks me, "You'll go with us, right? I don't really get baseball and Griffin needs someone there who understands what's going on."

"I'm a Yankees fan, Erin," I remind her.

"Eh, baseball is baseball," she says.

Jenna and I share a look. We giggle at Erin's naiveté about team loyalty. Erin is beautiful. She's smart. She has a lot of hidden talents. But sports to Erin is like rocket science to a goldfish.

Jenna says, "Oh, that should be fun. I'm sorry I'll miss it." She knows what a die-hard fan I am, so I'm sure she thinks it will be amusing watching me sit next to the enemy.

"Fine." I roll my eyes. "Get three tickets."

Erin claps her hands like a giddy schoolgirl. "Griffin will be ecstatic!"

I hear, "Hey girls," in a familiar voice. I turn my attention to the laptop screen to see Piper smiling, holding her own daiquiri. Baylor introduces Piper to Erin.

Erin looks from Piper to Baylor to me. "Wow," she says. "Piper, you look exactly like Baylor except you have Skylar's green eyes."

"You don't say," Piper says, sarcastically.

The three of us laugh and roll our eyes. People say that about us all the time. Piper is twenty-one, three years younger than me and five years younger than Baylor. We were all very close growing up. The only time we weren't together back then was when Baylor went to UNC for a year and when Piper spent a semester abroad her junior year of high school. Piper liked traveling so much that after she graduated, she decided to make it a lifestyle. Every once in a while she'll come home, but we see a lot more of her on a computer screen than we do in person.

"When can we expect you to grace us with your bodily presence, little sister?" I ask. "We haven't seen you since Baylor's wedding."

"Yeah, if you only come back for your sisters' weddings, we'll probably never see you again," Mindy teases. She points to me. "It'd take a miracle to get this one married off."

Piper laughs. "If you work that miracle and get my big sister to take the plunge, not only will I show up, I'll plan the whole damn thing." They all share a laugh when she mumbles something about pigs flying.

"Can we move on to more realistic topics?" I ask the group.

Obliging my request, Mindy raises an eyebrow at Erin. "So, Griffin's friend, Mason. Is that the same Mason you told us about before?"

Erin nods, smiling.

Mindy's lips curve up in a devious smile. "As in, Mason Lawrence, the young smoking-hot backup quarterback for the New York Giants? He's out with your husband. Right now?" She sighs and I can just picture the fantasy going on in her head.

Erin must notice the same thing as she quickly says, "He doesn't do hookups. Not since one led to him becoming a dad."

Mindy gives her a deflated look and announces to all of us, "A film producer, a photographer and a professional quarterback. Holy shit—I almost feel sorry for all the women who'll get shot down tonight."

I giggle thinking about it. Even though I haven't met Mason yet, I've seen pictures. And, of course, I've seen him play a few times. Mindy's right. Not only do their jobs ooze sex appeal, but they've got the looks to match. It's a deadly combination, the three of them together.

Erin refills everyone's glasses. The four who aren't drinking virgin daiquiris get more interesting as the night goes on. It's staggering the insight you get being one of the only sober girls at girls' night.

Jenna gets funnier the more she drinks. She tells us some of the horrible manuscripts that get submitted to her from writers looking for an agent. "One lady actually thought a book about a woman who falls in love with her cat would make her a million dollars." She quotes some excerpts that have even the sober among us rolling on the floor.

Piper's eyes get droopy the more she drinks. She looks like her head might fall down right onto her keyboard. Of course, that might simply be the six-hour time difference and not the alcohol. It's 3:00 a.m. where she is.

She slurs her words telling us how close she came to touching the Dalai Lama on her stint in Tibet. Her friend, Charlie, who has been traveling with her from the start, broke her leg, postponing their planned climb up one of the smaller Alps in Austria. And their latest adventure to help free some animals from a testing facility in Germany almost landed them in jail. Conspicuously absent from her adventure tales is any mention of men. I briefly wonder, not for the first time, if she isn't into them. Maybe there's more going on with Charlie than meets the eye.

Mindy gets horny when she drinks. She's busy texting some of her past conquests to see who she can meet up with later on. I think she's silently sulking over the fact that Erin won't facilitate a hookup with the hot quarterback.

Erin is about as drunk as I've ever seen her. And dammit, all she wants to do is talk about her husband.

"Griffin is a remarkably considerate lover," she throws out randomly, stopping all other conversations.

All eyes turn to Erin with raised brows. All except mine, that is. I wish my ears had ear lids that I could close and block out any Griffin stories that could have the potential of reappearing in my future fantasies.

"Did I ever tell you about the night he took my virginity?" she asks.

Mindy raises her drink. "Awesome!" she slurs. "Virginity-losing stories are the best. Let's hear 'em."

Jenna and Baylor smile and nod, concurring with Mindy. Piper looks as if she swallowed a bitter pill. She claims she's tired and signs off.

"Buzzkill," Mindy says to the now blank laptop screen. Then she turns to Erin. "Okay, spill."

Erin gets comfortable in her seat, holding out her half-full glass to Mindy for a top-off. "I was nineteen," she says. "My hair had grown in a few inches after chemo was done, making me look like a young Jamie Lee Curtis. Of course, I'd had my... my hys... uh, my..." —she shakes her head— "my surgery, several months prior." We all nod our heads in empathy. "Griffin went through chemo with me. We had been together almost a year. He was nineteen, too. A nineteen-year-old man who was a virgin. I still can't believe someone as hot as my husband wasn't sexually active before me. Especially considering how sexually talented—"

"Together almost a year, so then what?" I interrupt her rudely, earning me a hard stare along with a kick in the shin from Baylor.

"Oh, sorry," Erin says. "I was kind of getting off track."

"What?" a drunk Mindy squeals. "I *love* off track. Get off track!"

Thankfully, Erin leaves out tales of Griffin's sexual awesomeness and sticks to the basics. "Well, we had just gone away to college. Our dorm rooms were in the same building, so he would sometimes sneak onto my floor even though guys weren't allowed after midnight. Some nights when my roommate was gone, he would stay in my room all night and hold me. We would cuddle in my small twin bed." She laughs, her face looking all dreamy and nostalgic. "It wasn't easy. You know how big he is. Even back then, he was six-foot-three and built like a quarterback.

"I knew he was afraid to hurt me after all the chemo, radiation and surgery. But we were young. And we were horny. So one night,

I finally convinced him I would be fine. I joked about the fact that he didn't even have to use a... um... use a..."

"Condom?" Jenna asks.

Erin closes her eyes for a beat as she lets out a troubled sigh. "Yeah, a condom."

I snicker at Erin. She keeps stumbling over her words. I wonder if that's how I would get when I used to drink a lot.

Erin continues, regaling us with a romantic encounter that would rival even Baylor's story. When she's done, we all stare at her. Even *I* sigh, and I usually despise that sappy shit.

"Who's next?" Erin asks.

"Well, mine's no secret," Baylor says. "You've all read the story about Gavin and me."

"You know," Mindy says to Baylor, "we'll never be able to look Gavin in the eyes again now that we know he was the guy that did all those deliciously nasty things in your latest book."

"Yeah... just, eww," I add, not needing to be reminded of the visual of my brother-in-law bedding my sister in the many explicit sex scenes she wrote.

See—now why can't I simply look at Griffin that way? As a brother-in-law. Gavin is hot, too. Male-model hot. But he's never once been the object of my fantasies. That would be wrong on so many levels. If I could only get my mind to view Erin's husband the same way.

Mindy tells us about her high school boyfriend and the awkward deflowering in the back seat of his mom's car. Jenna's was equally awkward, but with her brother's best friend.

All eyes turn to me. I'm pretty sure I've told the story before, haven't I? It's no big secret. It's just not anything special. It wasn't with the love of my life like Baylor and Erin. It wasn't even an awkward moment with a boyfriend. It was with a complete stranger.

"My story sucks," I tell them. "I was at some underground club. A rave. It was in the city. My friends and I danced with these guys who had fantastic moves. It was like they were fucking us right there on the dance floor." I wince. "Sorry," I say to Erin.

"Don't fucking worry about it," she deadpans.

Every jaw at the table drops. I don't think any of the others have ever heard Erin cuss before. Apparently alcohol makes her talk about Griffin *and* cuss.

"You'd better not let Griffin hear you say that," I remind her. "He hates it when women curse."

She narrows her eyes at me, forming a wrinkle in her smooth brow. "Huh… it never bothered him before. Girls curse in front of him all the time."

Man, I really must rub that man the wrong way. Of course, maybe that isn't such a bad thing after all.

After the giggles die down and the drinks have been refilled, I continue. "So anyway, I was young. I was drunk. So me and this guy went and found a closet or something and we just did it."

Baylor shakes her head in sadness. She's heard the story before. As a romance writer, I know she wanted more for me than a quickie with a stranger.

Jenna says abhorrently, "You lost your virginity in a dirty closet at a rave?"

"It's no big deal. It's just not very noteworthy," I say. "And I didn't say the closet was dirty. But I don't really know because it was pitch black."

"What was his name?" Jenna asks.

I shrug.

God, I was such a tramp. Who doesn't know the name of the guy who took their virginity? I put a hand on my barely-there belly, glad once again to have a reason to change my ways.

Baylor puts a gentle hand on my arm and we lock eyes. She feels guilty, like she broke me somehow. As if my inability to get close to a man is her fault. It's true, it was shortly after she came home from college, dumped and devastated, when I made the stupid decision to sleep with what's-his-name in a closet so tiny we didn't even have room to remove our clothes. And I suppose it doesn't take a shrink to tell me that watching my big sister get destroyed by the love of her life somehow wrecked me. But it's most definitely not her fault. Hell, it's not even Gavin's fault. It just happened. Shit happens. Not everyone gets a happily-ever-after like Baylor's novels. Not everyone is meant to find their one true love. Not everyone is destined to be happy.

Erin looks at me with sad eyes. "You need someone like my Griffin," she says. "He's very easy to love. And so darn sexy, too."

I roll my eyes at the millionth reminder of how great her husband is.

Baylor winces and her hand goes to her large belly. "Ouch! This little one can really kick."

Erin's eyes grow large. "Baylor, could I... would you mind if I..."

Before she can finish, Baylor grabs Erin's hand and places it on her stomach. Erin stares at it like it's the Holy Grail. I know the second she feels the baby move because her eyes instantly tear up and spill over.

"Oh my God, Baylor," she says. She stares at Baylor's pregnant belly in disbelief, muttering, "Oh my God," over and over.

Then she cries. I mean—she ugly cries. She sobs unabashedly while keeping her hands firmly glued to Baylor's stomach.

Finally, she pulls back, mascara smeared down her face. Her eyes are glazed over in an alcohol stupor. She speaks incoherently as her sobs wane. She hiccups, "I'm gonna miss this."

I put my hand on hers. "Erin, having a baby doesn't mean you will have to miss anything. We'll still get to do stuff all the time. You and Baylor can even bring the babies to girls' night if you want. Don't worry. You're going to be a great mother."

She nods, wiping her tears. She stands, picking up one of the empty food trays to carry over to the sink. We all jump off our seats when we hear it crash to the ground.

I run over, not wanting her to cut her hand in a drunken attempt to clean up the shards of glass scattered about the kitchen floor. "Erin, I've got this. You go lay down. It's getting late anyway and we should be going."

Baylor walks Erin upstairs to her bedroom as I sweep up the floor. She comes down a minute later saying she'll escort Mindy and Jenna home safely, but that maybe I should hang around to make sure Erin doesn't puke. We say our goodbyes and I head up to the bedroom.

Erin's bedroom is a contradiction of sights and smells. I'm instantly hit with Erin's flowery perfume when I step through the door. I walk over to their large four-poster bed that is draped with white linens, making me feel like I'm approaching Sleeping Beauty.

When I sit beside her on the bed, I'm overcome by Griffin's rugged scent. I silently wonder if the side of the bed I'm sitting on is the side where he sleeps. Then as if drawn there by instinct, my hand wanders to his pillow, stroking the soft linens that are fortunate enough to reside beneath his gorgeous head of hair night after night.

I look at the nightstand to find it messy with a John Grisham novel, a cell phone charger, some loose change, and a picture of Erin when she was much younger and mostly devoid of hair. I guiltily cease my intrusive caress of his pillow. I have to hand it to him; he's got the romance thing down pat. He keeps a picture of his mostly-bald wife by his bed to remind her that he thinks she's beautiful no matter how she looks.

I've been jealous of women plenty of times. Jealous of their looks. Jealous of their jet-setting lives. Jealous of their clothing. But for the first time in my life, I'm jealous of a woman because of the relationship she has with a man. Then I wince, as part of me wonders if it's solely because of the man himself.

Erin moans, turning over to place a hand on me. "I love you, Skylar," she mumbles. "Promise me. Promise me you'll take care of them."

I run my hand down her arm to comfort her. "Of course," I say. "Don't worry about Jenna and Mindy, Baylor is making sure they get home safely. We've got this."

chapter nine

Sitting on the bench outside Yankee Stadium waiting for Erin and Griffin, I try not to think about how I finally broke down and opened 'the basket' Saturday night after Erin's get-together.

I stayed with her until Griffin came home that night. Drunk. Disheveled. More gorgeous than I'd ever seen him. Drunk Griffin was even hotter than pissed off Griffin. I gave him a brief synopsis of our evening, not wanting to be in his torturous presence a minute longer than necessary.

He thanked me for taking care of Erin, kissing me on the cheek when I left. It was an innocent kiss. A kiss of gratitude. A kiss much like a brother might bestow on a sister. A kiss that absolutely wrecked me. I have replayed that moment over and over in my head. The smell of him—his usual scent combined with a tinge of cigarette smoke and alcohol—was a sexy mingling of aromas that had even my sober head swimming in fantasy. His shirt was slightly untucked on one side and he had undone a few of the buttons when he arrived home. I wanted nothing more than to stick my hand inside and feel the heat of his chest. Did he have chest hair, I wondered? And would it be as dark as the hair on his head? Would his abs ripple and harden under my touch as they always do in my dreams?

When his lips pressed onto the flesh of my cheek, time stood still. My eyes closed as I imprinted the moment in my memory. I wanted to remember his breath on my face, his soft, confident mouth on my skin, his hard body as it momentarily brushed against mine. I wondered if he had any idea what that one small gesture did to me. It fueled my fantasies beyond anything I'd ever felt before. My body hummed with desire the entire cab ride home. I squirmed on my seat to get some needed friction in all the right places.

I went straight to my room. Nothing mattered to me but relieving the tension Griffin had built up inside me with that one innocent kiss. If his kiss could affect me that way, I wondered what his hands on my body would do. I was certain they would incinerate me.

After my wildly inappropriate tension-relieving session with a new 'toy,' the guilt came. I knew I was the shittiest friend in the history of the world. How could I fantasize about Griffin after spending the evening with his wife? *My best friend.*

I skipped Sunday brunch. Griffin and Erin were going to be there. I couldn't face her, knowing what I'd done the night before. I punished myself all day. I even considered telling Erin what I'd done, knowing that she would hate me. That's how guilty I felt. I couldn't have felt more ashamed if I'd actually been with him. I was a terrible friend and I knew it.

When Baylor called to check on me after I'd missed brunch, I told her what happened. She made me regurgitate exactly what he'd done. Did he put a hand on me when he kissed my cheek? *No.* Did he look into my eyes after? *No.* Did he say anything even mildly suggestive? *No.*

After the third degree, she laughed at me, saying my pregnancy was to blame. Griffin did nothing wrong, and my fantasies are perfectly normal. She told me not to beat myself up about them. I thanked her and assured her I wouldn't. Then I wallowed in my hormonal guilt and self-pity for the rest of the day.

I saw Erin the next day. She came by the restaurant to get the tickets, saying they would meet me here. I didn't say a word. I would keep my fantasies to myself. I didn't want to risk losing her. I would never do anything to hurt her. Griffin was off-limits now and forever. I just had to get through the next twenty-six weeks of pregnancy hormones and then I was sure everything would be okay.

The clearing of a throat startles me, pulling me from my thoughts as I look up into the steely-gray eyes of Griffin himself. I feel the heat rush up my cheeks and I hope it's not written all over my face how he affects me.

I crane my neck to look around behind him. No Erin. Great, we'll have to sit here in a sea of awkwardness until she arrives. I fail miserably trying not to notice his tight athletic shirt that clings to his broad chest then tapers nicely to his tight waist. He is blatantly sexy and heart-stoppingly gorgeous.

I plaster on my best you-are-*not*-the-man-of-my-dreams smile. "Hey."

"Hi." He appraises my wardrobe choice. Of course I'm wearing a Yankees jersey. I have a team hat on as well, with my ponytail pulled through the opening in the back. I'm wearing my favorite jeans, but I had to leave the top two buttons undone, so I left my shirt hanging over my waistband. The jersey is big on me and I'm sure he thinks I look ridiculous. "We're not going to have a problem with this, are we?" He points between our opposing jerseys.

I laugh. "No. Especially not when we kick your ass."

He smirks at me. Then he gives me the bad news. "Erin couldn't make it. Her sub cancelled at the last second. Looks like it's just you and me."

My heart beats wildly. *No!* Erin is our buffer. She would have sat between us. I wouldn't even have to look at Griffin all day with her there. I could pretend he wasn't even at the game. Does she have any idea what she's done?

I should go. I can make an excuse to leave. My mind works to find the right one without worrying him that it's something to do with the baby.

Before I can say anything, he reaches his hand out to help me up. "Come on, let's go."

I stare at his hand like it'll burn me if I touch it. I know for a fact that it will. Maybe I can get through this day if I just don't let him touch me. I can focus on the game. The crowd. The food. Anything but him. I give him a venomous stare. "I'm not *that* big, Griffin. I think I can still stand up without anyone's help." Ignoring his hand, I stand and shove my own hands into my pockets.

"Sorry. Just trying to be helpful." He snickers when he takes in my oversized jersey, now that I'm standing up. "You look like a young schoolgirl wearing that thing."

Not sure how I should receive the comment, I shrug it off. "Well, this schoolgirl is hungry. You're buying me a hotdog."

"You know those things are full of nitrates, right?" The edges of his mouth curve up. Erin and Griffin have never been overbearing about what I eat or drink. They don't ever question me about it and they don't make me monitor it. So either he's teasing, or he likes to fight with me.

"Just for that, you're buying me two." I stomp off ahead of him. I hear him laugh behind me.

We stand in the crowded line for concessions and I start to feel the excitement. There's nothing like attending a live sporting event. Doesn't matter what. Baseball. Football. Soccer. They all have the same feel. The camaraderie of the fans. The smell of popcorn, nachos, and grilling meat. The hustle of everyone trying to find their seats before the main event. It's intoxicating. And by the expression on Griffin's face, he loves it just as much as I do.

Someone pushes from behind, causing Griffin to run into me, toppling me over. He catches me before I face-plant the counter. "You okay?" His concerned eyes look my body up and down as if perhaps the baby had gotten hurt.

I try to form words, but all my brain can comprehend is his strong hands on my arms, holding me steady. His large hands encompass my biceps almost entirely from shoulder to elbow. The heat from them is coursing through my body. I know it's not an intimate gesture on his part. He's protecting me, the incubator that houses his child. But it doesn't keep my body from reacting to his touch.

"Sky, are you okay?" His voice comes out insistent and worried.

I nod my head. I silently will him to remove his hands from me. I silently beg him not to. "Yeah, sorry. Just stunned."

He looks relieved as he lowers his hands to his side. We inch closer to the counter when it dawns on me that he called me Sky. Or maybe I'm imagining things. Whatever. It's probably my stupid hormones again.

A few minutes later, we walk away with more food than two people should be allowed, and I know an extra fifty miles on the bike is in my near future. We go find our seats, arms full of hot dogs, salty pretzels and milk duds, along with a bottle of water for me and a beer for Griffin.

Jake was able to get us into the section reserved for family. I smile, knowing that Griffin will be surrounded by the enemy. When we approach our seats, he raises a knowing eyebrow and shakes his head in mock disgust. This may turn out to be fun after all.

It's interesting sitting next to someone rooting for the other team. One or the other of us is always yelling, cheering, or disagreeing with a call. But we never have the same emotion at the same time. I find it quite comical. And, apparently, so does Griffin. While we are both passionate about our teams, we each laugh at the opposite reactions we have to what happens down on the field.

I have to wonder what it would be like with Erin sitting between us. Would she cheer at all, and if so, for what team? Would she understand the game? Would she be having as much soul-feeding fun as we are right now? Would she find her husband extremely irresistible despite being outfitted in enemy garb?

Tension is high in the game. The score is tied and a fast grounder down the line to right field gives the runner on third an opportunity to make it home. The Yankees' right-fielder makes an incredible throw to home plate, omitting the cut-off man, putting the ball directly into the catcher's mitt just in time for him to get the tag.

"Heeeeee's OUT!" yells the umpire, as he makes the signal with his arms, prompting massive cheers and high-fives from most of the stadium.

Griffin springs up from his seat and all but climbs over the people in front of us. "Better have your fucking eyes checked, Blue. I could tell from here, he was under the tag."

Everyone in our section turns to us, looking at Griffin's uncharacteristic outburst. Several fans light-heartedly disagree with Griffin's statement. I'm not so nice about it, however. "*You* need to get your eyes checked. He was clearly tagged at least a foot off the plate." We're still standing, so I put my hands on my hips for emphasis. "And why is it okay for *you* to cuss?" I raise my brows at him.

I push aside the realization that I secretly like the fact that he spontaneously cusses, too. Some guys sound crass or childish when they cuss, but the way he does it makes my insides tingle.

He ignores my question. "The guy was safe!" he argues, loudly.

"No, he wasn't!"

"And you're the expert?"

"I have eyes. It was the right call, Griffin." I point my finger at the catcher. "He has an impeccable record. He hasn't missed a tag at home in thirteen games."

Griffin stares at me in wonder. Then his eyes harden once again. "What the fuck does that matter? Just because he's good, doesn't mean the call should go his way. The guy was safe, Sky."

"He was out!" I shout in his face, not even caring that I had onions on my hot dogs. "So fucking out. And don't call me Sky."

"Don't say fuck!" he shouts back at me.

The seats in the stadium are spacious, but we're standing with mere inches between us as we yell back and forth. We continue shouting ridiculous absurdities at each other until we realize everyone else is sitting back down and we're the only ones still standing. And all eyes are on us.

Our eyes simultaneously go wide and I could swear I see the hint of a blush cross over his face. I hastily sit down and he follows, crossing his arms in a huff, clearly still pissed off about the call. Or our argument. Or both.

I hear a low belly chuckle come from behind me. I turn my head to see an older man with a burly white beard. He's wearing a Yankees cap and a large foam finger. "How long y'all been married?" he asks.

Griffin chokes on the sip of beer he was taking. He looks at the guy and then back at me and I'm sure I'm bright red. He shakes his head. "We're not married."

"Oh." He looks back and forth between us. "Well, you sound just like me and Bess did forty years ago. Ya got that same fire in ya for each other. Maybe someday you'll be expecting your sixth grandbaby like we are."

I vehemently shake my head at the man. "No, we're not together. He's married." Foam finger guy raises a questioning brow. "To my best friend," I add. He shakes his head and chuckles as he puts his hands up in defeat and leans back into his seat.

I open my mouth to explain, but Griffin puts a gentle hand on my knee and shakes his head. I know what he's telling me. It's not worth trying to explain to the stranger. Our situation is complicated. How it must look to other people can be confusing. Just wait until the pregnancy is showing—we'll really start to turn heads then. I roll my eyes, silently agreeing with Griffin. He removes his hand from my knee and I'm all too aware of just how much I miss it.

There are several more controversial calls in the game, but quite conspicuously, Griffin and I remain silent. We simply eye each other and laugh. Fortunately the 'bad' calls evened out in the end. And although my team won by two runs, Griffin doesn't whine about it, so I decide not to gloat.

All in all, it was a fantastic game. If you take the fight out of it, I'd even go so far as to say Griffin and I have become friends.

We follow the crowd up the stairs and through the tunnel and I head to the nearest bathroom while Griffin leans against the wall to wait for me. A few minutes later, I emerge, looking for Griffin only to find him absent from the spot where I left him. I turn around to search for him and smack right into someone's chest. "Sorry," I say, looking up at the large specimen.

Suddenly, my eyes and the stranger's eyes spark in recognition as a slow and steady grin crawls up his face. "Well, looky what we have here."

I cringe at his heavy Boston accent. I assess his fiery-red hair and wonder what I ever saw in the guy. "Oh, hi." I look around for Griffin, conflicted on whether or not I want him here. On one hand, it might diffuse the situation if the guy thinks I'm here with another man. On the other hand, I really don't need Griffin witnessing my past indiscretions.

As I look around, the man—whose name I never did find out—continues talking, saying something about going back to his place for a repeat. His accent grates on my every nerve. It's not that I dislike people from Boston or anything. I blame Mr. Hewitt, my fourth-grade teacher. He was the meanest teacher I ever had. I also think he disliked me because he once dated my mother, before she met my father. I was doomed with him from the start. He had an incredibly thick accent that haunted my dreams. To this day, I'll occasionally have a nightmare about Mr. Hewitt singling me out in the class, telling everyone what a poor student I was.

So, it's not really this guy's fault that I hate him because of his voice. I just know deep down, I could never be with a guy who talks that way. Gorgeous or not. If Griffin could only sustain a minor head injury that would result in him speaking like Red, all would be well in my world.

"You up for it?" his eyes question me along with his words.

"Uh, no thanks," I answer politely, even though I'm not sure what the question was. I was pre-occupied looking for Griffin, who I now see exiting the men's bathroom.

Griffin comes up next to me, but that does nothing to keep Red from eyeing me seductively. He asks again, right in front of Griffin, "Aw, come on, we had fun, didn't we?"

I narrow my eyes at him. *What the hell?* "You're a douche, you know that? You have a wife and kid. Or are you choosing to ignore that little fact again?"

He laughs. "That didn't seem to bother you six months ago when you were riding me for the third time."

I'm sure my stunned face pales. I can feel the burn of Griffin eyeing me speculatively as I spit out, "I didn't even know you, you asshole."

"Right. You were too wasted to ask," he says.

I don't think I've ever been so mortified in my entire twenty-four years. Griffin must think I was a complete slut. A bottom-dwelling whore who would pick up any guy in a bar. Then I close my eyes briefly, because he'd be right. That's exactly who I was. Maybe it's even who I would still be if I wasn't hiding behind this whole surrogate thing.

I see Griffin shift around defensively. He takes a step closer to me and says to the asshole, "You need to leave. The lady isn't interested."

"Lady?" Red smirks. "Okay, if you say so. What are you, today's piece of meat?"

"Hardly." Griffin puts a possessive arm around me.

Red raises an eyebrow. "Yeah, I guess I can't blame you, man. I'd have gone back for seconds, too. Had I known her name, that is." He's clearly trying to humiliate me further to get a rise out of Griffin. "But, I'm not sure one man is enough for that pussy, so don't count on the little whore being faithful."

In a split second, it all happens at once. Griffin's face turns as red as the guy's hair. He balls up his fists and lays the dude out with one punch to the jaw. He carefully pushes me aside and prepares to go after the guy's friends if any of them are stupid enough to jump him. His friends are decent sized, but they're no match for Griffin. I think after watching their extremely-well-built friend go down after one punch, they wisely decided not to defend him.

"Pick up your asshole friend and get him out of here before I do some real damage." Griffin hovers over him, ready to act on his threat. He keeps me well behind him and the other guys in front of him. Everyone around us thinks he's just protecting what's his. They'd be right, but not for the reason they think. He's watching out for his child. He probably couldn't give a rat's ass what some random guy thinks about me and my sexual past.

The crowd dissipates after Red is helped away by his friends. Griffin stares after them on the defensive until they're out of sight. Then he turns away. "Fuck!" He grabs his hand and cradles it in the other one.

I'm about to call him on his choice of words when I look at his hand and see it's already starting to swell. "Oh my God, Griffin." It looks bad. He must have cut it open on the guy's face. Blood is running down his arm and dripping onto the dirty concrete floor. "Wait here." I run over to the concession stand and step in front of the patrons to ask for a bag of ice and some paper towels. I quickly return and place them on Griffin's hand. "We should get an X-ray of your hand."

"I'm sure it's fine." He shakes his head at it. I'm sure he's thinking he shouldn't have done it. He should have walked away. All the guy was doing was calling a spade a spade.

"I am so sorry," I tell him.

He shouldn't have to defend me like that. My actions put him in that position. I can't pull my eyes from his mangled hand. My vision gets blurry from unshed tears.

"Hey." Griffin puts his good hand under my chin to raise my head to his. "This is not your fault."

I lower my head in shame as wetness travels down my cheeks. "You're wrong. It is." I close my eyes, squeezing out the remaining tears. I'm no longer worried about being embarrassed. He's heard the worst things about me. Things I can't defend. Ugly things. "Everything he said is true." Even though I'm talking in nothing more than a whisper, I can tell he hears me. "You punched him, but you didn't need to. He was right. And now your hand... I'm so sorry."

"I punched him because he was being an asshole." He puts his good hand on my shoulder and lowers himself to look at my face. "I don't care what you did in the past. He had no right to say those things about you as if you aren't a human being."

All I can do is nod. I silently wonder how many other men out there think the same terrible things about me. I lost my chance to find a guy like Griffin. I lost it long ago. This is me. This is my life. I'm tainted now. No decent guy would want a girl with my history. And now I'm carrying a kid that isn't mine—well, not really. That probably ruins my chances even more. What kind of guy brings a girl home to his parents after she rented out her womb? I'm destined to end up alone. Or with a scumbag like Red.

Suddenly, it dawns on me what I've been thinking. *A man?* I want a man like Griffin? A good guy to spend my time with? My *life* with?

And now I know for sure. As I stand here and help Griffin tend to his wounds, I find the answer to the question that has plagued me for months. Not only am I jealous of Erin's relationship with her husband—I'm jealous of her specific husband. The man who stands up for sluts on virtue. The man who can go to a ballgame with a pretty girl and not betray his wife. The man who I know will protect his child at all costs.

The man I'm completely in love with but can never have.

I quickly excuse myself and run back to the bathroom where I can break down without having him witness how pathetic I really am.

chapter ten

On the ferry over to Liberty Island, I watch Erin absorb everything she sees as if she were a child. She told me she's been here before, but never took the time to appreciate it.

Guilt overcomes me each time I look at her. I spent the better part of the week since the baseball game trying to figure out how to turn my feelings off, but I keep going back to what Baylor told me once—you can't choose who you fall in love with.

Well, why the hell not?

After Gavin and Baylor got back together, she admitted she always loved him, even when she didn't want to. Even after the horrible thing he'd done to her. She told me her heart wouldn't let go of him. She tried to date other people. She even had actual relationships with men, one lasting almost a year. But they never worked out in the end. She told me how hard it was to live her life knowing she would never be with him.

Is that what I'm destined for? A life of longing? Comparing every man to Griffin, knowing they could never measure up? How ironic but maybe somehow, befitting, that a slutty girl who has always proclaimed she'd never love, falls in love with someone who is forbidden.

Maybe it's not really love I'm feeling. Maybe Baylor is right and it's my hormones gone amuck. Lust—that's what this is. That's what I feel when he touches me. Looks at me. Exists in the same world as me. Can you really blame me? He's gorgeous. Any woman would feel the same. Then again, as my mind pages through the throngs of attractive men I've hooked up with in the past, I know that what I felt for them doesn't even come close to what I feel for Griffin.

Prohibited. Off-limits. Banned. Maybe it's the challenge—the certainty that I could never be with him that has me wanting him. Yes, that's all this is. I take a deep breath and then blow out the tension, realizing this is all a childish game of wanting something I can't have.

I smile watching Erin's eyes fill with excitement as we approach the monumental statue that most New York City natives take for granted. "You know, they do allow babies on this tour. It's not like you're going to roll over and die when you become a mom."

She closes her eyes and lets the strong mid-afternoon sun warm her face on this chilly day. She sighs, taking in one last ray of sunshine before opening her eyes and turning to me.

"What's up with you, Erin?" I ask, when she looks at me through hauntingly dark eyes, filled with some unnamed emotion. "You've been dragging me all over the city for a month now. You can do all of these things with a baby. Well, maybe not hit the clubs we've gone to, but there are plenty of people willing to babysit."

Her sad eyes betray the smile curving her lips. "I've heard that you have to give up a lot of stuff, even if you promise yourself you won't. I'm simply trying to cram in as much fun as I can while I have the time. You got a problem with that?"

I stare at her and get an idea. "You know, I've heard of people taking a 'babymoon.' One last hurrah before their kid is born. Something you might not be able to do after. Why don't you and Griffin do that? Go to Europe, or Australia—places that are too far for an infant to fly. I'm sure Piper could give you some great advice on where to go and what to do." I look down at my growing belly that is still pretty much inconspicuous beneath my clothing. "And since you don't have to worry about carrying around this extra load, you could do something exciting, like climb a mountain or go surfing."

I smile, proud of myself for coming up with the idea that not only will have Erin doing something fun, but it might just get Griffin away from me long enough for these feelings to ebb. Heck, maybe I could even try to date someone. Not that anyone would want me in the state I'm in. But it's not completely unheard of. Plus, the guy wouldn't have to worry about dealing with a kid when it's all over.

Unexpectedly, my heart hurts and for the first time in my life, I wonder if, just maybe, at some point in the future I will be able to have something that resembles a family. The thought takes my breath away and all I can do is gaze down into the inviting blue water that effortlessly parts as the ferry slices through it.

Erin threads her arm around me, pulling me close to her side. "No. That's not in the cards for me. I like hanging around here where I can be with my friends. I don't want to miss a minute of your pregnancy. And Baylor is due any second. I want to be here for that." She looks off into the sea with a blank stare. "It will be incredible. Do you think she'll let me hold her baby?"

I smirk at her absurd comment. "Of course she'll let you hold her baby. She would trust you with its life. We all would. And soon enough you'll have little Bean's life entrusted to you." Saying that makes me remember how protective Griffin was last week and I laugh. "Griffin is already in full dad mode after what he did for your baby at the game."

She smiles and her face brightens. "I'm so glad he did that. You have no idea."

I momentarily wonder if she's gone completely insane. Why is she giddy over the fact that Griffin all but broke his hand defending a woman who shouldn't have been defended? "You're glad he hurt his hand?" I ask incredulously.

"Of course not, silly. I'm glad he's as protective of you as he is of me. You are part of our fa… family now and it's ob… uh, ob… uh… it's apparent he feels that way." I can see tears well in her eyes as the emotions she's feeling have her stumbling over her words.

"He wasn't protecting *me*, Erin," I remind her. "He was protecting his kid. I guess I can't blame him for that, even if I did deserve everything the creep said to me."

She stops looking at the water and forcefully turns me so that we are facing each other. "Don't talk like that. I don't ever want to hear you talk like that again, Skylar. You've changed. You are a wonderful person. From what I've heard, you were a wonderful person even then. You were misguided, that's all. If you were a man, nobody would fault you for your philandering ways. It's a double standard that's completely unfair to women. I know you never deliberately hurt anyone and you were always safe in your… practices. What you did behind closed doors is nobody else's business.

"But you have changed. I can tell you're no longer that person. Whatever you were missing in your life back then that caused you to behave that way, you've obviously found it. I see wonderful things in your future, Skylar. And you deserve every single one of them.

"And as far as who he was protecting, he wasn't just protecting his baby. He was protecting his family, because that is exactly what you've become to us."

She pulls me into a hug. And for the first time, I wrap her in a full-on embrace, squeezing her tightly against me, hoping she understands how lucky I am to have her in my life. I don't hold back. I'm not embarrassed when people pass by and see our display of affection.

When her arms go limp around me, I laugh when I become the one holding on longer for once. Then, all of a sudden her weight falls into me. I brace myself against the guardrail as her body slides down to the ground. *Is she fainting?*

No, she's not fainting; she's still looking at me, but she's not really there. Then her eyes roll upwards and her entire body starts to shake violently. I scream out, "Erin! Oh my God. Someone help!"

A crowd quickly gathers around. Someone puts their coat under her head while gently moving her away from the guardrail. "Does she have epilepsy?" the stranger asks.

"Epilepsy? Uh… no, I don't think so. She had cancer once." It might be a lame thing to say, but I don't understand what's going on with her.

Another man breaks through the crowd. "I'm a doctor," he proclaims. "Please, everyone give her some space. And someone call 911."

Tears stream down my face and my hands are shaking almost as badly as her body as I watch him put his fingers against her neck. Then, he just watches her like the rest of us. Her jerking body reminds me of a fish when taken out of water. Her neck snaps back. Her arms and legs are rigid, yet jerk with her torso as it violently convulses from front to back as she lies on her side. Like a fish out of water, I wonder if she's being deprived of oxygen. I gasp in horror.

"Do something!" I yell at him. "You're a doctor!"

He gives me a sympathetic look. "Ma'am, your friend is having a seizure. Without the proper drugs, there's nothing I can do except see to it that she doesn't hurt herself. It should be over very soon." He eyes the crowd. "Did someone call for an ambulance?"

A woman cries, "Yes! I have them on the phone. They're asking questions." The doctor tells the woman what information to relay to the dispatcher as I helplessly watch my friend in the most terrifying moment of my entire life.

Drool dribbles from Erin's mouth. Her hair whips around on top of the stranger's coat under her head. Her clothes become dirty and sodden from the morning dew that hasn't yet evaporated off the deck of the ferry. I watch in utter disbelief as I'm sure she's dying. I can't comprehend how all anyone can do is stand here and witness it. I scream out a few more times for someone to help. Arms come around me when my legs fail and I start to fall to the ground.

Then, in what was probably only a minute or two, but seems like hours, Erin stills completely. She lays lifeless on the ground as my heart gets ripped from my body. I instinctively touch my stomach, horrified at the thought of this baby losing its mother before they even get a chance to meet.

I hear sirens in the background and wonder how an ambulance could get here. We are in the middle of New York Harbor.

The doctor arranges her so she's lying on her back. He leans over her face, putting his ear close to her mouth while he presses his fingers to her neck again. "She's breathing," he says. I hear a collective sigh of relief from the large crowd behind us.

The next ten minutes of my life are a blur. Men in orange jackets scuffle around us, putting Erin on a backboard while they strap an oxygen mask over her face. She and I are taken aboard a smaller boat that heads back towards the city. I try to keep my hand on her, but they're working over her and I'm forced to step away. They ask me questions to which I have no answers.

All I can think of the entire time we're racing to the hospital is that this is my fault. I did this. I fell in love with her husband. I allowed myself to wonder for one brief moment what it would be like if Erin weren't around. I caused this with my selfish ways. Nothing has changed. I haven't changed. I'm the same horrible person I was six months ago. I tried to camouflage myself as something else. Pretend I'm someone I'm not. But this is proof.

I pray to God that I haven't just killed the best friend I've ever had.

chapter eleven

Other than my prayers on the rescue boat, I've never done this before. I sit in the hospital chapel wondering if there's some sort of protocol for talking to God. Do I simply tell Him what I want? Do I have to fill out some kind of form? Will He even bother listening to someone like me?

Not that I didn't attend church as a child. I did. My parents took me to Sunday School when I was younger. But when they opened the restaurant, we didn't go very often. Owning a business took up every waking moment, and devoting time to church fell low on their list of priorities.

Still, I'm pretty sure I believe in Him. Especially after seeing Bean's ultrasound. How could something as remarkable as the ability to grow another human inside oneself even be possible without a powerful being to drive it all? I believe there are things in the world that can't be explained away with science. I believe that if you're a good person, good things will happen to you.

That last belief is pretty much shot to hell as I think of Erin lying lifeless in a bed somewhere in the hospital. She's the best person I know, inside and out. She wouldn't hurt a fly. She accepts people with all their faults. She doesn't deserve to have this happening to her. I would trade places with her in a minute if I could do it without hurting their baby. I make all kinds of deals with God if he will let her be okay.

I recall the horror in Griffin's voice when I calmed down enough to call him on our way to the hospital. I selfishly wondered if there would ever be anyone in this world who would care about me enough to have the reaction he did if anything happened to me. I could hear the helplessness. I sensed the tears spilling out of his eyes. I knew he was having flashbacks to all the horrible moments he'd already lived through with Erin and his mom.

While Griffin sits in the waiting room, ready to be called back at a moment's notice, I remain holed up in the chapel. I know with her husband and most of her family here, I'll be the last one to get to see her anyway.

Erin's family members come and go, putting a comforting hand on my shoulder or commiserating with me for a quiet moment before they silently pray. I try to offer them comfort, but strangely enough, it seems it's me they think needs comforting. They all look to my belly when they talk to me. Every one of them knows our situation. Every one of them feels as bad as I do for the child who may grow up motherless. They all still praise me for what I'm doing. Not one of them understands I don't deserve it.

When the chapel is empty except for me and Erin's older sister, Jane, she comes over to sit with me. "Some of your friends are waiting out there with us. Erin sure has met a lot of wonderful people since you came into her life. I've never seen her surrounded by such a following. Not since high school. You are very special to her and not just because of the baby."

I shrug off her un-deserving words. "Can you tell me about that?" I ask. "I've always wondered how someone as great as Erin doesn't have people knocking down her door to be her friend. She's so nice to everyone. But she seems like somewhat of a loner, I guess."

Jane nods her head. "She is a loner. Well, until you came along. But she wasn't always that way."

"Yeah, she told me that her looks intimidate other women and because of it, she doesn't make friends easily."

Jane laughs. "Is that what she told you?" She shakes her head, amused. "Erin could have all the friends she wanted. Women would line up to be accepted into her world. But ever since high school, when her large group of friends couldn't run away fast enough from the girl with cancer, she's been hesitant to let anyone in. She's nice to people, and they always attempt to friend her, but she pushes them away. You're the first one she's let in for long time."

I look down at my belly. "Well, she kind of had to, Jane."

"No, she didn't. Just because you're her surrogate doesn't mean she was forced to make friends with you. The way she talks about you, it's like you're her female soul mate. I know you two lead very different lives, but she feels a connection to you. One she hasn't had with anyone else. Maybe not even Griffin. She loves you like a sister, Skylar." Tears spill from each of us as she continues to speak. "And no matter what happens here, we will always welcome you as part of our family."

A sister. Erin considers me a sister? I look at the cross perched in the corner of the room, along with symbols of some other religions. A sister would never do to her what I've done. A sister would never, for one second, want what she has. A sister would never sink as low as I have.

"Erin has an uncanny ability to see things in people." She puts a comforting hand on mine. "Sometimes she sees things that they don't even see in themselves. Don't sell yourself short, Skylar. She believes in you."

As she rises to leave the chapel, I wonder if I said all those things about sisters out loud.

I reflect upon the past months that Erin has been a part of my life. They've been the happiest I can remember, despite my inappropriate longing for her husband. I vow right now, right this very second, to do everything I can to become the person she thinks I am. I will force myself to accept Griffin as a friend, to no longer look at him or think of him in ways that make me a bad person. I make a promise to myself and God to be worthy of her and the way she sees me. To be her very best friend. To be her sister.

I don't even know how long I've been sitting here when someone sits down in the empty pew behind me. Someone who I can tell is quietly sobbing. I know who it is. I always seem to know when he's near.

I turn around, shocked at what I see. I gasp, thinking the worst. Griffin's eyes are red and puffy, the lines of his face etched in deep concern. His cheeks are wet with tears he's tired of wiping away. He looks broken.

"Oh, God... is she—"

"No," his voice breaks. He clears his throat. "She wants to see you."

I have a momentary feeling of elation that relaxes my whole body before I realize something is wrong. If she's okay, why does Griffin look utterly wrecked? "What's going on?"

"She asked to see you before anyone else," he croaks out, his voice hoarse. "I've been in to see her, too. But now she wants you. Room 817. Just go."

He offers no other words before he gets up to leave. My mind doesn't know what to do. Should I jump up and down because she's alive? Should I be wary of what I might find in room 817? I tentatively rise from my seat and take slow steps towards the door. I glance down at my watch to see I've been here for hours. I look back at the cross and send up one last prayer.

I ride the elevator with others going to see loved ones. I chastise myself for not stopping at the gift shop for flowers or balloons like they have. In my haste to get to her, I've forgotten all about visitation protocol dictating I bring a symbol of my well wishes. I vow to send her the biggest arrangement of white lilies I can find as soon as I leave here.

I find my way to room 817 and stop at the partially opened door. I listen for a beat to see what I can hear that might prepare me before I walk in. Silence. I take a deep breath and blow it out. Then another.

When I walk through the door, I'm stunned at what I find. Erin is sitting up in bed, looking like her usual self except she's in a tawdry hospital gown instead of designer clothing. Her hair has been done and makeup applied. She looks completely different from how she looked mere hours ago. When she sees me come through the door, a smile brightens her face. It's a smile that tells me everything Jane said is absolutely true. The only other people who look at me this way are my family. I know for sure now. Erin *is* my family.

My legs propel me over to her so quickly I almost fall over the bed. I wrap her in an uncharacteristically-tight hug. "You scared the shit out of me, Erin."

She nods into my shoulder. "I know. I'm sorry, that must have been terrible for you. It's only happened once before, the week Griffin was in Africa. I'd hoped you wouldn't have to find out this way."

I pull back, but keep my hands on her arms. "Find out what? Do you have epilepsy?"

She sighs.

I probe her eyes for an answer. I don't get the one I want. The answer I want is that she has some strange virus that made her have a seizure, and they gave her antibiotics to make her better. Or that she hit her head a while ago causing some sort of brain bleed they've now found and corrected. But the answer I see burning deep within her eyes is neither of those things. It's so much worse. "What is it? Tell me, Erin. I could see how wrecked Griffin was. I know it's something bad. Is your cancer back?"

She grips my hands, one of mine in each of hers. "Yes and no." She releases one of my hands and pats the bed next to her, scooting over to make room for me. "I do have cancer again, but it's not the same cancer I had before."

I gasp. "Oh, God, Erin. No!" Tears roll down my cheeks only to be absorbed by her hair as I pull her in for another hug. I remember everything she told me about the first time she had cancer and I regurgitate it back to her. "You beat it before. You're such a strong person. And this time, there are so many more of us who will be here for you. We're not going anywhere. You can count on it."

She nods. "I know. And I love you guys for it. But this time is different, Skylar."

"Different how?" I ask.

"Let me start from the beginning." She leans back into her pillow to get comfortable. She holds my hand in hers as if it's a lifeline. "Back in high school, before my diagnosis, I knew something was wrong. It wasn't anything big, just little things like a twinge here and an ache there. But still, I was young and I thought it would go away and I'd live forever. So when I started having those same feelings a few months ago, I was not ready to hear that I'd have to go through it all again."

"A few months?" I close my eyes tightly, wishing it all away. "You've known about this for a few months and didn't tell anyone?"

"Can I finish?" she scolds me with a playful wink.

I nod and give her hand a squeeze.

"A couple of weeks after we found out you were pregnant, I started getting headaches. I'd had some headaches before, when I went through menopause, so I didn't really think much of it. Then other things started happening. I experienced weakness in my right arm. I started having occasional trouble recalling words. And I would sometimes get lightheaded."

My brain cycles through all the times I was with her when I simply ignored those things happening to her. When she almost fainted on my couch. The missed words I'd attributed to drinking or emotions. The trouble she had with her wallet at the maternity store. "I should have said something. I noticed all those things, but made excuses for them in my head. I'm sorry. If I had mentioned it back then, maybe you would have been checked out sooner."

She shakes her head. "No, I wouldn't have. I was in denial. Even when things progressed and I knew for sure there was a problem, I still didn't go to the doctor until the week Griffin was away. That's when I had my first seizure."

My hand comes up to cover my sob. "No! I'm so sorry. I should've been there. I should have been around for you while he was away."

"It's not your fault, Skylar. Anyway, Jane was with me when it happened. She took care of me and made sure I went to the hospital."

"Jane knows?"

She nods. "My whole family does. I swore them to secrecy."

My brow furrows in confusion. Then it dawns on me that Jane didn't seem nearly as wrecked by all this as Griffin or I. She was comforting me in the chapel when it should have been the other way around. "Griffin didn't know either, did he? I saw him just now, and there's no way he's known about this for six weeks. Why didn't you tell him? Why didn't you tell me? I could have gone to chemo or radiation or whatever with you." I admire her long, thick head of hair. "At least you aren't losing your hair this time. That's something."

"First off—no Griffin didn't know, not until today. That's the way I wanted it. I didn't want him feeling sorry for me and treating me with kid gloves like he did last time. I didn't want you guys to know until you had to. I didn't want to burden you.

"And there won't be any radiation or chemo this time." She closes her eyes and takes in a deep breath. "What I have isn't curable. It's terminal, Skylar."

Terminal? Tears stream out of my eyes faster than I can wipe them. "God, no!" I sob, turning my head into her shoulder. I wrap my arms around her once again in an attempt to hold on to her. To keep her here with me in this world as long as I can. I hold her until my arms give out, the whole time silently screaming my apologies for all the horrible things I've done to make this happen.

Erin allows me to cry until my tears dry up. I heave and hiccup before my breathing steadies again. I look up to see her cheeks wet with tears. "Tell me more. I want to know everything. Maybe there's something we can do."

"There is nothing to do. I have a grade four glioblastoma. An inoperable brain tumor. It's one-hundred-percent fatal."

I tense up next to her. "You are twenty-seven years old, Erin. You're still so young. There has to be something we can do. Did this happen because of your other cancer? Did it spread to your brain?"

"Glioblastomas are a medical mystery. Most often there's no explanation for them. They don't appear because of another cancer. There's a small possibility it was caused by the radiation I had when I was eighteen, but there's no way of knowing. It's just one of those rare, unexplained things that happens."

"Can't they operate and remove it?"

"They could operate and remove some of it. But it will grow back. They always do. And recovering from brain surgery is not how I want to spend the last few months of my life."

"Months!" I gasp, now sobbing again.

She nods.

"Why aren't you falling apart?" I yell at her. "Why aren't you fighting this? There has to be some way to extend it. Can't they give you drugs or something? How can you sit here and calmly tell me you only have a few months to live? What's fucking wrong with you?"

Erin smiles. She actually smiles at me. She's dying, but she smiles anyway. "Skylar, I've had six weeks to accept this. I grieved already. I went through all the stages of accepting death. I spent weeks wallowing in anger, denial and self-pity to get here. You and Griffin are just now finding out, so it will take you time to get where I am."

I realize what she's been telling me and my mind goes back six weeks. She became withdrawn right after the ultrasound. The week Griffin went to Africa. I thought she was freaking out about the baby. Griffin noticed the change as well. It lasted for a few weeks and then she started doing all kinds of crazy things. Dragging me around to places she'd never been. Making vague comments about missing out on things.

"I'll never get to where you are. I'll never accept that there is nothing we can do. There has to be something. Don't you even want to *try* to be here when the baby comes? *Your* baby?" I grab her hand and stick it on my small baby bump.

"There are chemotherapies I could try that might add a month or two to my life. *Might*. But they come at a price, Skylar. I don't want to spend what time I have left gorked out on drugs, throwing up, and losing my hair. There are so many side effects from chemo that my quality of life would be awful. Even if by some miracle I made it as far as the birth, I may not even be alert enough to realize it."

"But it's a chance," I plead. "Don't you owe it to the baby to have a chance to meet you?"

"No," she says emphatically. "I want to feel good for as long as I can. They've got me on steroids to reduce any swelling caused by the tumor. That should help alleviate some of my symptoms. But it won't prolong my life; it'll only make it a little less unpleasant until the end."

Still in shock, and barely able to get out my words, I say, "And how exactly will we know when that might be?"

"They tell me it could happen any time, but when it happens, it'll happen quickly, probably over a period of a couple weeks. That's the way I want it. I don't want to stretch out my suffering—*your* suffering—on the potential for a few more days or weeks. Even if it means I'll never get to see the baby. I want to die peacefully and quickly. I don't want Griffin remembering me like some vegetable. It was like that with his mom. It took her months to die. He watched her waste away to nothing. I don't want that. And I expect you to respect my wishes. My family has. I'm going to die and everyone needs to accept that."

My hand covers my sob once again as I recall what I said on the ferry earlier. *It's not like you're going to roll over and die.* "Oh God, Erin. I'm so sorry about what I said this afternoon, about you dying. I'm such an inconsiderate bitch. Can you ever forgive me?"

"There's nothing to forgive. It's not your fault. It was a perfectly valid comment based on my behavior. Don't beat yourself up about it. Don't beat yourself up about *anything*, Skylar. But please, I need your support on this. I need your support more than anyone's."

I look down at my stomach. "But what about—"

"Don't worry about anything. It will all work out," she says. "We can talk more tomorrow. Right now, I want to rest and then I'm going to make some plans. There are things I want to do before I go. Things I need you to help me with."

"Anything," I say through my tears. "I'll help you with anything, Erin."

"I need you to talk to Griffin. You two are going through this together. My family will be there to support both of you, but you need to lean on each other. Go. Find him and work your way through this."

I nod my head and give her one last hug.

"Now get out of here. I'm tired. I have to get my strength back for all the shit I'm going to make you do with me."

I force a grin at her choice of words. Then I get up and hope my trembling legs can carry me across the room. I take one look back at Erin as her heavy eyelids close and she falls into a peaceful slumber. She's so beautiful. Even the way she's handling this is beautiful. I vow to do everything in my power to make sure her time left is filled with love, laughter and friendship. I will do anything she asks of me.

Anything.

chapter twelve

I somehow end up back in the waiting area, unsure of how I got here. I'm numb. I can't believe one person can have so many bad things happen to them. One very wonderful person. It doesn't make sense. Maybe there really isn't a God after all. How could He allow Erin to go through cancer, lose her ability to have kids and then find a way to have a baby, all to have it ripped away from her?

It's obvious to me that Baylor and all our friends have now been told. Muffled sobs, puffy eyes and looks of sheer disbelief are plentiful. Erin's parents and four sisters have taken it upon themselves to comfort her friends and Griffin. Like Erin, they've had time to accept this. But I wonder if they tried hard enough to get her to try some life-extending options. I can't imagine there being a disease that could take someone so quickly. She seemed fine this morning. She even seemed fine just now. Is there really something growing in her body that could kill her in a few short months?

I make a mental note to research brain tumors when I get home. After I talk to Griffin. Because that's what she asked me to do. And I'll do whatever she asks. I will be the perfect friend for whatever time she has left.

It's heartbreaking to see Griffin and his best friend, Mason. Here are two very large, very tough alpha males, and they've been reduced to a quivering mess of tears. Erin has grown close to Mason since he and Griffin became friends four years ago, when Griffin shot a spread for Sports Illustrated on promising college athletes featuring Mason. Despite their almost five-year age difference, Griffin and Mason forged a quick friendship. Where there's one, you'll usually find the other. And Mason has become the brother Erin never had.

Aside from the whole cancer thing, you might say Erin is lucky. She may not have a lot of friends, but those she does have would die for her. I think any one of us would take her place right now if we could. The world needs more people like her. The world has an over-abundance of people like me. Once again, I vow to change and become the person she believes me to be. A person who deserves to have a friend like her.

Griffin spots me in the place where I quietly leaned against a wall to watch him. He nods at me and then says something to Mason. He gets up and crosses the room looking like I've never seen him. His shoulders are slumped. His feet scuffle along the floor. His eyes are to the ground. He's been beaten down by cancer so many times, I question his ability to be strong enough to help Erin.

He has to be strong. We both have to be.

He comes up beside me. "Can we take a walk?" His words are shallow; his voice hoarse and tentative.

"Sure." I follow as he walks ahead of me, down the main hallway and out the building to a courtyard. The first thing I notice when we walk outside is the smell of flowers. I look around and it's beautiful. The area is adorned with benches surrounded by lovely budding flowers, vibrant bushes and colorful trees. *Life*. It reminds me of life. I suppose that was the objective. Something to bring hope to people who may not have any.

Griffin walks over to a bench and signals for me to sit down. I sit and then he joins me, head still hanging, hands still shaking. "Erin wanted us to talk."

I nod. "Yeah."

We sit in silence. Every time I try to speak, the lump in my throat prevents words from emerging. The same thing must be happening to him. He wrings his hands and clears his throat over and over. We both need a minute. So we just sit.

I'm entranced by the repetitious movement of his arms. He has on a short-sleeved shirt despite the chill in the air, and I'm able to see his tattoo more clearly than I've seen it before. It's a pink ribbon—the symbol for breast cancer awareness. There's some script, but I can't make it out. Maybe we could talk about that to ease us into talking about Erin.

I point to it. "Did you get that tattoo for your mom?"

He looks at it and studies it like he forgot it was even there. He nods. "Yeah." He holds it out for me to look at. It has his mom's name scripted on one side of the ribbon and what I assume is her date of death on the other side. "Looks like I'll have to get another one now," he says, choking on the words.

"I'm so sorry, Griffin. Erin told me all about your mom. I'm sorry you have to go through that again." I look up at him to see another tear roll down his cheek. "I'll get one, too. We can go together."

"You can't get one, Skylar. You're pregnant." As if suddenly reminded of the baby, he looks at my hidden belly and shakes his head.

"How do you know I can't get one?"

"Because I read the books Erin bought for us. Unlike someone, apparently."

I look down at my stomach, feeling sick over the fact that this little life has already been riddled with tragedy. "What are we going to do?" *About Erin. About the baby. About life.* All of these questions require answers I'm not sure we're prepared to give.

"I don't know. I can't think about anything other than Erin right now."

I nod my head in agreement. We have time to figure out the rest. We need to help Erin. She's our priority. Everything else can wait.

We fall into silence again. After a minute, I realize we're going nowhere fast and we don't have a moment to spare. "We have to make plans for what time she has left."

He nods. His elbows are resting on his knees, his head is slumped forward and I see a tear fall from his cheek. I follow it with my blurry eyes as it splashes onto the concrete patio of the courtyard.

"I want to make these last few months really s-special," I stutter though the frog in my throat. "I'll do whatever it takes."

He nods again. I wonder if he'll ever speak. After another minute of silence, he finally does. "Me too. Whatever it takes. Money is no object." His voice cracks again when he says, "I can't do it alone. I'm going to need your help. Do you think you'll be able to take some time off, work half days or something? I'll pay for your replacement. I know she wants you with her."

"I know she wants *you* with her," I say. "Yes, I can arrange for time off. And you don't have to pay for it. I don't want you worrying about money at a time like this."

He belts out a desperate laugh. "No, I'll pay for it. Money is one thing I have, Skylar. A lot of it. I may have shitty luck. I may have a wife who is dying. But, money I've got. And I plan to use it to make her life everything it can be until..." His chest heaves as he holds in a sob.

"What about you," I ask. "Can you take time off?" I know he's a freelance photographer and that usually means he sets his own hours and can pick and choose his jobs, but that doesn't mean he won't have pressing commitments.

"It's already done. I cleared my calendar indefinitely. I'll be here for her twenty-four-seven. It might take some convincing for Erin to let us pamper her. She hates that. She never wants me to spend money on her, either. That's one thing I won't budge on. I'm going to spoil her in everything I do. Will you help me?"

I elbow him and laugh to lighten the mood. "Will I help you spend a shitload of money to make a very special woman happy? You bet your ass I will."

He manages a hint of a smile before his face falls again. "Fuck." He takes a deep breath, studying his tattoo. "I can't believe this is happening again." His body starts to shake as more tears escape his eyes.

I scoot closer to him and wrap my arms around him. I hold him tightly against me. I let him know he doesn't have to go through this alone. He eventually wraps his arm around me, too. We hold each other for what seems like hours, until neither of us have any more tears to shed. And in that time, I realize I can do this. The embrace we shared was not intimate. It was not provocative. It was not enticing. I felt nothing whatsoever, except the overwhelming need to join forces with him to help my friend. I'm sure I've just overcome the first hurdle in keeping my promise to become a better person.

The sun set long ago and my watch, along with my stomach, tells me it's getting late. "We're no good for anything right now. We need to get some sleep and re-group later. Can you meet tomorrow?"

"I'm staying here tonight. They're bringing in a cot for me. I won't leave her." He straightens out his shirt and wipes his sweaty hands on his pants. He's trying to pull himself together. "They want to do one more set of scans tomorrow afternoon before they release her. That may take a while. Can we meet then?"

"Whatever you need. I'll spend the morning finding my replacement and then I'll head back to the hospital. We can talk more then. Why don't I bring over some food from the restaurant when I come? No point in torturing any of us with hospital food."

He flashes me a sad smile. "That would be great, Skylar. Thanks."

We head back inside to find friends and family congregating over a spread of sandwiches that Mindy had sent over from work. Nobody left. Not one person. They've been here all day, supporting each other. Supporting Erin. I survey Erin's family—who are now my family. I take note of my friends—who are now Erin's friends. I'm suddenly so grateful to be a part of this. It sounds twisted, but I'm genuinely honored to be included as one of the group who will get to witness her last moments in this world. Erin couldn't be surrounded by better people. Well, present company excluded. But I'm trying. And I'll get there. I swear to God I will.

My eyes become sore from all the research. Research that only tells me the same thing over and over. Erin was right. She's going to die. And soon.

I'm trying to prepare myself for what might happen as her disease progresses. I saw the list of the horrible things it will do to her body. The only solace is that it will probably happen relatively quickly. By the time she becomes bed-ridden, she may only have a matter of days to live. But what upsets me the most is that she may not have all her mental faculties about her. We may lose her before we lose her and I know that will be unbearable to watch. It's possible, however, that won't happen. From what I've read, it's different for everyone. There is only one exact similarity in every case. Death.

I close my eyes and curl up into a ball on the couch. I cry for Erin. I cry for Griffin. I cry for this little baby who won't know its mother. I cry for myself. When my tears dry up and I realize how selfish I'm behaving, I resolve to quit being reduced to a blubbering fool every time I think of Erin. Crying isn't going to help her. It's not going to improve her short life. There will be plenty of time for crying later. After she's gone. I'll mourn her loss then, not now. Now I need to focus on her life, not her death.

I pick up the phone to call Baylor. I need her help with something.

It doesn't even ring before she answers, "Skylar, how are you holding up?"

"I'm okay. I've been on my laptop looking up everything I can about her cancer." I sigh as I try to feign off more tears. "It's horrible, Baylor. We might only have her for a few more months. And of those months, we may only really have her for part of the time."

Baylor gives me words of comfort, letting me know what a good friend I am to Erin, but she doesn't know the whole truth. The truth that eats away at me like a leech sucking blood from flesh.

"Skylar?"

She's waiting for me to say something. But the lump in my throat is back and all I can do is sniffle.

"Skylar, talk to me."

I close my eyes. "Do you believe in fate?"

"Fate? Uh, yeah, I guess in a way I do. I think fate had Gavin and I run into each other in Chicago when we had moved to opposite sides of the country. I believe that we were meant to be together even though it took us a while to get there."

I nod my head, even though I know she can't see me. "Do you think people can change fate?"

She's silent for a beat. Then she asks, "What's this about, Skylar? What are you getting at? It's okay, you can talk to me. We're all grieving. Whatever it is that's on your mind, it's okay to feel that way."

I blow out a deep breath. "Erin believes in fate. She believes we were brought together so I could have their baby and improve my life in the process."

"Yeah, she told me."

"But I screwed up, Baylor. I messed with fate and now she's dying."

"What exactly do you mean by that?" she asks.

When I don't say anything, she presses on. "You don't mean because you think Griffin is hot and have had dreams about him, do you?"

"If only," I say. "It's so much more than that."

I hear a gasp over the phone line. Then I hear a door close. "God, Skylar, please don't tell me you slept with him," she whispers.

"No!" My eyes open but lower to the ground at my feet. "Of course not. I told you I would never hurt her like that. But I think somehow... I tried not to, but somehow I ended up... uh... in love with Griffin. I know it sounds crazy and I'm probably wrong, it's probably lust or something, but I couldn't help whatever it was and now this happened. I swear, Baylor, I would have never acted on it. And Griffin never gave me any indication that he was the least bit attracted to me. He loves her. I love her. I just couldn't help it." My sobs bellow out of me and I wonder if I'm making any sense at all. "I couldn't help it, Baylor. I'm such a terrible friend that I fell in love with my best friend's husband. Who does that? I'm so sorry. Oh, God, she'll never forgive me. She'll die and then she'll know. People know everything when they die, don't they? She'll hate me. I'm trying. I'm trying to stop, but it's hard to turn it off. Even with Erin dying. Even when I know it's wrong. Griffin and I hugged today and that was okay, so maybe it'll be alright. Maybe I can do this. What should I do, Baylor? How can I stop feeling like this?"

For the hundredth time in what only seems like hours, I come apart, already breaking my vow not to anymore. I sob and heave and hiccup into the phone while Baylor waits for me to calm down. I can only imagine what she must think of me. I'm ready for her to bite my head off. Tell me what a bad person I am. It's okay. I can take it. She won't be telling me anything I don't already know.

"Skylar, are you okay? Can I talk now? Will you listen to me for a second?"

"Okay." I scrunch my eyes tightly together and brace myself for her lynching.

"Listen closely, little sister. You did not cause this. What happened to Erin is not your fault. Not even in the tiniest way. Even if you had an affair with her husband, you still couldn't have caused her to get cancer. Stop beating yourself up about it. Secondly, you have to let go of this guilt you have over Griffin. I know I've told you before, but I'll tell you again. The heart wants what it wants. Yours wants Griffin. That's perfectly okay. Normal even. You never acted on it. You knew it would be wrong. You did the right thing. You are a good person and a good friend. A bad friend would have made a pass at him. You would never do that. As far as I'm concerned, you are the very best kind of friend. The kind who can fall in love with her friend's man but never act upon it out of love and respect for your friend. You are the kind of friend everyone should have, Skylar. You are kind, loyal and righteous. You've done nothing wrong. You've done everything right. Do you hear me? You are a good person and you did nothing wrong."

I let her words sink in. I let them sink into my soul. It may take a while before I can fully accept them, however. How is it that she knows exactly what to say to me, exactly when I need it to be said?

"I fucking love you, Baylor. Do you know that?"

She laughs. "I love you too, Skylar."

"I need your help with something."

"Anything, you got it."

We spend the next hour brainstorming ideas to make the next weeks or months the very best in all of Erin's twenty-seven years.

chapter thirteen

Having squared things away at Mitchell's, I arrive at the hospital with a platter of food just after noon. I didn't know who would be here, so I had our chef prepare extra. And although I don't normally recommend eating Chicken Piccata on paper plates, it'll have to do. We'll feed the nurses with whatever food is left over.

I smile when I enter the room and see the gigantic arrangement of white lilies I had sent over this morning. When I told the florist that the flowers were for my friend in the hospital who was dying, he reprimanded me for sending this type of flower. The flower used at funerals. He asked if I was playing a sick joke on her. I assured him they were her favorite. He didn't need to know more. He didn't need to know about the lilies and Bean. He wouldn't understand. Nobody else does.

I study Erin and see that she looks pensive today. I wonder if she's told me everything. Is she already having some of those symptoms that would indicate her progression is farther along than she let us believe? She looks between Griffin and me like she wants to say something. Maybe she's waiting for the right time. Maybe it's just not now, while we're going over the bucket list she made last night.

We laughed when I walked in the room and we handed each other a piece of paper with similar intentions written upon them. To cram as much fun into her last weeks as possible. Okay, so Erin's list may be a little less pretentious and wild than the one Baylor and I came up with.

Erin's list consists of things such as giving money to the less fortunate, sending an anonymous gift to someone in need and having a picnic in Central Park. I peruse the list, wondering how we can make some or all of these things happen. "Who's Mr. Segal?" I ask, referring to line item number four on her list.

"He was my ninth grade English teacher." She smiles as she talks about him and I can tell he's important to her. I silently promise to go to the ends of the earth to find him. "I became a teacher because of him. He showed me how much fun learning could be. He never raised his voice. He never got mad, he merely came up with ways to reach each student individually rather than bundle us all together, assuming we'd all learn the same way. I've always wanted to thank him."

I nod my head, continuing to read further down. "Skydiving?" I raise an eyebrow. Erin's never been an outdoor kind of girl, so this one surprises me.

"I know I can't really do it. My doctor says I shouldn't fly or do anything that involves a change in air pressure. So that kind of precludes skydiving and the next thing on the list, seeing the Eiffel Tower. But it's something I wish I would have done." She looks me straight in the eyes. "Don't ever wait to do things, Skylar. Promise me. Don't ever wait to live your life."

I pull her into a hug, crinkling the papers we're holding. "I promise. But you're not done either. We have a lot to accomplish and we'd better get busy if you really want to" —I look at her list— "ride an elephant?"

Griffin chuckles in the corner of the room. "Have you seen this?" I ask him.

He nods, looking up briefly from his laptop. Then he secretly winks at me and I'm sure at this very second, he's Googling places to ride elephants within a few hours' drive. I smile. We're really doing this.

The next item on her list surprises the hell out of me. "You want to get a tattoo and a body piercing?"

She giggles. "Sure. Why not? Everyone's doing it."

I make sure Griffin isn't listening when I lean close. I don't want to offend him. "Tattoos are scary, Erin. Who knows where those dirty needles have been."

She smirks. "It's not like it's gonna kill me, Skylar."

My face falls and I'm sure I pale at her words.

She puts a hand on my arm. "Too soon?" she asks.

"Yeah." I nod my head. She's joking about dying. How do you go from finding out you have a terminal brain tumor to joking about it in six short weeks?

"Sorry." She gives me a sad smile. "Okay, what's next on my list?"

"Try new, exotic foods," I read out loud. Bingo! This I can help with. I make a note to call Jorge, our head chef and get him on it. "Sounds reasonable."

I continue down the list. "Be a brunette?" My brows arch in amusement.

She nods emphatically. "I always wanted to, but my sisters would never let me. They always claimed I had such a unique shade of blonde that I'd be going against nature if I dyed it." She picks up a lock of her hair and examines it. "Screw nature—it obviously screwed me. I'm doing it. Will you help me?"

"Does your book say anything about pregnant women not being able to dye hair?" I ask.

"I don't mean for *you* to dye my hair, Skylar. I meant, will you go with me to the salon?"

"I know what you meant." I give her my best *I'm not stupid* look. "I was thinking maybe I'd do it with you—become a brunette. You know, if that's okay."

Her smile nearly reaches her sparkling eyes. "Yes!" she shouts. "That's going to be a hoot. Oh, let's do it tomorrow. Can we?" Then her eyes roll. "God, I'm being so selfish. Of course you have to work tomorrow. How about on your next day off?"

I sit down on the bed and pin her to her pillow with my stare. I need her to hear this and know I'm serious. "Erin, I'm not going to work tomorrow. In fact, I won't be working much for a while. I'm here for you whenever, however you need me."

Her mouth falls open. "But you can't just—"

"I can and I will. In fact, it's already been taken care of and there's nothing you can do or say to change my mind. You're going to have to get it through that thick head of blonde-for-one-more-day hair that I love you and will be here for you."

I glance over at Griffin, still pounding away on his laptop and I see him smiling at the words I've spoken. He looks up and gives me a nod. We lock eyes briefly. His eyes are filled with thanks. With gratitude. With hope that we can make something nice out of this horrible situation.

My gaze returns to Erin only to find her watching us. I momentarily wonder if she misconstrued our brief silent exchange. I swear I wasn't thinking inappropriate thoughts just now. I open my mouth to explain, but she pulls me close and hands me another piece of paper. There is only one thing written on it. "For your eyes only," she whispers.

I read the slip of paper. It says '*Get Griffin and his dad to reunite.*'

I lock eyes with her. I know what a falling out they had. His dad left his mom to die while he got drunk on the couch watching reruns of bad TV. He did this horrible thing to Griffin and his mom while she was going through what Erin is going through, yet she wants Griffin to forgive him?

"We'll need to get started on this right away," she whispers. She turns over the paper and points to a name and phone number. "Call him for me. Explain things. See if he will meet. I know he will. He's attempted to contact Griffin in the past, but a few years ago he stopped trying."

"What are you girls whispering about?" Griffin asks. "You aren't taking my wife to a strip club, are you?"

Erin and I both laugh. Maybe not a strip club exactly, but Baylor and I did put something on the list just as racy.

"One more," Erin says. Nodding to the original list she gave me.

My eyes fall to the bottom of her short list. "You want to perform a miracle?" I give her my most incredulous look.

"What?" She innocently shrugs her shoulders. "I can't skydive either, but I still put it on the list." She smooths out my list that was crumpled when we hugged. "Okay, now let's go over yours." She reads the first thing and tears instantly well in her eyes. "Are you serious? I could never ask Baylor and Gavin for this."

I shake my head. "It was their idea. They want you to have the experience of watching a child come into the world. They want you to be at the birth of their baby. To hold a newborn just minutes old. I know it's no replacement for Bean, but…"

"Oh, my gosh." Tears fall into her mouth that is now smiling. "Yes. Yes, tell them yes. And thank you. Tell them thank you. I can't believe they would do that. What an honor." She turns to Griffin, prompting my eyes to follow. "Did you hear that, Griff? I'm going to see a baby being born. Can you believe it?"

"That's incredible." He draws his lips in, forming a thin line where they meet. His gaze is on my stomach, where his baby grows safe and sound, blissfully unaware of his world changing before he's even born. Is Griffin, too, wondering about the fate of the child who is being left to deal with later?

It dawns on me that this is the first time I've referred to the baby as either sex. A boy. Yes, I think it's a boy. Suddenly, I can't wait to find out. Erin needs to know. I make one more mental note to speak to Griffin later.

Erin blushes as she reads the next item on the list. She whispers, "Watch a porn flick, really?"

Griffin laughs out loud behind us. Obviously Erin wasn't as quiet as she thought in her whisper. It makes me wonder if he heard what she said about his dad, too.

"Yes, really. That's assuming you haven't already watched one."

If her reaction is any indication, I'd say I was spot-on in calling this one. Everyone should see a dirty movie before they die.

She ignores my questioning stare and runs her finger down to the next item on the list. "Stay at… what?" She turns to me wide-eyed. "Isn't that New York's most expensive hotel?"

I glance over at Griffin. He immediately taps on the keyboard. Yeah, he's on board with that. Good for him. I guess he really did mean what he said. I look back at Erin and shrug.

"Drink expensive champagne?" she reads. "Oh, we've already done that. Griffin had some great stuff at our wedding."

I look over at him and he rolls his eyes. "Erin, that was forty dollars a bottle. We can do a helluva lot better than that."

"I don't want you spending money on me, Griff." She looks back at me. "You either, Skylar."

"I don't think you have much say in the matter," I tell her. "So best to just sit back and enjoy the ride. You asked us to accept your choices. Now you need to accept ours. We will do what we need to make things happen." I look her square in the eyes. "Okay?"

I can tell she's contemplating fighting me on this one. She lets out a huff, but I think it's only in mock exasperation, just for the sake of principle. "Fine," she says.

She continues down my list and reads aloud, "Learn to belly dance... shoot a gun... participate in a flash mob... walk a red carpet... buy a round of drinks for everyone in a crowded bar. Ooooo, I like that last one. That sounds fun!"

As we reach the end of both lists, my mind is swimming with ideas that I can't wait to get home and put into motion. A few of them will take much collaboration. Fortunately between Griffin's money and both of us having influential friends, I think we might be able to pull some of these off.

"Griffin, I have a favor to ask," she says.

"Anything, you name it." He looks up from his laptop ready to give his wife whatever she wants laced in gold and wrapped in silk if that's how she wants it.

"It's silly, but I've always wanted to sleep on a waterbed. Ever since I was little back when it was the trend. I'd really love it if you could get one set up for us. Today. Before I go home. I'll be busy getting my scans soon and Skylar can stay with me while you're gone."

He closes the laptop and stuffs it into his bag. He strides across the room and gives her a kiss on the lips. "You got it, sweetheart."

"You okay here?" he asks me.

"Of course. Go," I tell him. He mouths '*later?*' motioning between us. Oh, right, we were supposed to meet during her scans. I guess that isn't going to happen now. I mouth back '*my place?*' and he nods. Then I pale, thinking about what that must look like. I spin around to see a curt smile on Erin's face. Relief washes over me that she didn't catch our exchange and think we were hooking up instead of planning a meeting to go over these lists.

I think about what Baylor told me last night. *You're a good person, Skylar. This is not your fault. You didn't do anything wrong.* I play it over and over in my head. I might even almost believe it. Almost.

Erin pats the bed next to her. "Come sit. Let's have some girl talk now that he's gone."

I raise my eyebrows at her, but sit nonetheless.

"There's one more thing on my list. Actually, it's the only thing on my list that even matters. And you are the only person who can help me make it happen."

"Whatever you need, Erin. I'll do anything you ask. Just name it."

She smiles. "I was hoping you'd say that. And I hope you really mean it, because what I'm about to ask you is a tall order."

"Are you kidding? Don't even think twice about it. Spit it out already."

She takes a deep breath and blows it out. She closes her eyes and stretches her neck back. Then she looks at me with the most serious eyes I've ever seen. "I want this baby to grow up with two parents, Skylar. All babies need a chance at that. I want him to be in a large family with lots of people around. I want him to be loved and cherished. I want him to have a wonderful life."

A tear slips from my eye when I think of the picture she's painting. She can see her baby growing up in a household like she did. She wants that for him. He deserves it. I'll help her make it happen. I nod at her. "Okay. You want me to help you find the most perfect adoptive parents who ever walked the earth. I can do that. Of course I can do that."

She smiles at me. "No, Skylar. I already know who I want." She grabs my hand and holds it tight like I might try to escape from her. "It's you. You and Griffin. I want you to raise him. I want you to be his parents. I want you to be his family. I want you to love him and cherish him and maybe even give him some siblings down the road."

"What?" I'm not sure I'm hearing her. I think I know what she's saying but maybe the cancer has progressed further than we thought and is making her behave strangely. I read about this. "Uh… what exactly are you asking?"

"You know what I'm asking, Skylar." She pulls me closer to her. "I'm asking you to become the family that I'll never be a part of. I'm asking this completely outrageous and monumental thing of you. I know it's crazy. I know people will think I'm delusional. But, I'm not. I've seen you together. You guys are adorable. I know you are attracted to each other. I know you would never betray me by acting on it. And I know it may be the hardest thing you ever do in your lives, but I'm asking you anyway. Be the parents to the child who already has your blood running through his veins. Find a way to be with Griffin when I'm gone. Find a way to love each other like you both deserve to be loved. I'm asking you to take my husband and make him yours."

My mouth hangs open. I'm reeling from her request. I'm not sure I can even find any words. She wants me to be with Griffin and raise the baby as our own. She wants us to sleep together and have more babies. She wants me to… *be his wife?*

"You said anything, Skylar. You said you'd do anything for me. I don't care about all that other stuff. I want you to do this. I need you to do this. I'm dying. I realize it's petty and cruel, but I'm playing the cancer card. I'm asking you to fulfill my dying wish. I want you to be with Griffin. I want you to marry him and have a family. I want you to live happily ever after. Will you do this for me? Please?"

I pinch the bridge of my nose before massaging my temples. When I'm finally capable of forming words with my mouth, I say, "There are so many things wrong with this, Erin. You must know that. First of all, it's not only my choice." I freeze. "Oh my God. Have you talked to Griffin about this?"

She shakes her head. "Not yet. Today though. When he gets back."

"I didn't think so." There is no way he knew anything about this. He will freak out. He'll freak out worse than I'm freaking out. He'll want nothing to do with it. He loves her. He's loved only her. Since… forever. We seem to fight whenever we get together. It could never work. "You say you've seen us together, but you haven't. You weren't even around most of the time we were together. We fight all the time. We practically hate each other, Erin."

She laughs. "There's a fine line between love and hate. And sometimes it's called passion."

I gasp. "Passion? Is that what you think is between us? You *are* off your rocker."

"Are you going to sit there and tell me you haven't thought about my husband that way?" she asks. "That you've never fantasized about him when you were cooking together, or at the ballgame, or out to dinner? The blush on your face right now tells me all I need to know. It's okay, Skylar. Griffin is hot. He's nice and genuine and wonderful. And I know he'll do what I ask. He'll do anything for me. He's proven that time and time again. It's not him I need to convince. It's you."

I eye her skeptically. "You've been planning this." I think of all the times over the past month that Griffin and I have been thrown together. All the times Erin didn't show up, forcing us to be alone. "The dress, the cleavage, the sex toys, the baseball game, the suggestive talks about Griffin's penis and sexual awesomeness—this was all your plan to get me to fall for him, wasn't it?"

A tear trails down my face. All this time. It wasn't my fault. I was being manipulated into falling for a man who was unavailable. Or so I thought. All the guilt I felt over what I was doing to my best friend. I drop her hand and stand up, pushing myself away from the bed. "You bitch! Do you know how guilty I've felt over the situations you put me in with him? Do you know how much I hated myself every time I had an inappropriate thought about *your* husband? How dare you screw with my life like that?"

She's crying with me now. "I'm sorry. It's true. Everything you said. But I didn't know any other way. I had to find out if you were compatible. I had to know if there could ever be something there. I know that there can be, Skylar. And I'm asking you to let there be."

I feel dirty. Like I need to run home and shower and scrub filth from my flesh. "Doesn't it make your skin crawl thinking of Griffin with another woman? How can you even suggest it?"

"Yes, of course it does," she says. "Don't you think if I had my way that none of this would even be happening? But I can't have my way. It's not about me anymore." She motions to my belly. "It's about him. I chose to do this. It was *my* decision to bring this life into the world. And now I have to do what's best for him. That means making sure he grows up with loving parents. Parents who are already his biological mom and dad. People who I can trust his precious little life with."

"I don't want kids, Erin!" I shout at her. "I was never unclear about that and you know it."

She shakes her head, allowing another tear to spill over. "You may think that, but I see the way you are with them. With Baylor's son. With my nieces and nephews. I just think you've never let yourself try. You've always given them back when they cry or poop or need anything. You've never had one of them depend on you for more than a smile and a laugh. But I know you. I know you can do this."

"What about one of your sisters?" I ask. "I'm sure they would be happy to adopt him. It's the perfect solution."

"No, Skylar. He needs to be with his mom and dad. His real mom and dad."

"But Griffin and I... I just can't."

"You can. I know you can."

"You can't force us together, Erin. Yes, you can ask us to try, but you can't make us fall in love."

She looks at me and raises her brow. *Does she know?* How could she possibly?

"I've seen the chemistry between you. You need to understand that when I went into early menopause, I wasn't exactly the sexual person I used to be when Griffin and I first started having sex in college. I tried to be a good wife and keep him happy.

I try to be sexy. But sometimes it's hard to pretend when your body just doesn't crave it. He sees you as this fertile, sexual being. I can see it in the way he follows you, stares at you when you're not watching. You're carrying his child, and intentional or not, men are ingrained to be attracted to that."

I can only stare at her, shaking my head.

"Would you prefer the baby grow up without a mother? Because I know Griffin will do it. He'll be the best single dad he can. For me. But do you really want to burden him with that? You see Mason. You see how hard it is being a single dad. Children are meant to be raised by two parents. I know sometimes that doesn't always happen, but it doesn't have to be that way with this baby. You are perfectly capable of giving him a wonderful life. You are perfectly capable of loving Griffin and making a family.

"You know how much I believe in fate. Things happen for a reason. I'm here to bring you and the baby together with Griffin. You have to allow me to do that. Otherwise, my life will be in vain."

I narrow my eyes at her ridiculous statement. "Is that what you really think? That your fate was to die young and give your husband and child to another woman?"

"No. My fate is to be that precious baby's guardian angel forever. And I'm starting right now. Please, Skylar. It's my one dying wish. Do this for me. For him." She points to my belly.

I pick up my coat off the chair. "I can't... I have to go." I head for the door and without turning around to face her, I say, "I'll call Baylor or one of your sisters to come sit with you until Griffin gets back."

Then I walk out of her room. I walk down the hallway and get into the elevator. I ride it down and head for the entrance. My stomach churns. I know what that means and I run for the nearest bathroom only to make it as far as the sink before I lose my helping of Chicken Piccata.

I wipe my mouth and stare in the mirror. What's happening? This can't be happening. All this time, I've wanted him. I've wanted what she has. I've even envisioned myself in her place. In her life. And now, she's handing it to me on a goddamn silver platter. She wants me to live her life. Be her. Raise her kid. Fuck her husband.

And there's only one thing running through my mind at this moment. Something my dad used to say when I was young.

Be careful what you wish for.

chapter fourteen

Damn her.

I was supposed to be working on the list. Arranging for her
last months to be full of friends, family and extraordinary
experiences. Why did she have to go and ruin that with her
ridiculous request? All I can do is sit here and think about
everything she said. She doesn't know what she wants. It must be
her disease making her say those crazy things. The baby would be
much better off with an adoptive couple who would love it, not a
mom who doesn't even want it and a dad who will be grieving for
God knows how long.

If I weren't pregnant, I know exactly what I'd be doing.
Getting drunk. No, plastered is more like it. I want to forget
everything that has happened in the past two days. I want to go
back to the way things were. Life was easy then. All I had to do was
pick out what I was going to wear to work and make my customers
happy. Now, I have to help pick out a casket and grant a dying
woman her last wishes.

I don't know how long I've been lying here when I suddenly feel strange. My stomach flutters and I wonder if I'm going to puke again. I close my eyes and breathe, trying to stave off my would-be sickness when it dawns on me that something incredible is happening. These flutters I'm feeling, as light as a butterfly's wings, it's not nausea, it's the baby moving. *Oh, God.*

My hand instinctively goes to my belly as I concentrate on feeling the sensation. He's in there. There's actually a living, breathing human growing inside of me. I mean, I've known it all along. I even saw Bean on the ultrasound, but it was never truly real until this very second. Why now? Why did he choose now to let me know he's there? Is it because he knows I said I didn't want him?

A wave of guilt washes through me. Could I do this? Could I be a mom? It was never part of the plan.

Then, as quickly as it started, the flutters cease. I lay perfectly still for a long time, willing them to come back. Is he okay? Is something wrong because he stopped moving?

A knock on the door startles me, and I jump up to answer it.

I look through the peephole to see the top of Griffin's dark hair. He's slumped over, his head is hung low and he's supporting himself against my door with an outstretched arm. Did she tell him? Or is he just here to go over the list? My heart races thinking of facing him after the bomb Erin dropped on us.

I tentatively open the door and Griffin falls through it like he forgot he was leaning against it. He stumbles into my apartment, catching himself before he hits the floor. He looks up at me and it's written all over his face. He knows. He's defeated. Lost. Shattered. He's also drunk off his ass if his unsteadiness and his smell are any indication.

"Are you drunk?"

"Damn, I hope so," he slurs. He walks into the kitchen and starts rummaging through my cabinets.

"What the hell are you doing?" I follow him.

"Got any booze?" He opens the cabinet over the fridge and pulls out a bottle of champagne. The bottle Erin brought, but never opened, the second time we took a pregnancy test. I had forgotten it was even there.

I try to grab it from him. "You can't open that! It was from Erin."

His eyes go wide as he keeps the bottle from me. Then he turns so his back is to me and proceeds to rip the foil from the cork.

"Stop it, Griffin! Don't do this."

He laughs as the cork pops and a bit of liquid spills from the bottle. The laugh is desperate. Full of pain. Broken. "Well, it's only fitting it was from her. This way we can toast the happy fucking couple. To us." He tips the bottle at me and then takes a long drink from it.

I watch as he chugs the warm champagne. I worry that he's drinking too much on top of what he's already had. That won't do anyone any good. I rip the bottle from his lips, spilling some onto the floor as it trails out of his mouth.

"What'd you do that for?" he yells, looking at the puddle on the floor below. "You wasted some damn fine champagne. Not a very good way to start this thing." His cloudy, unfocused eyes find mine. "You always gonna tell me what to do? Already acting like my ball and fucking chain, aren't ya?"

"Griffin, stop!" I yell over his voice. "This isn't any way to deal with it. You're making it worse."

"Ha!" He all but falls over, slipping in the spilled liquid, but catching himself on the countertop. "Worse? How can I make this any fucking worse? My wife is dying. *Dying!* And she wants me to fuck her best friend. That's one hell of a parting gift, don't you think? How about you? How does it make you feel being my goddamn consolation prize?"

Tears collect in my eyes. I try not to let his words get to me. He's drunk. He's hurting. He's devastated. He's trying to cope with the unrealistic demands his sick wife is making. I can't fault him for getting drunk. I'd be right there with him if I could.

He tries to grab the bottle from me but I won't let it go. We struggle for a second and then his hand slips and the bottle falls, crashing into the sink, shattering into many broken pieces. We both stare at it. Then I feel a sting and look down to see that my hand got sliced from the bottle. "Fuck!" I scream out in anger. In hurt. In sheer heartache for our situation.

"Goddammit, Sky, don't say fuck!"

I spin around and reach for a towel, but slip on the champagne. Griffin catches me and pulls me into his arms. Before I even realize what's happening, his lips are on mine. He kisses me with such desperation, like a man who will never kiss a woman again. And for one small second, I let him. For one small second, I want to forget everyone and everything. I want to forget about dying and bucket lists and final wishes. Forget motherless babies, widowed fathers, and grieving friends. For one second I let myself live the fantasy of Griffin's lips on my body.

But when the second is over and I fully comprehend what's happening, I pull away. Then I slap him. Hard. "What the hell are you doing?"

"I'm doing what she wants!" he yells.

I grab a paper towel and hold it to the small cut on my hand. I throw a few more down on the puddle, so we won't slip on it again. Then I go into the living room. Away from him. I sink into the couch and pull my legs up to protect me. I watch him follow me. I see the moment he realizes what he's done as horror washes over his face and he closes his eyes. He sits on the chair opposite me. His body language says everything. His head falls forward and his arms rest on his knees. He shakes his head back and forth. "Jesus, Skylar. What the hell did I do?"

"I won't disrespect her like that," I say. "Even if she thinks this is what she wants. I would never do that to her."

He leaps off the couch and runs into my bathroom. I don't have to ask why. I take the opportunity to clean up my wound and the kitchen floor. I carefully throw the shards of glass into the trash and then I put on a large pot of coffee.

When I emerge from the kitchen, I find Griffin passed out on my couch. Good, he should sleep it off. We have a lot of planning to do. The rest can wait. I make a few phone calls while he sleeps.

Two hours later, when Griffin comes to, my apartment has been populated with friends and family. Mason, Baylor, Mindy, Jenna and a few of Erin's sisters are here.

Griffin looks around at everyone. His guilt-ridden gray eyes fall on mine and I see the regret. He stares at me until I give him a smile and a nod, letting him know I understand. That I forgive him. That everything will be okay. Well, almost everything.

"Who's with her?" he asks.

"Our parents are there," Jane says. "She's going to be released in a couple of hours, so if you want to be there take her home, we'd better get started." She gives him a look of disapproval.

I had briefly explained that Griffin showed up drunk. I left out everything else that happened. I'm not sure how much everyone knows. I'm one-hundred-percent sure, however, that Baylor knows everything. The way she's looking at me, at Griffin. It's as if she knows we've been put in this impossible situation.

Makes sense. I did text her to go sit with Erin until Griffin got back. Good. I'm glad she knows. This way I don't have to explain it to her. She can help me talk sense into Erin.

But that will have to wait. We have other things to deal with right now.

Griffin and Erin's family help add a few more things to our list and by the time we disband, we have several balls rolling in all kinds of different directions. The first of which will be Erin being whisked away from the hospital not to their townhouse, but to a pricy and pretentious hotel by way of limo. Waiting for her in the penthouse suite will be a spread of some of the finest, most exotic foods Jorge could whip up with an extra team of chefs we brought in at the last minute. Frogs legs, caviar, Ethiopian cuisine, black truffles, Peking duck. She will drink milk straight from a coconut and eat fresh oysters on the half-shell. It's a spread fit for a queen. Or a last meal. Take your pick.

If she likes that, I can't wait to see what her reaction will be to tomorrow's planned agenda.

Baylor hangs around after everyone else leaves. I wondered if Griffin would stay, too. But since my sister appears to be staking her claim on me, he and I will have to discuss our predicament some other time.

Sitting on the couch with Baylor, my eyes focus on her very pregnant belly. She's due any day now. As far as I'm concerned, the sooner the better. That way Erin won't miss the birth. "I felt the bean move earlier."

Her eyes light up and her face sports a knowing smile. "That's wonderful. Isn't it the most incredible feeling in the world?"

I suppose you could look at it that way. I simply saw it as a reminder of a huge problem that has to be dealt with. A guilt kick from a child trying to assert himself into the world without being forgotten.

"Don't you think it's kind of coincidental that the baby kicked today of all days?" she asks. "On the day that you officially become its mother?"

"What?" I snap my eyes to hers. "No. Are you crazy?" I shake my head vehemently.

"Are we going to talk about this rationally, Skylar?"

"I *am* being rational. I'm not cut out to be a mom. Erin is delusional." I lean my head back against the couch cushion and sigh. "She orchestrated this whole thing. Did she tell you that, too? Did she tell you that she *made* me fall for him? That she set us up and put us in situations where we'd be thrown together? That she deliberately fed my inappropriate fantasies? Hell, maybe my feelings aren't even my own. Maybe they are just manifestations of what she wanted me to feel."

Baylor eyes me skeptically. "Do you mean to tell me that now the door is open, you don't love him anymore?"

I silently pick at an invisible spot on my jeans.

"I didn't think so," she says. "So, what's the problem? It's the ideal solution, isn't it? It may be a bit unconventional, but you are Bean's parents after all. It makes sense. Plus, you already love Griffin. And he likes you a lot. Erin told me they talk about you all the time and that Griffin seems to be enamored."

"I'm sure she brainwashed him, too," I spit out.

"You can lead a horse to water, Skylar." She raises an eyebrow.

"Would you quit with all the idioms, Baylor? I don't need that shit right now. How can you be on her side? This is ludicrous. Would you be able to give Gavin away to Jenna if you were dying? Could you even think about him touching another woman?" I shake my head. "He kissed me today. Fucking kissed me. Do you think I should run back to Erin and tell her how wonderful that is? Maybe he should just fuck me now to give her a nice going away present. Maybe we could videotape it for her enjoyment. Is that what you think we should do? Is it?"

"No. Of course not." She lays a hand on my arm. "Calm down."

I take a few deep breaths while she goes to the kitchen and comes back with a bottle of water for me. She hands it over to me saying, "To answer your question—yes."

I look at her in confusion.

"I spent a lot of time this afternoon trying to put myself in Erin's position. I thought about what would happen to my husband. To Maddox. To our baby if I only had a few months to live. And the answer is an emphatic yes. I would absolutely want someone I love and trust to take care of my family." She gives me a look of compassion, the look only a big sister can share with a little sister. The look that tells me I'm not alone in this. "Let this sink in. Give yourself a chance to accept it. It seems as if Griffin is on board, although I have to say I don't agree with him kissing you."

"Me either. I know he did it because he was drunk. And angry. And confused over the whole situation."

"And that's understandable," she adds. "But you need to show Erin the respect she deserves. You need to let this play out separate from her, when she's not watching. After she's gone even."

"Play out? I still think you're all crazy. How can we be together? Even if I do love him, and I'm not even sure I do anymore, he hates me half the time. Heck, sometimes I think I even hate him. We seem to fight constantly when we're together."

"Hate isn't the opposite of love, Skylar, it's just its twisted cousin." I eye her speculatively, thinking of something similar that Erin said earlier today.

"You can do this, little sister. You owe it to Bean to at least try. You owe it to Erin. But most of all, you owe it to yourself." She gives me her best big sister smile. "It wasn't so long ago when I remember you telling us that you wanted to do something meaningful with your life. That's what got you here today. What could be more meaningful than fulfilling a dying woman's last wish? What could give your life more purpose than allowing this little baby to grow up with both his parents? You said it yourself, Skylar. You wanted to change in a fundamental way. This is your chance. This is the ultimate test. This will define who you are and direct the course of your life. But, most importantly, I want you to think about this—if you walk away, will you be able to live with yourself?"

Her words are profound. They swirl around in my head like a damn tornado eating up everything in its path. I never looked at it that way. I've been consumed by thoughts about how I can't do it, how I'm not cut out for it, how I'm being forced into it. But I never for one second stopped to think how I would feel down the road if I walked away. Walked away from my best friend. Walked away from this baby. Our baby. *My baby.*

I put a hand on my stomach and for the very first time, I allow myself to feel. I allow myself to feel the connection to the life growing inside of me. And as if responding to a question I'd sent up to heaven, my tummy flutters as the little bean answers back.

chapter fifteen

As we wait for Erin to emerge from the dressing room, Griffin tells me how wonderful last night was at the hotel. He again thanks me for the food I had sent over, saying they enjoyed tasting all the exotic cuisines as they sipped champagne that cost as much as my first car. He was even able to arrange for them to set up a king-sized waterbed in their suite.

We stand off in a corner, trying to remain out of the way as dozens of people rush around in a flurry of activity, shouting this and moving that. I find a 'Mad Max Productions' director's chair to sit in while we wait. Gavin was able to shuffle a few things around last minute which resulted in Erin getting cast as an extra in the movie being shot under his studio label. It's not anything big and fancy. No Brad Pitt or Julia Roberts. It's an indie film that Gavin's company bought as one of their first projects when he started his company early this year.

I smile thinking how grateful I am to be able to be a part of moments like this. Yesterday, one of Erin's sisters had mentioned that before Erin decided to become a teacher, her life's dream was to be an actress. Star in a movie and walk the red carpet. When she was little, she had a large roll of red felt her mom bought at a flea market and Erin would spread it across their living room and dress up like a princess while prancing around on it, thanking her many fans.

It was sheer luck that Gavin's production was shooting locally today. He was able to get her added as an extra and as a bonus, she even gets to say a few words in passing to one of the lead characters. Because of the speaking part, and the fact that the cameras will be focused on her, even for just a few seconds, she had to be done in full hair and makeup. And apparently, even for an extra, that takes a lot of time.

So Griffin and I sit and make small talk while we wait for Erin's film debut. We talk about the weather. It's getting chilly. It makes me wonder if Erin will be able to hold on until the holidays. We talk about the restaurant. It makes me think of the first time I met her, looking larger than life and ready to take on the world with me. We talk about Baylor and how she's ready to pop any day now.

It's then that I notice him staring at my belly.

He looks around to make sure we're alone. "Are we going to talk about this?"

"Talk about what?" As if I don't know.

"The elephant in the room," he says, nodding to my stomach.

"Are you calling me fat again?" I tease.

He laughs. It's nice to hear him laugh again. "I wouldn't dare. Not after the new asshole you ripped me last time."

Now I laugh, thinking about the fight we had during his one and only cooking lesson. He studies me, looking between my face and my pregnant belly that is just beginning to become obvious to the world.

"She couldn't give a rat's ass if you learn how to cook," I tell him. "You realize that now, right?"

He nods his head. "Yeah. Listen, I'm so sorry about what happened yesterday. I know my being drunk is no excuse. It won't happen again. I was just so pissed at her."

"Pissed?"

"Yeah, aren't you? She took away our choices, Skylar. She took away the chance to be with her these last six weeks. I mean, if I had known then, I would have quit working and maybe taken her to see the world. Paris. She always wanted to go. We said we would. Someday. And now, well, what we're setting up next week is great and all, but it's not the same."

I agree. Even buying out the entire Imax theater for a day and treating Erin to a visual experience in Paris that way, still won't produce the memories of actually being there.

"And the choice of who we should be with? After she... when she's gone. She's taken that away from us, too. So, yes, I'm pissed at her. I won't tell her that. I won't taint her last months with my anger, but that's the way I feel."

I can only nod in agreement with everything he's said. But I add, "We do have a choice, Griffin." I motion to my belly. "We don't have to do this."

"You don't want to?" he asks. His eyes trace the outline of the chair I'm sitting in.

"Do you?" My heart braces for his answer. And even though I know that if he says yes, he'll be doing it for Erin and not for me, I still wait with bated breath.

"I want to honor her wishes. And it's not like I don't find you attractive. Of course I do. Any man in his right mind does."

It's hard to enjoy the compliment when I feel a *'but'* coming, and it sends a spear straight into my heart. I'm not sure if I want to do this either, but hearing him say he doesn't will crush me.

"But, I just can't say for sure what I want right now. My wife is dying. It's all I can do to hold it together and get through this. I'm sorry I can't give you a better answer."

I'm not sure what I expected him to say, but I respect him for what he said. If he'd said *'hell, yeah, let's get it on,'* I'd run the other way. If he'd said *'hell, no, I don't want my kid,'* I'd think he was just as much a low life. He said the perfect thing. Which happens to be the only thing he could have said to make me fall for him even more.

"We don't have to figure it out right now," I say. "This little guy isn't going anywhere for a long time. But Erin is going to want answers. And we don't have them. What are we going to do about that?"

He bites the inside of his cheek and stares at the ceiling. "We're going to tell her what she wants to hear, I guess. We'll not bring it up unless she does and when she does we'll just say we've agreed to try. Nothing more, nothing less. Sound good?"

"Sounds good."

We sit in awkward silence for a few minutes. How the hell can this be taking so long? It's only a little hair and makeup. Erin's already beautiful, they don't have to do much. I search my mind to think of anything to say to pass the time.

I glance over at Griffin to see him rubbing his tattoo. "Do you think she'll really get one?" I ask.

He chuckles. I understand. The idea of Miss Prim-and-proper getting a tattoo is laughable. "Who knows. But I'll be there to hold her hand if she does. I'll do anything for her, Skylar."

Is there hidden meaning in that statement? He just told me a minute ago that he isn't sure he can honor her wish, yet he's telling me he'll do anything. Maybe he means he'll do anything while she's alive, but then after, all bets are off.

"It's started already," he says.

"Started?"

He nods. "I missed all the signs before. The slurred or missing words. The fatigue. The headaches. I never once thought they meant anything. And now, for the past two days, I notice every little symptom. They scream out at me and are as obvious as her eyes are blue. And I notice new ones, as well. The way her hand falls away from mine when she loses feeling in it. The way she will sometimes ask the same question twice. It's starting. And it kills me."

It kills me, too. But I'm trying not to think about it. There will be plenty of time for that later. I try to lighten the mood. "Hey, would you mind if I steal Erin for a girl's day tomorrow? She wants to color her hair and I have a few other things that don't involve boys that I'd like to do with her."

He looks pained, like he doesn't want to let go of her for one second. But I can tell he knows she needs this. She needs time with her family and friends, too. He needs to share her with us. Even if it's the hardest thing he ever has to do. He scrolls though his phone and then grabs a pen and paper off the nearest table. He scribbles something and hands it to me. "This is a hair stylist who works with a lot of the models I shoot. I'm going to text him right now and let him know you'll be calling. He owes me a favor. If he's in town, he'll squeeze you in. I'm sure of it."

My jaw drops when I see Erin emerge from the dressing room area. They're directing her over to where she will stand with a large group of people. She's supposed to be part of a crowd at a concert.

They are pumping out dry ice to make it smoky. The lights dim after they've told everyone exactly how the scene will play out. She has one line. When the lead character walks by the crowd, she is supposed to stumble into him and say 'Excuse me.' That's it. That's all she has to do. And this took two hours of hair, makeup and costuming.

Griffin and I can't peel our eyes away from her. She's beaming. She's acting out every little girl's dream. The energy coming off her in the dimly lit studio is palpable. She's gorgeous. She's living.

His camera is immediately retrieved from a bag by our feet. He takes dozens, maybe hundreds, of pictures of her. He should. She's radiating happiness.

It takes over an hour and six takes to get the scene right. But not because of Erin. She was flawless. Every time. Every take looked the same to me. I wonder if Gavin asked the director to stretch it out, giving her more time to enjoy the experience. When I find Gavin, standing close behind some of the cameras, he winks at me. Just as I suspected.

I glance at Griffin. He's watching his wife with a look of awe. "She's so happy," he says, staring at her. "She needed this today, after the morning she had."

I stiffen and my insides tense up. "Did something happen?"

"We went by her school. She had to tell her students she's not coming back." He shakes his head and I can tell he feels bad for the seven-year-olds who no doubt think Erin walks on water. "She didn't tell them the entire truth. Only that she's too sick to be their teacher anymore. It was heartbreaking, Skylar. They swarmed her after she told them. They begged her not to leave. They said they would help her out and be really good. They said they'd do anything to keep her there. I knew exactly how they felt and it gutted me."

"I'm so sorry, Griffin." I put my hand on his and give it a reassuring squeeze. Then I momentarily wonder if it's okay to touch him. I stare at my hand that rests on his. I quickly look up to see that Griffin is doing the very same thing. He catches my eyes, holding them with his. He gives me a small nod. Then, at the same time, we withdraw our hands from one another.

I look over to see what's happening on set only to find Erin striding towards us. I'm positive that she saw me touching him. Her gaze is fixed on the arm of the chair our hands just vacated. I also don't miss the fact that it seems to make her happy.

This is truly twisted.

She flings her arms around me. "Thank you so much, Skylar. You and Gavin are absolutely wonderful to have set this up on such short notice. I'll never forget this."

"I'm glad it all came together so nicely. You were wonderful. A natural, Erin, really."

She waves her hand up and down her body like a game show model, showcasing the dress they outfitted her in. "Isn't it fabulous? They're letting me keep it. Cancer perk, I guess." She giggles. Griffin and I wince. "Anyway, I don't want to waste this look. I think I have a gallon of makeup on. I'm freaking hot, don't you think? Let's go out."

"Sweetheart, you'd be hot in a burlap sack," Griffin says. "But, yes. We can go out. What did you have in mind?"

She looks at me. "How about your number nine?"

Griffin looks confused, but I know exactly what she wants. I know because Erin and I have this connection. This understanding of each other. This inexplicable bond that allows us to communicate without words. Well, and also because I know that

163

number nine on the bucket list that Baylor and I concocted will have Erin walking into a crowded bar, shouting 'Drinks are on me!'

"This is going to be so much fun," I say, as Erin and I hook elbows and walk out of the studio with Griffin trailing behind.

chapter sixteen

I stare at the brunette in the mirror. Her green eyes stare back at me, then fall upon the growing baby bump that strains underneath my now-too-tight Yankees t-shirt I'm lounging around the apartment in today. It takes me by surprise each time I catch a glimpse of myself. I let Erin pick out the color and she chose dark brown. Really dark, almost the color of Griffin's. It makes me wonder what color hair Bean will have. Will he have dark blonde hair like I normally do, or will he inherit Griffin's darker, wavier locks?

I had a dream about the baby last night. It's the first time that's ever happened. I was holding the hand of a little boy and he was swinging between me and someone else. But when I looked at the other person, it wasn't Griffin, it was Erin. What does that even mean?

I shake off the bad feeling of Griffin conspicuously missing from my dream and I finish brushing my hair, happy that I chose not to get the permanent color, but the kind that will completely wash out in about four weeks' time. Erin did the same. I'm glad she did. I really didn't want to tell her that I couldn't imagine her not looking like herself her last weeks on earth.

Especially considering what happened the day we went to the salon. When we were out for lunch, after Griffin's hairstylist friend gave us the gold-star treatment, Baylor and Mindy came to join us and Erin asked if I was going to introduce her to my friends. It was hard to hide the shock from our faces, but within a few minutes she was herself again, asking when Baylor and Mindy had joined us. Then she proceeded to drop her fork repeatedly. And she cried in my arms when she almost didn't make it to the bathroom in time to pee. It was the first time I've seen her cry sad tears since we shared tears the day she told me she was dying. The headache that came on that afternoon sent her to the doctor who promptly increased her steroid dosage. Still, she ended up in bed for a couple of days.

Today, we're shopping for baby clothes while Erin's family and our friends make last-minute arrangements for this afternoon's surprise. I realize we don't know the sex of the baby yet. Well, not for sure. But Erin insists it's a boy and she knows her taste in clothing far outweighs mine. I think this kid will have a wardrobe large enough to clothe a small village by the time she's done. She wants to shop for furniture next. She's having everything delivered to her townhouse. I haven't asked why and she's failed to tell me. Some things are better left unsaid at this point. I'm grateful she hasn't pushed. I don't have the heart to tell her nothing has been decided. She hasn't come right out and asked if we're going to honor her dying wish, and Griffin and I are only too happy not to talk about it.

She seems her regular self today. There have been no lapses in memory, no slurred words, no headaches. The only thing I've noticed is her right arm hanging limply at her side. The steroids are doing their job and I'm grateful she'll be able to enjoy the afternoon we have planned. This is by far the largest undertaking and it's taken dozens of people to be able to pull it off.

As we exit the last designer baby store, she looks at me, questioning the horse-drawn carriage sitting at the curb out front. When a grin takes over my face, she bounces up and down like a little girl and takes the driver's hand, hoisting herself into the carriage. We had done this once before, and she was so enamored with the horses, I thought it was only fitting this be her transportation to the ball—so to speak.

'The ball' is actually a picnic in Central Park. Well, picnic is not really an accurate description. Party is more like it. Everyone will be there. All of Erin's family. Aunts, uncles, cousins, you name it. We had them all flown in from various locations around the country. Her former colleagues are coming, along with many of her students. Everyone who has touched her life will be there. Why wait for them to come to her funeral where she wouldn't be able to appreciate each of them?

When we get closer to the party, her eyes go wide as she takes in the tents, the inflatables set up for the children, the endless tables of food and drink, the local band we hired that she said was her favorite a while back when we were at a club together. "Tell me this is not all for me, Skylar."

I smile. "You said you wanted a picnic in Central Park, didn't you? We just thought we'd invite a few other people, that's all."

"A few people?" She looks around at the hundred or so people that line up along a path as the carriage makes its way to our final stop. "Do I even know this many?"

I laugh. "Yes, you do. And they all love you. You have no idea the impact you've had on so many lives, do you?"

Her mouth falls open and tears stream down her face as we pass by the familiar faces of her students, her extended family, her friends. The carriage finally stops and Griffin is waiting to help her down. He takes her into his arms as she thanks us for putting this together for her.

He leads her over to the large grassy area where every food you'd expect to see at a picnic and more is set up in the biggest catering spread Mitchell's has ever done. She greets everyone in her path along the way before Griffin seats her at the table of honor. He nods at someone in the tent and over walks an older, distinguished looking man, carrying a plate of food. He places it down in front of Erin and says, "Miss Hudson, I trust I won't have to give you detention for participating in a food fight again, will I?"

Erin jumps out of her seat. "Mr. Segal! Oh, my gosh! How… where…?" Tears flow out of her dancing eyes as she draws him into a hug.

"You'll never know what an honor it is to be here." He holds her at arm's length and looks her over. "My star pupil. You did it. You followed your dream. Look at you." His eyes glisten as he fights to hold back the tears. "When your friend, Skylar, called me and told me your story, it knocked the wind out of me. I'm so sorry, Erin. But I feel so privileged to be here with you and to have been a small part of your life."

They sit and talk over lunch, being politely interrupted from time to time as long lost friends and relatives offer Erin a hug or a kind word. All the while, Griffin hangs back and captures the moments on film.

Watching Griffin take pictures is fascinating. It makes me feel like I'm a voyeur, as if I'm seeing something private like an intimate dance between lovers. He walks around his subjects quietly, stealthily, and with grace, taking in the scenery, lighting and ambiance, making it all become a part of a story that he plans to tell with his photos.

There is dancing, there are toasts. There are children running about and grown-ups getting drunk. To a bystander, it might even seem like a wedding. The beginning of a life together between two people. Nobody would ever guess that it's quite the opposite.

I'm dancing with my father when I hear Erin squeal. I look over to see another bright smile on her face as she shakes hands with a familiar-looking handsome man who looks to be in his forties or fifties. She pulls him into a one-armed hug and the poor man is squished against her, Erin style, whether he likes it or not. His hands hesitantly come around her as he looks to Griffin who is watching them intently. Then it hits me. He looks like Griffin. Or, rather, Griffin looks like him. It must be his dad. But how? I tried to reach him days ago, leaving messages with little success. Perhaps one of her sisters?

I watch the three of them talk. I see Griffin's demeanor change from hesitant to amenable. I watch in awe as Erin works her magic, pulling father and son together like nobody else can. I wish Griffin could see himself like this.

Without thinking too much about how pissed Griffin might be if I touch his equipment, I sneak over to where he's stashed it and remove one of the cameras that looks like I can just point and shoot. I use a nearby tree as camouflage and zoom in on the three of them. Then I snap a few pictures of Griffin and his dad. His dad looks so happy to be here with his son. I hope when Griffin sees these, he'll be even more accepting of him. Everyone deserves a second chance. No one knows that better than I do. Like Griffin, I take dozens of pictures, hoping that among them will be the one that shows the perfect emotion of the moment.

I try not to push my luck and quickly put the camera back before I head over to join the conversation. Erin pulls me to her side. "Jack Pearce, meet Skylar Mitchell. My very best friend who also happens to be carrying your grandchild."

Mr. Pearce looks between Erin, Griffin and me. It's apparent nobody has filled him in on this little piece of information. He stammers, "Uh... okay... hello, Ms. Mitchell. You called me the other day, right?"

Erin laughs at the awkwardness of the situation then proceeds to explain the surrogacy to Mr. Pearce.

Out of the corner of my eye, I see a bit of commotion and then I watch Gavin run over to us looking happy yet completely panicked. "It's time," he says, looking from me to Erin.

Her eyes light up in understanding. "It's time! Oh my gosh. It's time!"

As Gavin gets Baylor to the hospital, we politely excuse ourselves from the party, Erin giving last-minute hugs and kisses to those she may never see again. Then Griffin, Erin and I hail a cab. The smile on Erin's face says it all, and I'm so grateful this is happening now and not when she's having one of her bad days. Who knows how many good days she has left?

Griffin and I sit in the waiting room, along with my parents and some friends. Baylor had Maddox pretty quickly, so nobody expects this to drag on for too long. The big question is, boy or girl? They refused to find out. As a result, they got a lot of yellow shit at their baby shower.

I look down at my barely-there belly and wonder again about the baby's sex. Like Erin, I feel that it's a boy. I'm not sure why. Maybe just because she wants it to be. As if on cue, the little bean flutters inside me and my hand instinctively goes to my stomach.

Griffin gasps beside me. I glimpse over to see his eyes go wide. "Is the baby moving? Can you feel it yet?"

I nod and smile. "Yeah. For about a week now."

He looks around the waiting room and I follow his eyes. Everyone is busy chatting or reading a magazine. He looks back at my belly. "Do you think I could feel it? I mean, um... would you mind if I...?"

Griffin is adorable. I'm not sure I've ever seen a man blush like this before. It looks like he's completely mortified, asking this of me, yet I can tell how badly he wants to feel it. I grab his hand and place it on my belly. "I'm not sure you'll be able to feel it. The book says it can take other people a lot longer to feel any movements."

With his hand gently on my stomach, he looks up at me. "You're reading the books?"

"I'm reading the books," I say. I nod to my belly. "Did you feel that?"

He shakes his head and then holds still in intense concentration as if that will help him in his quest to feel the baby move.

All I can do is watch his face. I see the wonder on it. I see the fascination in his eyes. I wish I could will little Bean to give his hand a kick. I wonder if this gesture means anything. Is he simply trying to forge a connection with his child? Or is there more to it?

Griffin may not feel anything yet, but I'm more than aware of the sensations coursing through my body from the mere touch of his hand. I try to control my quickening breaths and I hope he can't hear my pounding heartbeat that I'm sure must be audible through my chest wall. This is the first time he's touched me since the day he drunk-kissed me. He's been purposefully keeping his distance, despite Erin's attempts to get us as close as she can. But the lines have become blurred and there always seems to be a question lurking about how to show respect for Erin while at the same time honor her dying wish.

Here in this moment, with his hand on my belly, I can almost picture us as a family. I can almost picture what it would be like when we're the ones in the hospital about to give birth and the same people who are here now will be waiting to find out the sex of our baby.

Our baby.

It's the first time I've thought of Bean as Griffin's and mine. Could it be? Could we really do this? Or am I just fooling myself?

After another minute, Griffin withdraws his hand and I instantly mourn the loss of it on my body. Then, of course, I feel guilty for feeling that way when I think of Erin right down the hall. Would she approve of his hand on me? Or would she smile and pretend it's what she truly wants when in reality, it's killing her inside?

"I want to do an ultrasound for Erin," I whisper to Griffin. "I want to have one of those 3-D ones so she can see as much detail as possible. I want her to know what sex the baby is."

He nods. "Set it up and let me know when. It's a great idea, Skylar. Thanks."

I make a note in my phone to call the doctor's office to make an appointment. In my phone, I see the reminder to reach out to Griffin's dad. I turn to him. "Who called your dad? Was it one of Erin's sisters? I tried to a few days ago, but all I could do was leave a message."

"I did," he says.

The look of surprise on my face makes him laugh. "You didn't think I heard you that day in the hospital, did you?"

"I wondered," I say.

"I did it for her. I'm not sure I ever would have done it otherwise. He was a jackass. A drunk. A loser. I mean, who checks out on their sick wife and fifteen-year-old son?"

"But you did it anyway." I smile at him. "Whatever the reason, you did it and now the door is open. He seems like a really nice guy. Obviously he's changed, Griffin. I can tell he wants a relationship with you. I know it must have been hard for you to reach out to him. You did the right thing. You're going to make a great father."

He eyes me speculatively. "I don't know about that." He motions to my belly. "I never wanted kids, you know. Erin spent years talking me into it. I did it for her." He shakes his head as if something has dawned on him. "Everything I've done since high school has been for her." The way he says it isn't spiteful, just matter-of-fact.

"Well, maybe it's time you do something for yourself then," I say.

"Yeah, maybe. I just wish I had a goddamn clue about what that is." He lowers his eyes to the ground and my heart sinks along with them.

Did he just admit he doesn't want me? The baby?

As if hearing my silent questions, he looks back up at me. He puts his hand on top of mine. "Don't read too much into that, Sky. I'm just trying to figure out which feelings I'm having are mine and which are Erin's."

Feelings? He's having feelings? I stare at his hand still resting on mine. I'm afraid if I move a muscle, he will withdraw it. And I really want it to stay where it is. I want to savor the feeling of the heat of his touch. The sensation of his large hand encompassing mine. The feeling that maybe he wants me, too. Even if only in some small way, tucked down deep under lock and key where it can't hurt Erin.

A door opens and he jerks his hand away. We both look up with guilty eyes as we stare at Erin's smiling face as she comes across the threshold. Gavin looks happy, but utterly frazzled, walking next to her. He turns to her and says, "Go ahead."

She blurts out, "It's a girl!"

Everyone jumps to their feet with cheers and congratulations. We all share hugs and tears as we listen to Gavin and Erin tell us about the birth of Jordan Christine McBride. Sometime during all the elation, I notice Griffin's eyes trained on my belly. When I catch him staring, he smiles up at me and gives me a nod. I could swear he says more with that nod than he ever has with words. I could swear he's just told me he's willing to try this. That after hearing the story of another baby entering the world, he can't imagine not being present for his. That he may even be willing to put up with someone like me if it means making his wife as happy as she is in this very minute.

Or maybe I'm just reading way too much into it.

chapter seventeen

The past three weeks have gone by fast. Too fast. It's been a whirlwind of activity. So much has happened. A lifetime worth of experiences jammed into twenty-one days. Some days were better than others, and it amazes me what we were able to pull off with the help of friends, family and even strangers.

I sit here in Erin's newly-appointed room on the main floor of their townhouse. A study that Griffin turned into her bedroom when she stopped being able to climb stairs last week. We've tried to pretty it up with flowers. We've taped an endless stream of cards from her second graders to the windows. We've put pictures of loved ones where she can see them. But you still have to call it what it is. It's a makeshift hospital room. A place to succumb to her unrelenting disease. It's where she's going to die.

I'm practically living at their house now, at Erin's request. I try to give her and Griffin plenty of alone time; however, it's me she wants to spend most of her days with. I hope Griffin doesn't hold it against me or somehow think I'm trying to monopolize her time. But it's an unspoken rule that Erin gets whatever she wants, so when the medical delivery guys were setting up her new room, I set up mine in the guest room down the hall from Griffin's.

It makes me wonder where we would live if we were to make a go of it. Could either one of us live in a house that bleeds Erin from every wall, decoration and tchotchke? I try not to think about it as I listen to Erin tell me stories of Griffin. It's her favorite pastime these days. I think it's her goal to tell me everything there is to know about her husband so I will know him as well as she does.

We reminisce about the past few weeks and the wonderful things we've done such as her Parisian Imax experience, the red-carpet premier of a blockbuster movie that Gavin got us into, the exotic elephant ride, even a skydiving experience. No, we didn't go up in an airplane, but we did get to experience a simulated sky dive. It was more of a vertical wind tunnel with air pushing you upwards so that you have the sensation of flying. Her doctors weren't thrilled about it, as they said there would still be air pressure issues that could cause increased swelling, but at that point, Erin had already started the final decline in her health and figured it couldn't make things worse. Watching her experience something she never thought she'd get to do was one of the highlights of my life. I will never forget these things we've done together. Griffin will make sure of it. I think he must have taken a thousand pictures over the past few weeks.

Today she got a thank you note from the anonymous donation she made. Only the hospital knew who made the donation, so they were able to forward the note to her. Several weeks ago, when Baylor had little Jordan, there was a woman who was in labor with triplets. She was about to have a C-Section and we learned her husband had recently been laid off. Not only did Erin pay their hospital bills, she outfitted them well into their second year, paid for a year's worth of diaper service, and set up a college fund for them. The pleasure I watched flow through her when she placed the phone calls to make it all happen is a memory I will keep with me forever. In typical Erin style, it was all about everyone but her. She didn't want thanks, she didn't seek acknowledgment. Just knowing she had made someone's life better was all she needed. Little does she know, every day she's around, she does that very thing.

Sherry, Erin's hospice nurse, comes in to get Erin ready for our outing. Sherry has been here for the past few days. We all know what that means. They don't bring in hospice unless they think you are going pretty soon. Between Sherry, Griffin and I, one of us is always by Erin's side.

Erin has been confined to a wheelchair for the past few days. Her legs are too weak to hold her now-frail body. She can no longer control her bladder and her right hand stays curled up close to her body. Thank God she still has her mental faculties about her. Yes, she has moments of confusion and they do happen more and more, but for the most part, she's still Erin. And she hasn't detached from us yet so we're making every second count. Sometimes she stares across the room, looking at nothing. She tires very easily and she keeps making mention of getting the baby's room ready, something she completed last week. Griffin hired a decorator to cater to her every whim and it was touching to see all the effort she put into it.

Nobody will come out and say it, but we're all aware that today will most likely be the last time Erin ever sets foot outside her house. We're going to my obstetrician's office to have a 3-D ultrasound. Erin doesn't know about it yet, it's a surprise. Today is the day we find out if Bean is a boy or a girl.

While Sherry gets Erin ready to go, I wander the walkout basement of the townhome. There's a large sitting room next to the laundry area. It's perfect for reading and I've spent a lot of time down here when I'm not with Erin. But the most interesting part of the lower level is Griffin's photography studio. It's truly remarkable. Lining the walls are numerous pictures he's taken over the years; photos depicting animals in the Congo, architectural masterpieces, and famous bridges. The man is as talented as he is gorgeous. Conspicuously absent are pictures of models he has photographed. You won't find any pictures of women lining these walls, not unless they are Erin.

Or apparently, me.

With my mouth hanging open, I walk towards a wall that displays the pictures he's recently taken. They are held up by a massive system of clips, allowing him to see many at a time. I presume this is where he puts his work while he decides which pictures to use professionally. It's one gigantic display board.

Hanging on the board are pictures from the picnic in Central Park. But what surprises me is the number of pictures he took of me. They are so intimate. I remember being exhausted after our shopping spree that morning and I had wandered off to lie on a grassy mound. Little did I know he had taken a picture of me, hand on my belly, looking up at the sky as if I didn't have a care in the world. Another picture was shot when I was watching Erin talk with her favorite teacher. A third shows me standing with my eyes closed, absorbing the mid-afternoon sun on my face on the unseasonably-mild October day. I look over the dozens of others and realize in each picture I'm touching my baby bump. I didn't even know I did that. And I certainly didn't know anyone was noticing. I wonder what he was thinking when he took these.

"That one is my favorite."

I jump at Griffin's words. He must have snuck up behind me and I momentarily wonder how long he was standing there while I was mesmerized by his photos.

"They are wonderful, Griffin. I didn't know you were taking them."

He looks embarrassed. "Sorry. I didn't mean to spy on you that day. You just looked happy. It was a good day and I wanted us to remember all of it. I hope you don't think I'm creepy."

I laugh. "No, not creepy. Just incredibly talented."

He nods. Then he walks to a drawer and opens it, pulling out a stack of photos. "You're not so bad yourself." He hands them to me.

I look through the photos of father and son that I took of Griffin and Jack Pearce. They captured exactly what I'd intended, his father's pure joy of being able to see his son again. "Thanks. I needed to see this," he says. I smile at him until he holds up a hand to scold me. "Now if you ever touch my equipment again, I will cut off your right arm. Nobody touches my shit, Sky."

I give him a sheepish look and shrug my shoulders, as I secretly love the way he uses my nickname.

"But listen, seriously, I have so much to thank you for. These past weeks. Hell, these past months, despite the situation, they've been the happiest months of her life. You know I was actually jealous of all the time she was spending with you. I mean, before you it was just Erin and me. Then you entered the picture and it was like she found the other half of herself. You represent everything she's always wanted but was afraid to be. It sounds corny, but you complete her. And I'm so grateful for you, Skylar. You'll never know how much."

He leans in to hug me and I melt into his arms. I let tears stream down my face at his words. Everything I feared; everything

I wondered about; everything I second-guessed—he's somehow… validated my life. And for a split second, I wonder if I believe in fate. Maybe Erin was right. Maybe I was put on this earth to find her and become her friend so we could have this time together. Maybe what I've been doing is… meaningful.

Sherry shouts down that they're ready to go and he releases me. Then he kisses me on the cheek and my heart flutters. My eyes briefly close and I try to enjoy the sensation without feeling the guilt that usually follows. "Let's do this," he says. I nod my head, reeling over the words that have come to mean so much more than when I first said them over six months ago.

There's not a dry eye in the room. Even the ultrasound tech picked up on what's going on and is silently crying with us. Four pairs of eyes are focused on one tiny baby on the screen. It's incredible what you can see on the 3-D ultrasound. I had no idea that at eighteen weeks, the baby would be this perfectly-formed tiny human. All it does for the next twenty-two weeks is grow bigger. Every finger, every toe, every curve of his face is already in place. And when the screen fills with Bean's boy parts, Erin screams out.

"I knew it!" she cries. "It's a boy. You're having a boy."

I grab her hand. "*We're* having a boy."

She nods her head, eyes still glued to the monitor as we watch him squirm about. At one point, it looks like he's even sucking his thumb. I'm grateful the ultrasound tech allows us to watch much longer than I'm sure is the normal time for the procedure.

"We should name him after you, Erin," I say, squeezing her hand.

"What? You can't name a boy after me."

"Sure we can. A-a-r-o-n," I spell it out for her. "It's perfect."

Her eyes finally snap away from the monitor to meet up with mine. Her hand goes over her heart and the look of gratitude on her face overwhelms me. Then she sighs. "No. You can't. It's morbid. You'd think of me every time you call his name."

I laugh as I look between Griffin and Erin. "Yeah, that's kind of the point. I *want* to think of you. You are the best friend and best wife anyone could ever ask for. You would have been the best mother, too. Everyone knows that. You are the reason for all of this. He wouldn't even exist without you. He may be growing inside me, but he's *your* creation. Of course I want to name him after you. That is, if you guys agree."

She looks at Griffin who winks at her. Then she puts a hand on my tummy while she looks back at the monitor. "It's a pleasure to meet you, Aaron Pearce."

Even though I'm sobbing with everyone in the room, I don't miss how she assigns him Griffin's last name. I peek at Griffin who, no doubt, heard the same thing. He shrugs it off and proceeds to plant a kiss on Erin's head. Then he puts his hand on top of hers as they both rest on the side of my belly, out of the way of the ultrasound wand as we enjoy a few more moments with our son.

Our son.

Holy mother of God. I'm going to have a baby.

When we arrive back at the townhouse, Griffin carries Erin effortlessly up the front steps and into her new bedroom. I don't miss her look of longing as she passes through the front door. She knows it's the last time it will happen. She clutches onto a few pictures the technician printed out for her as he lays her down on the hospital bed.

More flowers have been delivered in our absence. It's become somewhat of a private joke between Erin and me that nobody else has been bold enough to send her white lilies. The sympathy flower. The flower of death. Not even Griffin will bring them. He chooses the more traditional roses, and sometimes orchids, like Baylor. Not me. I'll never get her anything but white lilies.

An hour after arriving home, Baylor and Mason show up at the townhouse, and along with Erin, they send Griffin and I on pointless errands with strict instructions not to return home until asked. I'm not sure why we've been kicked out, because none of them would discuss it. The only thing I can think of is that Erin is enlisting the help of those closest to Griffin and me so they can carry on her mission once she's gone.

Shortly after dark, Griffin and I are beckoned home. Erin calls me into her room. She's got that look on her face. I know that look. This is it. This is when she's going to ask what my plans are. This is when I'm going to break her heart because I don't know in all certainty what the future holds. This is when we have a heart-to-heart for quite possibly the very last time.

She pats the bed next to where she reclines. I climb on and lie down with her, silent tears welling up in my eyes when I hear her wince in pain next to me. We do this every night after she has her glass of wine on the patio. We lie here like teenagers at a slumber party, talking about everything and anything. Well, except that one thing.

"Do we have to do this now?" I ask, like a petulant child.

She smiles at me like an all-knowing mother. "It's now or never."

My heart sinks at her declaration. "You know I love you, right, Erin? You know I'd do anything for you and I want to do this. I really do, I just need to know I'm doing it for the right reasons."

"Disney World," she says randomly.

I shake my head, thinking she's gone into another state of confusion. "Disney World?" I repeat.

"Take Aaron there. Don't wait. Take him when he's little. It will be magical to watch his face light up when he sees Mickey Mouse and Donald Duck in person. And Santa Claus—please, do everything in your power to make him believe for as long as you can. Don't send him to private school—it's for snobby rich kids. And even though he'll be rich, don't ever let him act like it. Make sure he's a giver, not a taker. Then again, seeing who his mom is, I know that won't be a problem. You're the biggest giver I know, Skylar." All I can do is roll my eyes at her statement. She's delusional, but I'm not about to call her on it now. "Make sure he knows how to treat a lady. Griffin is a great example, but you need to remind Aaron of it every day. Don't let him get lazy. Teach him how to drive. Even if you live in the city, every kid needs to feel the freedom of getting a license when they turn sixteen. Hug him and kiss him. Even when he says he's too old. Even when he says it embarrasses him. No matter what he says; he needs to know you love him. And kiss him for me. Every day. Tell him his guardian angel will always watch over him."

I listen intently as Erin rambles on, slurring her words as she lists everything she wants me to do with Aaron. Things I never would have thought of. Things only a good mother would be sure to do for their child. How can she entrust him to me? When she finally becomes exhausted from talking, I take her hand. "Erin, I promise to try to do all those things, but what makes you think I can live up to your expectations? Everything you've said makes me see just how different I am from the mother you would have been. How can you be so sure I'm the best one to raise Aaron?"

She shakes her head at me as if I'm crazy. "Skylar Mitchell, I've known you for exactly six months. It only took you all of about two seconds of that time to work your way into my heart. The heart I thought was closed to new friends because of how I was treated back in high school. But the second you fell off your stool, I knew we were going to be great friends. You've opened up my world to new people, new experiences, new love, and I'm not just talking about this larger-than-life thing you did for me, either. You've proven that your capacity for loving another human being is endless. Look at what you've done for me these last weeks. How can you doubt, for one second, your ability to completely give yourself over to another person and make their world a wonderful place?

"I know you don't think you're worthy of being a mother. I know you don't think you're worthy of Griffin. You're wrong on both counts. I wouldn't ask you to be their family if I didn't think you could do it. If I didn't think you were the only one who *should* do it. If I didn't think Griffin could love you."

Her voice cracks when she says it and I know it must kill her to think of us together. "Erin…"

She pulls me tight with her good arm. "No, Skylar, it's okay. I want him to love you, but you need to allow him to. I've seen you together. You're drawn to each other. But you're fighting it because of me." She touches my tummy. "You have this incredible connection that will bond you for life. I see what it does to him. He may not have been on board with having a baby at first, but I watch him watch you. You are the mother of his child. And you're beautiful and fun and sexy as hell. You are what he needs. He is what you need. But more than anything else, you're both what Aaron needs.

"Promise me, Skylar. Promise to live life to the fullest and don't let a day go by with regrets. If you want to see the Eiffel Tower, go to Paris. Don't say *someday*. Say *today*. Don't wait to love Griffin. Love him *today*. I need you to show him it's okay. You need to be the one to let it happen. He won't do it. He won't do it out of respect for me. I need you to do it, Skylar. Don't wait another minute. Let me die knowing you are going to take Griffin and Aaron and make them your family."

I cuddle into her, spooning her from behind, not wanting to let her go. Not wanting to let her down. I say the only thing I can. The only thing a true best friend could possibly say in this impossible situation. "Okay, Erin. I promise. I swear to you I'll do everything in my power to honor your wish. You are the best thing that's ever happened in my entire life, do you know that?"

She goes limp in my arms. I pray that she heard. I pray that if those were the last words she ever hears from me, that she believes them to be true.

I hear a noise in the doorway and turn to see Griffin leaning up against the frame. A tear rolls down his face as he stares at me. Then he turns to walk away without a word.

chapter eighteen

Turns out, those were the last words Erin heard me say. At least the Erin I knew. Later that night she slipped into a light coma. Apparently it's not uncommon for this to happen the last few days. She's withering away quickly. Erin signed the papers refusing a feeding tube when the time came. She didn't want anything prolonging her life just so we didn't have to deal with her death. I see now, I see why she did it. It's horrible. When she's not sleeping, she's completely incoherent. Belligerent even. She doesn't know who we are or who she is.

Still, Griffin and I keep vigil at her side. Family members come and go, but other than me, she didn't want any friends with her near the end. She knew how it would go. She didn't want everyone remembering her the way she's been these last few days. Family, that's who she wanted here. I'm now lucky enough to be considered a part of that.

Griffin and I take a break, both of us exhausted from lack of sleep. Neither one of us want to leave her for more than a few minutes, knowing we could miss being with her at the very end.

Her instructions were clear. When the time comes, she wants Griffin and me and no one else with her. We leave Erin with Sherry and some of her sisters while the others make more arrangements for what will inevitably happen soon. We open a bottle of Erin's favorite wine out on their back porch. It's cold out here. It's wet, too. But this was her peaceful place, her area of solace, the spot she would come every night and share stories of her childhood and her hopes of the future. Aaron's future. We came out to toast her. I take one sip of wine in honor of my friend and then I laugh at what happens next.

Little constant flutters riddle my belly. The bean has decided to protest my forbidden drink by getting the hiccups. The quick and soft little jerks make me smile. He gets them all the time and so far, it's my favorite thing about being pregnant.

Griffin looks at me as if I've lost my mind. I know he's wondering how I can possibly laugh at a time like this. But all of a sudden, in some twisted way, I'm happy. I feel this little life within me. In the other room, life is slipping away, yet here is Aaron, growing big and strong and reminding me every day that life is precious.

"Aaron has the hiccups," I say, looking down at my belly. I sit on the porch swing and close my eyes to savor the moment.

I feel the swing shift under Griffin's weight as he sits next to me. "Can I feel?" he asks in a whisper.

I nod and with my eyes still closed, I reach out and grab his hand and place it under my coat onto my belly. We sit like this for a silent minute.

I know the second he feels it because he chokes up. I keep my eyes closed and let him quietly enjoy the first time he feels his son move. I hear him murmur '*Incredible*' over and over. His hand is frozen in place on my belly. I can tell he doesn't want to move it for fear of losing the moment to the past.

But the hiccups stop and then Sherry sticks her head out the door and says the words we have dreaded for the past month. "It's time."

We both belt out a pained whimper into the darkness of the night. Then we compose ourselves and do what we have to do. We go say goodbye to the woman who has single-handedly changed our lives.

We walk past her family as they quietly sob, all gathered around the kitchen. I try not to look at them. I want to be strong in these last moments. I know Erin probably won't be able to hear me. She won't even see me, but I need to be strong for her anyway. I can fall apart later. Once she's gone. Right now, I need to be here for her. For Griffin.

I'm stunned at what I see when we walk into her room. Her eyes are open. They're as clear and as blue as I've ever seen them. She follows our movement to the side of her bed. I take one side, Griffin the other. I've read about this. I've read how some terminally ill patients have one last moment of cognizance before they die.

Her body is relaxed and I immediately notice her hand is not curled up in front of her. Her hair has finally lightened back to the glorious blonde spirals that I love. Her face is peaceful, despite the dark circles, faint lines, and hollow cheeks that have come from a lack of nutrition. Her respirations are slow and the time lengthens between each gurgling breath she takes. She doesn't speak but her eyes say volumes. I nod at Griffin. He needs to say goodbye.

"Sweetheart, I'm here. Skylar is, too," his shaky voice cracks. "God, I love you so much. You have brought such joy to my life. I can't even begin to explain what you mean to me. When I had no family, you took me in and made me part of yours. You believed in me when nobody else did. Even now, when I thought I could never forgive my dad, you managed to bring us together." He can barely get the last words out, but I know he needs her to hear him so he pushes through. "You've done everything that you needed to do. You let us take it from here. Thank you, baby. Thank you for being my wife."

He bows his head and gives her a kiss on the lips. Then he nods to me through his tears.

I take a deep breath and pray I get through this without breaking down. "Erin Pearce, you are the best friend I've ever had. I could look to the ends of the earth and never find another friend like you. You see the good in people. You look past what others can't. You have changed my life in the short time I've known you and I will never be the same. Heaven will be a better place because you are in it. Aaron will have a better life because you are his guardian angel. I will be a better person because I've known you. You don't have to worry about anything now. We've got you covered. I love you, Erin. Thank you for being my very best friend."

I can't tell if she's heard us. Perhaps the words we've spoken are more for us than they are for her. We continue to praise her with our love. We tell her it's okay to leave, that we'll be fine, that Aaron will be alright. But her eyes dart between us like she's not quite done with us yet. Like she isn't ready to let go. Her eyes fall onto our hands. Each of us has one of Erin's hands in ours. She fixes her gaze on them as if willing her limp hands to move within ours. Then, Griffin reaches across the bed with his free hand and grabs mine. We hold hands on top of her chest, forming a circle, each of us holding the hands of the other.

Erin lets out a deep sigh as the life exits her body along with her final breath. She peacefully closes her eyes and slips away. As I watch my best friend leave this world, I try not to drown in my loss. Instead, I rejoice that she is once again whole. She's no longer confined to the broken body she was sentenced with. She is free to be Aaron's guardian. She can go to Paris and free fall from a plane. She can dance on the clouds and have dozens of babies.

Staring at her lifeless body, I realize her face looks different. It looks younger. Even the dark circles and lines that riddled it moments ago seem to be gone. She's as beautiful in death as she was in life.

I put my hand on my belly and feel Aaron shift around inside me as I think how one life has been traded for another.

Griffin silently cries into her dressing gown as I make my way out to the family and give him one last moment with her before they come take her away. I slowly walk as far as the kitchen when I feel my legs collapse out from under me. But before I hit the floor, strong arms come around me from behind and pick me up, carrying me up the stairs to the room that has become mine.

The last thing I remember is Griffin telling me everything will be okay.

chapter nineteen

I sit and stare at the urn on the table. The urn that has been entrusted in part to me, in the house that has been given in part to me. What the hell did she do this for?

I curse her for the millionth time since Baylor read Griffin and me the letter with Erin's final wishes. It was only yesterday, the day before her funeral. The letter stated that her body was to be cremated, not buried. We knew this, but it went on to say her ashes were to be given to Griffin and me. That we were to decide together when and where to spread them. She was explicit about it being a place of happiness and life. That when the time was right, we would know what to do.

The letter also went on to explain that the townhouse, which was solely in her name—a wedding gift from Griffin—was deeded to both Griffin and myself. We know what she's doing, of course. She's made it perfectly clear she wants us to keep, and live together in, the townhouse.

Along with Erin's parents, I've stayed here the few days since she died. At first, I was too exhausted to do anything else. Then, her family asked me to help with the reception being held here today, just hours after her funeral. The funeral that was adorned with what I'm sure was every last white lily in the city. I loved it. Nobody else would understand. Nobody else had that connection. When I walked into the service to see every available space draped with Erin's favorite flower, I saw life, not death. I saw life and boy babies and long pistols. I saw Erin's smiling face. For one very brief second, I may have even seen hope for the future.

Other than making an appearance at the reading of Erin's letter and the funeral, Griffin has been holed up in his bedroom. I don't know how to console him. If I touch him, he may think I'm trying to take Erin's place. If I don't, he may think I'm not interested. I desperately want to honor Erin's dying wish. Even if I wasn't already in love with him, I'd want to. But I'm just not sure what the proper amount of time is to grieve your best friend before shacking up with her husband.

Maybe we need some space. Some time to grieve separately before we try to be together. I decide to pack up my suitcases and head home tonight. It's the right thing to do. Erin's family will be leaving and heading back to White Plains after the reception. I don't want it to be awkward with only Griffin and me in the house.

The Mitchell's catering van arrives, followed by Baylor's clan. Friends and family trickle in all afternoon. We do our best to make it a celebration of Erin's life, so I take it upon myself to bring up pictures from Griffin's studio. Pictures that depict Erin at her happiest moments during her last weeks.

Baylor hands little Jordan to me. She's barely a month old. I know what Baylor is doing. She's trying to get me comfortable with babies. But babies don't like me. Jordan squirms and cries and looks freakishly uncomfortable in my arms. Knowing this doesn't come naturally to me just feeds my anxiety.

Griffin comes downstairs, making small talk with whoever engages with him, but he has closed himself off. He sits in the corner of the living room watching me with his pensive slate-gray eyes. Is he wondering how he's going to do this? Or maybe he's wondering how he's going to let me down. I try to ignore his punishing stares as I mingle with Erin's loved ones.

The setting sun has most of the mourners leaving. Erin's parents pack up their car as her sisters and nieces help clean up, sealing the leftover food in freezer containers that will feed Griffin for a month. Everyone says a tearful goodbye as we promise to get together soon. Even though the bean is not their blood relative, it has never crossed their minds not to treat him as such. They've taken me on as a daughter, an aunt, a sister. They've become my second family and one more support system for Aaron.

I close the front door after the last of her family leave. Suddenly, the house feels huge. I have no idea where Griffin is. Back in his bedroom I presume. Being here by myself feels wrong. I've never needed another person as much as I do now. I've never felt so utterly alone in my entire life. I touch my growing belly and remind myself that I'm not.

I make my way up to my bedroom and pack up my belongings. I put my suitcases by the front door and go in search of Griffin to tell him I'm leaving. His bedroom door is cracked open. "Griffin?" I gently push the door open wider. I let my eyes wander over the room. The suit he had on at the funeral is crumpled in a pile on the floor. There are pillows and a blanket on the couch in their sitting area and I realize that's where he's probably been sleeping as my eyes find the perfectly-made bed. He couldn't get himself to sleep there without her. I wonder if he's slept on the couch since she moved downstairs. Maybe now that everyone is gone, he can sleep in a guest room instead. Part of me hopes he chooses the room I was in. Part of me hopes he will lie on the same pillow I did and inhale my scent. All of me hopes Erin isn't damning me from heaven for wanting these things.

I pass by the nursery and wonder for the hundredth time if this is where Aaron will grow up. Erin didn't leave out a single detail. She had a mural painted on the wall. A baseball mural. She hated baseball. Another selfless move on her part. Knowing the sport is very near and dear to Griffin and me, she probably hoped that we would share our love of it with Aaron. She conspicuously left any specific team names out of the decorating and it's obvious to me Griffin doesn't visit this room or he'd have noticed the array of tiny Yankees outfits I had already purchased.

I descend the stairs and look out on the back porch to find it empty. I sadly think how maybe Griffin won't frequent Erin's favorite spot anymore. There's only one other place he could be. I make my way down to his studio. He doesn't notice me standing in the doorway so I silently watch him. He's holding a picture in one hand. And a bottle of Jack in the other.

He stares at a picture of Erin on the display board. He yells, "What the fuck do you want from me?"

I turn to walk away, but my heel catches the doorway and he turns, seeing me before I can escape. "I wasn't yelling at *you*, Skylar."

"I know. I'll leave you alone. I just wanted to say goodbye. I'm moving back to my apartment." I walk away.

"Wait," he calls after me. "You have every right to stay here. It's your house, too."

I shake my head. "I don't know what she was thinking."

"Yes you do." He walks towards me. "We both do. But what I want to know is how the hell she left us that generic letter. A fucking business deal. Did she have no parting words for us?" He takes a swig of Jack and I'm pleased to see the bottle is still mostly full. He paces around the room. The tension rolling off him is palpable. "Split my fucking ashes. Split my fucking house. That's it?"

I've never seen him so mad before. Except maybe the time he hit that guy at the baseball game. No, this is worse. He's mad at Erin and she's not here to defend herself. "That's not fair, Griffin. She spent the last month giving us her parting words. You know how much she loved you. You know what you meant to her. Did you really need to see it spelled out in some letter rather than remember the words that came directly from her lips?"

"Yes!" he shouts. He points his fingers between us. "You and me, we poured our hearts out to her that last day. We didn't want her to leave without knowing everything we felt." He takes another drink. "What if she changed her mind? How am I supposed to know what to do? Where the hell do we go from here? Why the fuck did she think it was okay to leave us without telling us what she wanted? How could she be so selfish?"

I walk over and slap his face. For the second time in my life, I slap him. *How dare he?*

The picture he was holding flutters to the ground when his hand comes up to feel the reddened flesh of his cheek. I follow the picture to where it settles on the floor only to see it's a picture of me. The one from Central Park. The one he said was his favorite.

"Selfish?" I shout at him. "You think she was selfish? I've never met a less selfish person in my entire life. She gave me her baby. She gave me her fucking husband. Who does that? She's a goddamn saint. I swear to God if you ever call her selfish again, I will knock a hole in your fucking teeth."

I've never been so mad and upset at the same time. Tears run down my cheeks, yet I'm too pissed off to wipe them. Through my blurry vision, I'm positive I see him experiencing the same two emotions.

He throws the bottle against the wall, shattering it and sending liquid spreading across the tiled floor. "Goddammit, Sky. Quit saying fuck!"

"Why, Griffin?" I draw my eyebrows at him. "Why do you always have such an issue with me saying fuck? What's your problem?"

He blows out a long breath. "My problem is that it makes me want you, okay? When you talk like that, all I want to do is throw you down and screw the hell out of you."

My jaw drops. I'm stunned into silence. We stare at each other for about two seconds before our feet propel us forward and our bodies crash into each other right before our lips do.

When our lips meet, I could swear we both cry out in pain. Pain because we hurt that Erin is gone. Pain because we worry that we are hurting her. We pull back slightly and our glistening eyes meet. I can tell he needs this. I need this. Maybe this is how it's supposed to happen. Rip off the bandage.

He cups my face in his hands and brings his mouth back to mine. Our lips mold together in a perfect, albeit hesitant, sensual dance. But once we allow our tongues to mingle, I lose myself in him. I know our mutual grief is driving this. I know the alcohol he consumed is allowing this. I know my heart craves this. I permit myself, in this moment, to let go of the pain and I hand myself over to him completely.

He picks me up and wraps my legs around him. With our lips still together, he carries me up the two flights of stairs to my bedroom. When he sets me down, we tear at each other's clothing as if the world is about to end and we have one last chance at being together.

He pulls my shirt up and over my head. His large hands cup my breasts and I moan at the feel of a man's hands on my body after all this time. Did it ever feel this good to have a man's hands on my bare flesh? I tremble as he removes my bra and stares at my breasts as his fingers work over each of my nipples. *Oh, God.* They are so sensitive. I can't keep my pleasurable groans to myself as I feel my entire body respond to his touch.

I tug on the button of his jeans and he removes his hands from my body only long enough for us to rid ourselves of our remaining clothes.

We stand naked, our eyes wandering over each other. His heated gaze goes cold when it stops on my belly. He briefly closes his eyes when he sees my bump that is now protruding enough to let the world know our secret. Did he forget about it, I wonder? Is he about to stop whatever it is that we're doing?

Almost immediately he resumes the assault on my nipples, only with his mouth this time. He walks me backward towards the bed and lowers me down, never breaking contact with my breast. At the same time, a hand finds its way to my throbbing clit and I cry out, "Oh, God, yes!"

My pleas make him work harder. His tongue swirls around my nipple. He licks, sucks and nips at it. He inserts a finger inside me and murmurs something about how wet I am. The sensation of his fingers inside me drives me higher. His hot breath against my breast as he speaks deliciously dirty words, telling me what he wants to do to me, makes my insides start to quiver as I ride his fingers, his mouth, his words to an earth-shattering orgasm.

When my eyes are capable of focusing again, I find him staring at me in complete awe. "Shit, Sky. I have to see that again."

I smile and then find my way to his hard-as-steel length. How can something so soft be so incredibly rigid at the same time? I yearn to put my mouth on him. It's something I've never been a fan of, but the thought of tasting him makes me burn with desire. I rub my hand up and down, taking time to pay attention to his tightening balls as his fingers resume exploration of my well-pronounced curves. I climb down his taut body, making my intention clear while enjoying my tactile perusal of each ripple on his torso. When I glance up at him, I see that his eyes are lidded and full of carnal need.

I take him in my mouth and he shouts my name. My nickname. As I pleasure him he shifts me around so he can fondle my heavy breasts. I work my tongue around the tip of him, then I sink my mouth over him and take him in as far as I can without gagging. My fingers play with his balls and the silky-soft skin of his perineum. He lets out the hottest groan I've ever heard. "I'm gonna come in your mouth if you don't stop."

His words incent me to work harder. I pump my mouth around him. And in a bold move, I allow my fingertip to press against the pucker of his ass. He bucks his hips, shouting out as powerful shots of semen flood my throat.

I lay my head down on his thigh, watching him recover. His chest rises and falls with such intensity you'd think he'd just run a marathon. He throws his arm over his head and takes some deep breaths. Then he locks eyes with me, his rough voice strained and taut with need. "My turn," he says.

My insides quiver at his proclamation. He plants his mouth on my breast and I revel in the sensation radiating from my over-sensitive nipple. Every flick of his tongue sends a shot of electricity to my needy clit. He works his way down my body, kissing along my protruding belly as he goes.

When his mouth meets my pulsating bundle of nerves, my body shudders. I feel him smile against me. His tongue finds my opening and he tastes me before returning to the very spot I need him most. His fingers slide effortlessly in and out of my slick walls. My insides are coiled so tight, I feel I will explode if I don't orgasm this very second. As if hearing my silent plea, he brings his free hand up to pinch my nipple, sending me over the cliff and falling into a fit of spasms as I pulsate around his fingers. "Griffin! Oh, yes!" A stream of tangled, incoherent words come out of me as I try to express what he's doing to my body.

"Holy fuck, Sky. I have to be inside you. Now." Before my body has even recovered, he's pushing his cock inside me, filling me up so completely. When he hits the end of me, we both gasp. He stills. "Don't move. I need a minute."

I press my lips together and try not to laugh. He doesn't want to come yet. I bask in the knowledge that he is so turned on that he has to will himself to stop. That even after coming not ten minutes ago, he's almost there again. After a long pause, I can't help but move my hands over him. I explore the ridges of his back with my fingers. I take the globes of his ass into my hands and knead the soft skin over the strong muscles underneath. I work my way up and over his shoulders and finally into his glorious hair.

God, I love his hair. It's so inherently Griffin. It speaks to everything about him. Unruly, yet in a perfectly kept way. I never realized until now how much I love his hair. I wonder if I could orgasm again merely by running my fingers through it.

"You're killing me, Skylar," he breathes into the crook of my neck as he begins to move his hips up and down, back and forth in a slow and controlled motion that has me slowly building up yet again.

I can feel beads of sweat trickle down his back. He's doing his best not to put his weight on me and squish my tummy. His thrusts become more demanding and he grabs my wandering hands, putting them beside my head as he takes control of me completely. I look into his eyes and we share a moment. A moment of pain. A moment of sadness. A moment of pure unadulterated elation. A moment of emotions so mixed I'm not sure we can fully understand them.

"I'm gonna come," he says, squeezing a tear from his now-closed eyes. He puts his weight on one elbow and reaches a hand between us to stroke my clit. "I need you. You feel so damn good. Come with me. I need this. God, Sky, I need you."

His words push me over the edge once again as he stakes claim on my third orgasm. I milk him with my pulsations as we groan into each other's shoulders. Our groans turn into mutual sobs and we grip each other as if we will slip away if we part. I don't even know how long we cry in each other's arms before we both fall asleep out of exhaustion.

Light dancing through a seam in the curtains wakes me. Not ready to get up yet, I roll over and bury my head into the pillow. When I take a breath, I immediately stiffen. The undeniable smell of sex permeates the pillow, sending flashbacks of last night through my sleepy head. I had sex with Griffin last night. I had earth-shattering, no-holds-barred, life-altering sex with my best friend's husband.

On the day of her funeral.

My heart sinks into my stomach and I wonder if I will need to run to the toilet. Nothing has changed. I haven't changed. I took the first opportunity I saw to jump into bed with him. I cry into my pillow that still smells of him as I silently beg my friend for forgiveness.

I lie in bed for hours, listening for any noises coming from outside my room. What must Griffin think of me now? He'd been drinking. He was clearly upset. He was grieving. I took advantage of that. I became the exact person I was trying to leave in the past.

I get up and throw on my robe, going in search of him so we can fix this. I open my bedroom door and almost trip over my suitcases. I could have sworn I put these by the front door last night. Upon further inspection, I see a key and a note perched on top of them. As my heart races, I open the folded paper and read it.

Skylar,

I'm sorry I took advantage of you. It was a mistake. Stay here—the place is yours. I can't do this.

Griffin

chapter twenty

It's been two weeks now. Two weeks since Erin died. Two weeks since Griffin left. Two weeks since I've set foot outside the townhouse. Two weeks and I've not breathed a word to anyone about what I did with Griffin.

I haven't heard from him. Complete radio silence. Nobody knows where he is. Not even Mason. He didn't take his phone. He didn't take any clothes. He didn't even take his camera bag. Griffin never goes anywhere without his camera bag.

I can't do this. His words echo the way I feel. I'm still mourning Erin. I don't know if I can mourn Griffin, too. But every time the phone rings, my heart stops. Will this be the call where they tell me his body washed ashore after he jumped off the Brooklyn Bridge?

My only hope is that he simply needed time away to deal with Erin's death. I just wonder how much worse I made things by sleeping with him. I can't say how many times I've re-read the note he left. *A mistake.* Making love to me was a mistake.

No—not making love. *Fucking.* That's what it was. There was no exchange of feelings, no real emotion on his part, other than the obvious grief. Let's at least call it what it was.

The phone rings and I jump. Then I see it's just Baylor's daily phone call. It's always the same thing. She'll try to get me to go back to work. She'll say it will help. But all I want to do is sit in Griffin's studio and stare at the walls and think of how I can't do this. I can't be a mom. What kind of mother will I be if I can't even resist my best friend's husband long enough for us to properly mourn her? I screwed up. I ruined everything. And now he's gone and I'm alone.

"Not today," I say in lieu of hello.

"Why not today?" she asks. "Do you really think tomorrow will be any better than today for you to go back to work?" I hear baby noises in the background, reminding me of tough decisions ahead. "Listen, Skylar. I know it's only been a couple of weeks, but you had six weeks before that to prepare for Erin's death. We all grieve in our own way, and I'm willing to respect that, but you need to realize you didn't die with her. Do you think Erin would want you to sit there wallowing in tears over her?"

I shake my head and before I can stop it, it comes out. I blurt it out like a volcano percolates and boils to the point of eruption and then spews all over everything in its path. "Erin wouldn't give a shit. She would hate me. I slept with him. I slept with Griffin. I couldn't even wait until the day after her funeral, Baylor. Who does that? You know who—*me.* Because I never fucking changed. I tried to. But a leopard never changes its spots. I'm a leopard, Bay. Face it. I couldn't even help myself. I have no self-control. And now I ruined everything. For a quick lay."

My throat is thick with unshed tears. I swallow the gigantic lump and continue before she can get a word in. "But the thing is, that wasn't what it was for me. It was the best sex of my life. Nothing has ever come close to what I experienced that night with Griffin. I dream of it every night. I think of it every day. I will compare every future encounter to it, already knowing how disappointed I'll be. What would even be the point of being with anyone else ever again?"

More damn baby noises on her end of the phone. "And what the hell am I supposed to do about Bean? I thought I could do it. I thought it might be possible. With Griffin. With the two of us trying to figure it out together. But now it's just me. He could be dead for all I know. He doesn't want this. He doesn't want Aaron." I take a breath and say the words that utterly destroy me. "He doesn't want me."

I close my eyes as guilt consumes me. "I don't think I can do it, Baylor. I don't think I can raise a baby. I'm going to have to find someone to adopt him."

Silence. I've shocked her with my confessions. I'm sure she's trying to think of something sisterly to say, but can't. What could she possibly say to make this any better?

"I have to go, Skylar. I have a meeting. But I'll call you later and we can talk, okay?"

I nod. Of course she wants to go. She probably doesn't want to regret the words she really wants to say. "Later then," I say. I hang up the phone and make my way down the stairs. I avoid looking at pictures of Erin. I know she's staring back at me. She knows what I've done. What I'm going to do.

I look at the pictures of Griffin with his dad. They are the only pictures of him in his entire studio. He's usually behind the camera, not in front of it. His dad was so happy to be having a grandbaby. I wonder if he'll hate me, too.

I walk over and take Griffin's favorite camera out of its case. The camera is an extension of him and it makes me feel closer to him when I hold it. I carry it over to the sitting room and curl up on the couch with it. I fall asleep dreaming of him taking pictures of his son with this very camera. Taking pictures of me. Of the family we were supposed to be.

The doorbell rings. Three times. Someone's impatient. "Geez, I'm coming." My sleepy legs carry me up the stairs from the basement while I wonder who's been sent to be on 'Skylar watch' today. I look through the sidelight. Baylor. And, oh great, she's brought the baby with her. Just what I need.

I open the door and then walk to the kitchen to put on a pot of coffee.

"Don't bother helping or anything, little sister," Baylor pouts as she pushes Jordan's stroller through the door and then leans down to retrieve a bunch of other crap. *How does one tiny baby need so much shit?*

She parks the stroller, checking on her daughter who is perfectly happy staring at the ceiling of the townhouse. "Slight emergency," she says. "I need you to watch her."

No need for coffee. I'm fully awake now. "What? No!" She should know better. I don't babysit. Kids hate me. I never have any idea what they want. I look down at my twenty-two-week belly and apologize to little Aaron that he was dealt such a shitty hand.

"You have to, Skylar. Nobody else can do it. I've called everyone. I can't miss this meeting with my publicist." She checks her watch. "If I'm not there in thirty minutes, he will drop me. He's the best publicist in New York. I've put him off for weeks and now he's pissed. You have to help me."

She pulls a notepad out of the gigantic baby bag. "I've written everything down. Just follow the schedule. Jordan is very easy." She pulls some bottles out of the bag, putting them in my refrigerator. "I pumped just in case I can't make it back for her next feeding in two hours."

My eyes go wide in horror. "Two hours? You're leaving her for two hours? What am I supposed to do with her, Baylor?"

I try to remember the few times I babysat Baylor's son, Maddox. But all I remember is my little sister, Piper, holding him, feeding him, changing him. I think I would just play with him until he needed something and then I would pass him off to her. I suck at this. She can't possibly trust me with her six-week-old baby. She's lost her freaking marbles.

"Oh, I don't know. Hold her maybe?" Baylor looks at me like I'm a dimwit. "She's a newborn, Skylar. She doesn't need much. If she cries, check her diaper. Pick her up and walk around with her. And here's a thought—use the world's best rocking chair Erin got for the nursery. You have everything you need right here."

She looks at her watch and gasps. "Hell, I have to go. You'll be fine. Call Mom out in Long Island if you need any advice. I'll be back as soon as I can." She walks out my front door before I can get in another word.

I look around. Maybe I'm being punked. This is not happening. Nobody in their right mind would leave a little baby with me. Jordan makes a squeaking noise and I walk over to look at her in her stroller. "Your mom is nuts, you know that, right?" She just stares at me. I think she smiles. Can a kid that little smile? Then I hear an awful sound. It sounds like explosive diarrhea. I bolt to the front door and run down the front steps. "Baylor!" I yell, looking in the direction of the subway. I stand there and wait for something to happen. Anything.

I hang my head and go back up in the townhouse. Jordan is really squirming around now. And it stinks to high heaven in here. I grab her bag and put it on my shoulder. Then I lean down to pick her up and the heavy bag falls off my arm. I roll my eyes at my awkwardness. I deposit the bag on the couch and pick up little Jordan. I hold her tightly in one arm, supporting her head like Baylor showed me, while I put the bag over my other shoulder. I did it. Okay, I can do this.

Proud of myself, I head to the stairs. I stand at the bottom of them and look up. What if I trip and drop her? What if my foot slips and we both fall? Who the hell decided a baby's room should be up the fucking stairs anyway? How on earth did so many of us survive this?

I take one slow step at a time until we reach the top where I exhale the breath I was holding. I walk into the nursery and eye the ornate changing table. I decide it's too dangerous. She might fall off it. I put Jordan in the crib and get a blanket from the closet, spreading it on the floor. Then I get a diaper and a cleansing wipe from Baylor's bag and put them next to the blanket. Grabbing Jordan, I carefully place her in the middle of the blanket and proceed to take her out of her clothes. When I'm struggling to get her little arms out of the outfit, I curse the sadistic makers of the baby clothes before I discover the crotch snaps.

"You've got a lot to learn, Skylar," I mumble to myself.

I gasp when I remove her diaper. She must be sick. There's a gooey pile of greenish-yellow poop. Oh, God. I try to breathe through my mouth. I just have to do this and then I'll call my mom. Or a doctor.

I remove the diaper, but not before Jordan's little feet smear the disgusting poo all over her legs, my hands and the blanket. I reach over for the wipe, realizing I got out only one and the rest are tucked into the designer baby bag. I wipe her up the best I can with the one wipe and the blanket beneath her. I'll throw the damn thing away. Anything to get rid of the nasty poo she's spreading around.

I need to wash her. I get another blanket out of the closet knowing I'll ruin that one as well, but at this point, I really don't care. When I'm in the closet, I notice a small baby bathtub. I look at the picture on the box. It shows a little baby, about Jordan's size. It has this thing up by the head so she can't slump over and fall under the water. Yes, this'll work.

What seems like hours later, I have one clean baby, but a train-wreck of a bathroom. I leave it to deal with later. I carefully carry Jordan down the stairs, one step at a time, leaving the baby bag in the nursery. No need to chance it. I call Baylor but go directly to voicemail. I call my mom. She laughs at me. *Laughs.* She assures me that Jordan's poop was perfectly normal for a breast-fed baby. Good Lord, why would anyone choose to breastfeed if *that's* what it produces?

She starts crying and I check the clock. Two hours almost on the dot. Baylor thought she'd be back by now. I retrieve the notebook and follow the instructions for warming up the bottle of breast milk. After she eats, I curse Baylor for leaving out the fact that Jordan will vomit half of it back up, ruining one of my favorite shirts. I wonder if I should feed her again. Baylor did bring extra bottles, maybe that's why. But Jordan falls asleep before I can heat one up. *Thank God.* I'm sure Baylor will be back before she wakes up.

I run upstairs and clean up the bathroom and nursery while Jordan sleeps in her stroller. How can one baby cause this much of a mess? Frazzled, I change my shirt, grabbing an old t-shirt from the laundry.

I sit down to finally get that cup of coffee when Jordan starts to cry. I look at the clock and I could swear she just went down, but time tells me it's been over an hour. I sigh and take a few lukewarm sips before I walk over to see what's wrong. She's been fed. She's clean. I stick my head a little closer—nope, no more explosive poop. I pick up my phone and call Baylor. Voicemail. I call my mom again. She tells me to pick her up. Talk to her. Play with her—babies need attention, not just care.

I look in the baby bag and pull out some sort of play mat. I lay it on the floor and then put Jordan on it before I lay on my side and show her the rattles and bears that detach from the Velcro on the mat. This seems to mollify her for a while so I sneak into the kitchen and grab a quick bite to eat, running out to check on her every ten seconds in case she learns to roll over or crawl in the span of time that I'm gone.

I take my sandwich out and sit next to Jordan when my phone pings with a message from Baylor that tells me she's going to be a lot longer than she thought. Hours longer. She may not even be back until dinner time.

Shit!

I call my mom. "You need to come help me. Baylor may not be back for hours."

More laughter. "Honey, I'm here all by myself, waiting on a delivery. By the time I get someone to cover for me and take the subway all the way into the city, Baylor will be home. You're doing fine. You shouldn't doubt your abilities."

"Mo-om," I whine.

"Oh, gotta go. The delivery is here. Call me later if you need anything else. Bye, honey."

I stare at the dead phone. My own mother hung me out to dry. I try calling Mindy and Jenna, but both go to voicemail. I look at Jordan, happily sucking on her little fist and drooling like she doesn't have a care in the world.

"I know what's going on here," I tell her. "They can all go to hell. They're throwing me in the fucking deep end." I roll my eyes at my choice of words. "Sorry," I say to Jordan.

By the time Baylor comes back to get Jordan, it's after nine o'clock at night. I had to give Jordan two more baths and take a shower myself after her faulty diaper leaked and she got shit all over me. It was awful. I put her next to my shower in a bassinette from Aaron's room. Every noise she made had me poking my head out and checking to make sure she wasn't climbing out or falling over. How do people do this?

Baylor finds us sleeping on my bed. I had barricaded Jordan's side of the bed with furniture and pillows. I know I could have put her in Aaron's crib, but I was afraid to leave her in there. What if she woke up and I didn't hear her? What if she got sick or got her little arms stuck in between the slats? But I was exhausted. I had to lie down come hell or high water.

I'm only half awake when Baylor enters my room. I don't even have the energy to yell at her. I just tell her to get the hell out.

I wake up to discover a letter on the pillow next to me. It's labeled with only my name. There's a sticky note attached to it that reads '*I was supposed to give this to you when the time was right.*' It's signed by Baylor.

I open it and the first thing that comes to mind is that Griffin was wrong. She did leave parting words. It's a letter from Erin. My heart pounds inside my chest and Bean moves around as if he can feel the shot of adrenaline coursing through my body. I close my eyes and breathe. In and out. In and out. I settle into my pillow and read her words.

Skylar,

I'm not sure if this is the first letter you've been given, or one of the last. So if this is redundant, I apologize. Baylor and Mason have a series of letters written by me. They have been instructed to give them to you and/or Griffin in certain situations.

Right now, at this very second, I'm rejoicing. It doesn't matter if I'm still alive but unaware, if I've been dead for a year, or if I've only recently passed. It doesn't matter, because if you are reading this letter it means that you and Griffin have taken a step towards being together. A step towards becoming the family I so desperately want for you. A step towards the love and caring that radiates around you when you are together.

I'm talking about sex. You and Griffin making love. If you are reading this, it's happened. But if you are reading this, something has gone wrong. I wish I could see into the future. But I can't. I'm only human, or maybe an angel by this point. All I can do is try to put myself in your shoes. How would I feel if I had just slept with my best friend's husband?

I can only imagine that you are carrying a heavy load of guilt. Shame. Betrayal. How could you do this to your best friend?

I have one thing to say. STOP IT!

I put you there, Skylar. I put you in the very position you've found yourself in. I threw the two of you together with the sole intention for you to develop feelings for each other. If anyone is to blame here, it's me. You fell into the trap that I perfectly orchestrated.

I lied—I have another thing to say. GET OVER IT.

Let go of the guilt. You are doing exactly what I've asked you to do. You are trying to fulfill my dying wish. You are allowing yourself the chance at happiness. And let me tell you something, Skylar, you deserve it. You deserve every loving touch Griffin bestows upon you. Every tender word he whispers to you. Every wonderful child he gives to you. And I will be smiling down upon you every single second of it. You don't need it, but if for some reason, you think you do, I'll say it anyway—you have my permission. I give it to you wholeheartedly, now and always. I give you my blessing to love and live and be happy with him.

I don't presume to know if it's you or Griffin or both of you that are fighting your feelings. I don't presume to have any magical words of wisdom that will take down any walls you may have erected. I don't presume to have any heavenly powers that can fix what might be broken.

All I can say is this.

Have faith. And love them.

Love them hard.

Love them forever.

Your best friend on earth and in heaven,

Erin

I read the note again before folding it up and returning it to the envelope. Then I do something I haven't done in many weeks. I smile. A weight is lifted from my shoulders. From my heart. This may not change the fact that Griffin is gone and may never return. But I feel the guilt being drawn from me as if Erin has attached a string to it from heaven and is actively extracting it from my every pore.

Then it hits me and I take a breath so big, it feels like it's the first air I've allowed into my body in fourteen long days. Jordan was with me for twelve hours yesterday and she survived. *I* survived.

I put my hand on my growing belly. "You might have to cut me a little slack, Aaron. But I can do this." I look around my room. The guest room that became mine almost a month ago.

Moms don't sleep in the guest room.

I get up and walk down the hall and push open the door to Griffin's bedroom. His suit still lies crumpled on the floor. Erin's glass of water still sits, evaporating, on her night table. His pillows still lie on the decorative couch where he slept. I put my hand on the rich oak of the large bed. I pull up on it to see that I can't even begin to budge it. I grab my phone and make a call.

"Mason, I need your help at the townhouse."

After we hang up, I catch a glimpse of myself in the mirror and laugh. Yesterday after my shower, in my haste to get back to little Jordan, I had inadvertently put on one of Griffin's traitorous baseball shirts.

It feels good to laugh. It feels good to smile. It feels good to have the rest of my life ahead of me.

I call Mindy and tell her I'll be back to work at the end of the week, after I take care of a few things. The last call I make is to Baylor. I only have one thing to say to her. "Thank you."

I hear her relief come through the phone. "Anytime, little sister."

I head down the stairs and sit on the couch, staring up at the urn that resides on the mantle. I'm not sure why I decided to put it there. Maybe it's the best place for her to watch over us. Until we decide where she truly belongs.

I sigh. *We*. There isn't a *we*. There's only a *me*. And somehow, someway, I'm going to make the most of it.

I look up at the urn. "Don't worry, Erin. I got this."

part two

griffin

chapter twenty-one

Loud voices wake me, pounding through my skull like a sledgehammer. I cover my head with a pillow to drown them out, along with the light that's shining through the curtains.

Wait… voices?

I sit up, then immediately curse myself for moving too quickly, adding even more pain to my already piercing headache.

I glance around the now-familiar bedroom that is part of the suite I've been staying in for a while now. Something's different. And who's talking outside the door? I look around the room for answers. Unfortunately, I get them.

Shit. I finally did it.

I stare at the floor where there's a heap of women's clothing. A dress. A pair of high heels.

I lie back down, raising the sheet from my body. *Naked.* I shake my head. Is this rock bottom? First I leave my family. Well, my sort-of family. Then I lose myself in a bottle. And now—sleeping with a random stranger. Have I finally become my father?

My eyes search the floor for a telltale square wrapper. *Not there.* I slowly walk into the connecting bathroom and check the waste basket. *Nope.*

I lock eyes with myself in the mirror. I don't even look like me anymore. "What the fuck did you do?"

I splash some water on my face and then hold my mouth under the faucet and gulp down a long drink.

Throwing on some clothes, I hesitate before opening the door to the other room, wondering what I'm going to find on the other side. I listen for a second. Then, hearing a familiar male voice, I throw the door open. "What the hell are you doing here?"

Mason eyes me from head to toe. I know I must be a sight. My hand comes up to run over the long scruff on my face. I can't remember the last time I shaved. Hell, I'm not even sure I've showered lately. He shakes his head in disapproval. "Shouldn't I be asking *you* that question, man?"

I ignore him and look at the woman. She's wearing my shirt. It comes down to her knees and the collar is hanging off her bare shoulder. She looks like *her.* So much like her. Is that why I chose her?

She gives me a sympathetic look as she extends her hand. "Tammy. Nice to meet you, Griffin."

I look between her and Mason, confused. "Uh, we didn't make introductions last night?"

She just smiles, helping herself to a cup of coffee. "I hope you don't mind me crashing here. I was in no condition to drive, and the rooms here are way out of this working girl's budget."

My eyes go wide and my blood pressure shoots through the roof. *I hired a hooker?*

Fuck. I have hit rock bottom.

I fall back onto the couch and put my head between my knees. I feel sick. I look up at her. She doesn't look like a hooker. "Don't you girls insist on using protection?"

She giggles. "Honey, you were so wasted last night, you couldn't have hoisted it up with a sail. Hell, I thought your name was 'Finn' until Mason here set me straight."

I blow out a relieved breath. *Thank God.* I didn't know until this very second how bad I would have felt sleeping with someone else.

I hear Mason cracking up behind me. I'm about to ask him what his problem is when Tammy's face breaks into a devious smile. She laughs out loud, turning to Mason. "I'm sorry, I never was a very good poker player."

I look between them as they share some kind of private joke. "Wait, you're not a hooker?" I ask.

She shakes her head. "Sorry, no. Just a pharmaceutical sales rep you met in the hotel bar last night."

"Not a very good one if you can't even afford a room of your own," I spit out in misguided anger.

"Dude!" Mason chides me for my crassness.

Tammy holds up a hand. "It's okay. I deserved that. An eye for an eye."

"No, I'm sorry," I tell her. I run my hands through my dirty hair. "Can I call down for some breakfast? It's the least I can do."

She waves me off, taking another sip of her coffee. "Nah. Coffee's good. I have a meeting to run to. But I'll use the shower if that's okay."

"Of course." I watch her walk into the bedroom and shut the door.

Once I hear the water running, I turn to Mason. "Why are you here? And how did you even find me?"

"It took a while, brother. I'm not gonna lie." He pulls a chair over from the small dining table and straddles it, resting his elbows on its back. "I found a girl at the post office who recognized me and she gave me the address where you were having your mail forwarded. I had to give her some tickets to next season's opener because she said she could lose her job over it."

Irritation pinches my brows. "Isn't that some kind of federal offense?"

"That's not the point," he says.

"Well, what is the point exactly?"

"The point is, you ran away, Griffin."

I get up from the couch and pour myself a cup of coffee. My head is pounding and I'm in no mood for a heart-to-heart with Mason Lawrence. Or with anyone, for that matter. I just want to be left the hell alone.

He nods his head towards the bedroom. "She said you were so drunk you kept telling her she had eyes as green as the sky."

I stare at him blankly over the rim of my coffee cup.

"She looks like her," he says. "She looks just like Skylar Mitchell. Is that what you've been doing down here? Picking up girls who look like Skylar and fucking them to assuage your guilt for sleeping with her?"

"What? How do you—"

"You've been gone a long time, my friend. Too long. Skylar and I have become friends. She needs as many as she can get. You know, to give her a little support after losing her best friend and then being hung out to dry by your sorry ass."

"It's not like I didn't lose something, too, Dix."

"Of course it's not. We all know how much you loved Erin. Nobody is going to fault you for needing time to grieve your wife. But you have a kid to worry about now. Have you even stopped to think about that? Can you stop screwing your way around Miami Beach to give even a little thought as to how this might affect *him*?"

"I'm not screwing anything down here. I thought Tammy was the first."

"Well thank goodness for small favors." He laughs. "And limp dicks."

When Tammy comes out of the bedroom, I apologize to her while Mason orders breakfast. After he walks her out, he sits down again. He eyes my new tattoo that I'm staring at. "New ink, huh?"

I nod.

"Listen. I know you need time to get over this. But you should come back to New York. You have to face your responsibilities. I understand you're feeling guilty about sleeping with Skylar, it tore her apart, too."

My eyes snap to his. Then my heart settles in my stomach, making me feel like I've been kicked in the gut. She thought it was a mistake. "Shit, Dix, that's not it at all."

"You don't feel guilty about sleeping with her?"

I shake my head. I've been over this a thousand times in my own mind. I don't even understand it myself so how can I be expected to explain it to him?

"Whatever it is, you can tell me, G. We've been through a lot together, you and me. It's okay, man. I won't bail on you."

How much worse can I make things if I tell him? I close my eyes so I don't have to look at his reaction to my awful words. "I was relieved. All I felt was relief when Erin died." I rub my fingers across my new tattoo. I don't have to open my eyes to find it. I know exactly where it is on my arm.

"Of course you were relieved, Griffin. She was free of all the horrible things her body was putting her through those last months. It's normal to feel that way."

I shake my head. "It was more than that. Those first days after she died, when I locked myself in my bedroom. I wasn't in there grieving. I'd done all that before she died. I was hiding from her—from Skylar. From the way my body reacted to her when she was near me. I knew I wouldn't be able to be around her without wanting her. I also knew how wrong it was. I knew what a douche of a husband it made me that two seconds after my sick wife died, all my body craved was getting into her best friend's pants.

"Then after the funeral, I started drinking. And when Skylar found me in my studio, I couldn't even help myself. I had to be with her. I didn't even think of Erin. Not one time. Not until right after." I pinch the bridge of my nose remembering that night. "It was awful, Dix."

Mason nods as if understanding what I'm saying. "Bad sex, huh? Been there."

"No. That's not it at all. And that's part of the problem. It was the best goddamn sex of my life. I had just buried my wife and I ran straight into Skylar's arms and I loved every minute of it. Who does that? And worse, I've thought about it every day since. It's been two months and I haven't cried for my dead wife. Not since the night of her funeral." I hit the couch cushion next to me. "I'm such a jackass."

I blow a deep breath out. "I don't feel guilty because I slept with her, man. But at the same time, I do. My wife fucking died and the first thing I do is forget about her to be with her best friend."

He nods at my tattoo again. "But you haven't forgotten about Erin. She's right there on your arm. Just like your mom is. She'll always be with you." He laughs. "You're beating yourself up over nothing. She wanted this. She *wants* this."

He grabs his bag and sorts through some mail, pulling out an envelope and ripping off a sticky note that was attached to it. He walks over and shoves it in my face. "Here, you need to read this."

I immediately recognize the handwriting as Erin's. *Oh my God.* She did leave some final words for me. My throat becomes thick and my eyes sting.

Mason turns to leave. "Room service is taking too long. I'm going to head next door to that waffle place. You take some time to read that. And shower. You smell like a fucking pig, man."

With that, he turns and exits the suite, leaving me staring at the envelope with my name on it.

I put it on the table in front of me. I can't get myself to open it. Erin would be so disappointed in me if she could see me now. I decide to shower and shave before reading it. Maybe it's strange, but I feel cleaning myself up will somehow make me more worthy of her last words.

When I emerge from the shower, the food has arrived. Doesn't matter. I couldn't eat now if it was my last meal. I sit down and tear open the envelope.

Griffin,

I'm not sure if this is the first letter you've been given, or one of the last. So if this is redundant, I apologize. Mason and Baylor have a series of letters written by me. They have been instructed to give them to you and/or Skylar in certain situations.

If you are reading this letter, you and Skylar have taken a step towards being together.

You've made love. And I'm rejoicing whether I'm still alive or up in heaven. But if you are reading this letter, something's gone wrong.

First, I need to apologize. Since the day you entered my life, you've been my caretaker. I'm sure it came from what happened to your mom, but I was all too willing to let you care for me over and beyond what any seventeen-year-old boy should have been responsible for.

You were my best friend. My lover. My husband. But I'm not naïve. No matter how much we both wanted it, we were never soul mates.

Despite that, I know you would have stayed with me forever. I know we would have loved each other the best we could. And I'll always love you for that. Your loyalty is one of the most wonderful things about you.

I also know that if you've tried giving yourself to Skylar, you probably feel as if you've betrayed me. Well, listen closely, Griff. The only way you will betray me is by not following your heart. I've seen you and Skylar together. The way you look at her is how every woman should be seen. The way your face lights up when we talk about her and how your eyes follow her every movement—it's how every woman should be revered.

I may have planted the seed, but you know as well as I do there is something between you two. Something wonderful. Something huge. Something I want more than anything for the two of you to accept and explore.

You were never my soul mate, Griff. But in some strange way, I think Skylar is. I think she's both our soul mates. It's as if the three of us together make the perfect couple. Fate brought her to us. Fate allowed her to carry your child. Fate had her fall in love with you.

You remember what I always said about fate, don't you? DON'T MESS WITH IT!

Follow your heart, Griff. It will lead you in the right direction. Have faith. Let go of any guilt you may have over me. Go to her, go to your child. Be where love and life will surround you.

By taking care of them, you continue to take care of me. By loving them, you continue to love me.

So, please... love them.

Love them hard.

Love them forever.

Your best friend on earth and in heaven,
Erin

I put the letter back on the table and stare at it. How could she have possibly known I would screw this up?

I can't help but think about the letter my mom wrote to me that I was given after her funeral. I was only fifteen at the time. She asked similar things of me. She asked me to let go of the guilt I felt over her getting sick. She asked me to let go of the hatred I had towards my father. She said he was grieving in the only way he knew how. She asked me to repair my relationship with my dad and to love him. She said my life would be better for it.

What is it about dying that makes everyone want to forgive, forget and make the world one big happy fucking kumbaya? Instead of being pissed off that they're dying, they want to fix everyone else's lives.

I read Erin's letter once more. I try not to be upset that she waited two months to tell me this. Then again, it was me who ran away. If I'd stuck around, Mason could have given me the letter right away. I have nobody to be pissed at but myself. I could have avoided two months of self-loathing, self-pity, and God knows what else I could have gotten myself into.

My eyes focus on the words that could burn a hole in the letter. The words that contributed to the guilt, the self-abhorrence, the drinking.

It's as if the three of us together make the perfect couple.

The words she could have plucked from my own head because I've thought them so many times.

chapter twenty-two

When I first laid eyes on Skylar, I felt like the air was sucked out of the room. When her emerald-green eyes met with mine, I forgot to breathe. I had never experienced anything like it, not even when I met Erin. Not even when I've been around some of the world's top supermodels.

She looked so nervous. I could tell she tried to put on a front and project this rough exterior. But when she started talking and that soft, melodious voice came out of her full, pouty lips, I thought I had never heard anything sweeter.

Then when she fell off the stool and into my arms, I swear to God I felt all that shit you see in sappy chick-flick movies. I couldn't even begin to understand it. I was happy. I was happy with my beautiful wife and my dream job. I didn't need or want another woman. I wasn't ever looking for one. And no matter how strong my physical reaction to her was, I knew I would never act upon it. Erin was my wife. She was my life.

I realized I was being kind of a dick to Skylar at first, telling her my stare was innocent when I knew it was anything but. I even found myself getting jealous over the fact that she had a promiscuous past. It was ridiculous. I had no claim over this girl. But I knew I didn't want to spend nine months or more having the reaction I was experiencing. I mean, I'm only human.

I was about to put a stop to the whole meeting when Erin started talking about fate. She wanted a baby. She wanted it so badly. We'd been trying to adopt for a few years, and only after she'd worked on me for several before that. I was never fully on board with having a kid. I was an only child and look at what happened to my fucked-up family. Shit goes wrong. People die. Fathers leave. I didn't want to risk putting that burden on a child. But she wanted it so much. And who was I to deny Erin anything? From the day I met her, she garnered my complete loyalty. And I knew she would have it forever. No matter what.

So by the end of our meeting, I had decided to suck it up and be a man. I wasn't going to be involved that much anyway. Pregnancy was a woman's thing. I would simply keep my distance and then she'd be out of our lives after giving Erin the baby of her dreams.

I didn't count on Erin and Skylar becoming best friends. I'd never seen Erin become attached to anyone like that before. At first I thought it was because of the baby. But the more I was around Skylar, the more I understood the draw. In many ways, she was the opposite of Erin. And not just physically. She exuded adventure, independence and friendship from her every pore. She was feisty and candid. She spoke her mind without hesitation. And dammit, when she cussed, all I wanted to do was shut her pouty lips up with mine. It was torture.

I did a good job of staying away those first few months. But then Erin started throwing us together. I thought she was crazy making me spend time with the gorgeous woman who was carrying my child. I tried to rationalize I was genetically predisposed to be attracted to her merely because she was pregnant with my baby. However, the more time we spent together, the more drawn to her I became. And all Erin wanted to do was talk about her. Tell me how great Skylar was. How cute her growing body was becoming. How loyal a friend she had become.

Then when Erin dropped the terminal-cancer bomb on us and told us her dying wish, I was sure, that in some twisted way, I'd caused her illness by the inappropriate thoughts I never would have acted upon.

What kind of wife gives their husband and best friend permission to hook up? Then again, our situation was never typical from the very beginning. I understood her request. I'd seen plenty of kids raised by single parents. She didn't want that for Aaron. So I promised her. And then I failed her.

For the first time in my life, I failed Erin by running away.

The door to the suite opens, startling me. Mason walks through and I shake my head. "They gave you a goddamn key? Is there anything you can't weasel your way into?"

He laughs. "Can I help it that women throw themselves at me?" He shows me a second key card. "She gave me two, actually. She said her break was at noon if I wanted to meet her there."

My jaw drops.

"What? Like you've never been handed hotel keys before." He rolls his eyes at me and then tosses the second key in the trash. "Guys like you and me; we've been both blessed and cursed. These looks come at a price."

He doesn't have to explain. I know all too well what price he's talking about. It comes to visit him every other weekend and on Wednesdays. Even less during football season. I decide to change the subject. "So, no playoffs this year?"

"Well, what do you expect when I'm not out there throwing the ball?" It's a joke, but he's frowning. We both know he should've been the starting quarterback for the Giants this year. It's why he was drafted his junior year at Clemson. It wasn't his fault that Johnny Henley retracted his retirement at the last minute. But instead of throwing a fit or asking to be released, Mason accepted his position as backup quarterback, claiming he would earn his way to the starting position.

"It'll happen, Dix. One of these days, it'll happen."

He nods at me. "Makes for a very boring January. But hey, maybe I'll hang down here with you for a few days. Work on my tan."

"You can hang out here if you want. The suite is paid for until the end of the month." I get up and walk over to the table, suddenly hungry. "I'm heading home as soon as I can get a flight."

Mason gives me an award-winning smile. I know he's about to gloat. I hold up my hand to stop him. "It was the letter, not you, you dickwad."

He smirks at me. "The letter, huh? Has nothing to do with the 'best sex of your life'?"

I throw a dry waffle at him.

"You really didn't screw around this whole time you've been down here?" he asks.

I shake my head and then take a bite of lukewarm eggs. "I tried. But every time I'd start getting somewhere with them I felt like I was cheating on her." I lock eyes with him. "Cheating on Sky. How messed up is that?"

"Sky?" He raises an eyebrow. "I thought she hated that nickname."

I laugh. "She does. It's probably one of the reasons I use it."

"You two get off on rubbing each other the wrong way, don't you?" He smiles. "Sounds like true love to me," he jokes.

Love. I'm reminded of Erin's comment about Skylar being in love with me. I'm sure it was just another manipulation tactic on her part. Half the time I think Sky hates me. And I probably sealed the deal when I walked out on her, telling her it was a mistake. I wonder just how much work I've got cut out for me to make up for it. "Exactly how pissed off is she at me?"

"Pissed?" he says. "I wouldn't say she's pissed. She's trying to deal with things the best she can. You were both dealt a devastating blow, but now she's been left with a kid she never thought would be hers to keep." He lets out a long breath. "But, listen, it's best you get back there soon. Grab your stuff and I'll head to the airport with you."

"What happened to getting a tan?" I ask.

He laughs. "Are you kidding? I wouldn't miss a second of what you're about to walk back into."

I draw my brows in confusion. "I thought you said she wasn't pissed."

"Well, *she* might not be. But I didn't say there wouldn't be a shitstorm coming from everyone else you know."

I run my hands through my hair before heading into the bedroom for my suitcase.

Mason can fall asleep anywhere. Once, he fell asleep on the subway during rush hour. He just slumped over and started snoring. Me—I've got too much shit flowing through my head. What's it going to be like being in the city without Erin? Who am I if I'm not the man taking care of her? Where will I stay? Am I even welcome back at my townhouse?

But most of all, as I stare out the window at the pillowy clouds below, I think of Sky.

I remember what seem like the most inconsequential moments. Moments like when I held her hair back as she puked into her waste basket. Or when she reached her arms around me to tie an apron. And when I put my arm around her at the baseball stadium to keep that creep away. Every one of those touches was innocent, yet with each one, I felt some sort of electrical current making its way through my body. Each touch hit me in the pit of my stomach and had me questioning my sanity if I were to keep being around her.

Then, of course, there were the touches that almost wrecked me. When she put my hand on her stomach and I felt Aaron move for the first time. It was only minutes before Erin's death. Minutes that separated one of the best moments in my life from one of the worst.

And when we slept together—it was all I could do not to pour my feelings out like a pansy ass. Being with her was surreal. I know I was a little drunk, but that did nothing to dull the feel of her touch. It did nothing to lower the incredible sensation of her milky-white skin against mine. It did nothing to stifle the memory of every nuance in her face, every curve of her body and every taste of her skin.

I reach in my pocket and wrap my hand around the small rectangular box wrapped in holiday paper. I'm still not sure I'll give it to her. I'm not even sure it was ever my intention to give it to her, but it seemed too perfect not to buy.

I reach into my carry-on and pull out the ultrasound picture I swiped from Erin's room the morning I left. It's the picture of him sucking his thumb. I can see the wrinkles on his little face and the creases on his tiny fingers. I touch the picture, tracing his face with my thumb. I'm glad he hasn't been born yet. I'd hate for him to be old enough to understand what I'd done. I know what it's like to hate your own father.

As the plane descends to JFK, I can still see holiday lights lining the streets of Queens. It makes me think of Erin and how she loved Christmas. She would go all out every year, decorating our house as if we were hosting a gala and not just a simple family dinner. She would put beautifully wrapped presents under the tree and mark them *'from Santa.'* I'd roll my eyes at her every year, but she'd always pretend he was real. It didn't matter that we were the only ones in the room. It was her favorite holiday.

I was sad that she couldn't make it long enough to see one more. I spent the entire day drunk, lost in the crowd, sitting on the beach surrounded by the masses of vacationing families. I wondered how Aaron would spend future Christmases. Would Skylar carry on Erin's traditions? Would I send gifts, hoping that he'd get them and not deposit them directly into the trash as I did when my dad sent them to me?

Suddenly it hits me. It hits me so hard that if I weren't sitting down, I'd fall over. I will do anything to give my kid a good life. I'll do anything to make sure Skylar will be a part of it. I'll do everything I can to honor Erin's dying wish and become a family.

chapter twenty-three

As night falls, I stand on the sidewalk staring up the steps at the door to my townhouse. I watch as the crisp, cold New York air turns my hot breath into quick puffs of smoke, making me acutely aware of how nervous I am. The fresh snow lining the stoop is a far cry from the warm beach I was walking on just yesterday. I take in the exterior of the townhouse that doesn't even feel like mine anymore. It's only been two months. A lot can change in two months. The outside of the building looks the same, with the exception of a large wreath that still decorates the front door even though it's mid-January. I smile. Maybe Skylar likes Christmas as much as Erin did.

With as much trepidation as I've ever felt in my twenty-seven years, I climb the steps. There's a soft glow of light coming from the sidelights surrounding the front door, giving me hope that she's home. I gave her no warning that I was coming. I didn't want to give her a chance to stop me. I can only hope she'll accept my apology and allow me back into her life.

Despite the frigid temperature, I'm sweating. I shift the flowers from one hand to the other as I wipe my damp palms down the sides of my jeans. It's then I remember the box in my pocket. I'm not sure I'll give it to her. Christmas was weeks ago. Maybe I'll save it for her birthday.

Shit. I don't even know when that is. Just like I didn't know what kind of flowers to bring. There's a lot I need to learn about Skylar Mitchell.

I take a deep breath and look up at the darkening sky. I don't know why, but it makes me feel better to do it. Maybe I'm asking God to help me through this. Maybe I'm asking Erin. Either way, I probably need all the help I can get.

I ring the bell. I know I'm still part-owner of the townhouse, but after what I did, I think I lost the right to use my key. My body goes tense. I feel like a goddamn teenage boy calling on his first crush. What the hell is wrong with me?

I see movement when I peek through the sidelight. My breath catches when she turns on a light and comes into full view. My eyes instantly fall on her perfectly rounded stomach before making their way to her face. I'm not sure what I expected. I knew she'd be bigger by now, but I didn't expect her to be more beautiful. Her dark-blonde hair is long and down, bouncing around her shoulders with every step. Her legs look toned and shapely in the leggings she's wearing, and her tight green blouse is stressed by her growing breasts, accentuating her belly that's now the size of a small soccer ball.

In the darkness of the porch, I know she can't see me staring at her. It's a good thing, because I can't tear my eyes away. She's so damn beautiful. Shivers, that I'm positive aren't from the cold, run down my spine.

The porch light flickers on and she looks at me through the window. I can't tell for sure, but I think she gasps. Her hand goes to her belly and she glances briefly over her shoulder before locking eyes with me. Those eyes—the shirt she's wearing makes them an even more stunning green than they already are.

I have the sudden urge to photograph her. It's a desire I haven't felt in months. I haven't snapped a picture of anyone or anything since the days before Erin's death.

Right this second, I can't wait to wrap my hands around a camera again. My fingers ache to move their way around the focus and bring Skylar into frame. I want to capture this look she has on her face. I can't quite figure it out, but I think she's warring with herself. I swear I see two different emotions behind those emerald eyes. Relief and... anger? Whatever they are, they contradict each other.

Her eyes fall to the bouquet of flowers in my hand. Her gaze softens as she lets out a visible sigh and regards the white lilies with her head tilted to one side. She returns her eyes to mine as she reaches out to unlock the deadbolt.

She opens the door and I feel a rush of warmth graze over me. She wraps her arms around her body and I wonder if it's from the chill, or merely to protect herself. Both of us are quiet. I had rehearsed what to say a thousand times on the flight. But now, as I stand here, I'm not sure I can get my brain to form the words I need her to hear.

She raises her eyebrows in silence. She's stubborn. She's not going to give me the satisfaction of her saying the first words. She's right. She has nothing to apologize for. This is all on me. My mind races for the appropriate thing to say. What does one say to the woman you abandoned who also happens to be your dead wife's best friend who is carrying your baby? I step forward and shove the

241

flowers at her as my unfiltered words escape my mouth. "Let's do this."

Her face falls. She was expecting so much more and I've let her down again. Let *them* down. Her disappointed eyes flicker to the flowers in my outstretched hand. I momentarily wonder if it's the lilies that have made her sad, or the man holding them. Without a word, her arm reaches up to shut the door.

I put my foot in the doorway so she can't close it on me. "Wait! That came out wrong. I mean, yes, I want to do this, but I should apologize. I need to apologize first. I'm so sorry for running out on you that way."

She looks nervously behind her and then comes closer to the barely-open door. "You left, Griffin." She shakes her head. "I know you loved her and I have no right to claim my grief was any worse than yours. In fact, I'm sure it pales in comparison. But you left. You said everything you needed to say in the note. It was a mistake. You can't do this. So now, you show up after two months. After I've worried myself half to death that you would turn up dead. Or that you would leave the child that Erin so desperately wanted—that you'd leave him by choice. And now you come back and simply say 'let's do this?' Do you expect me to fall at your feet? What exactly is it that you want, Griffin?"

Before I can begin to answer her, I hear a grating male voice. A voice I already know belongs to a man I'll hate. "Everything okay, Skylar?"

"Yes, everything's fine." She opens the door to forge an introduction. "John, this is Griffin. He used to live here before his wife died."

I eye the man who may not even realize he just became the competition. He has short hair, cut precise and above the ears. His eyes are pale-brown and unassuming. He's shorter and stockier than I am. He's got a clean-cut military look and I momentarily wonder if she prefers her men that way. My hand comes up to run through my wavy mane as I finish my assessment of him.

John winces, and then reaches out to shake my hand. "Oh, man. I'm so sorry to hear that."

I get the idea he doesn't know the whole story. I want to stare him down and tell him to get the hell out. That Skylar is carrying my baby and what right does he have to be here. I'm not sure why I don't speak up. Hell, I did it to ward off men in the past. But common sense gets the better of me and keeps me from blurting out anything that could have the potential of upsetting her more than she already is.

"Thanks. I, uh… just need a few things. My cameras. My phone. Is it okay if I grab them?"

She breathes out a sigh of relief. She thought I was going to tell him. Ruin her date, or whatever this is. I stretch my neck around them to see the dining room table is set for two and there are candles lit in the center. *Date. Shit.*

Why did I think this wouldn't happen? Because she's pregnant?

She steps aside and waves me in. "Of course."

I suddenly remember the flowers I'm holding and feel like a dick intruding on her without warning. I nonchalantly place them on the entry table on my way by.

John walks to the back door. "I'd better check on the steaks. Nice to meet you, Griffin."

I nod my chin at him as a foreign feeling courses through my body. He's walking out of *my* back door onto *my* patio, to check on steaks he's grilling on *my* grill. I want nothing more than to follow him out and pummel his unsuspecting head into *my* concrete wall.

I've never before wanted to claim anything as badly as I want to claim her right now. She's carrying my kid, dammit.

Skylar's eyes find my fisted hands and she questions them with a raise of her brow.

It takes everything I have to relax them before I walk by her. "I'll just be a minute," I say.

I take the stairs two at a time and race to my room. The sooner I can get out of here, the better. I stop cold when I reach the threshold of the master suite. The room has been transformed. The furniture Erin and I had in here is all gone, replaced by some pieces from the guest room, the couch that was in my studio, and some stuff I recognize from Skylar's old place. I briefly close my eyes as the light scent of her flowery perfume hits me.

My eyes fall on her bed. The bed we made love on. The sheets are rumpled and I have a moment of unbridled anger wondering if John has been on it.

Then I see the picture on her nightstand. It's one I took at the picnic when Erin and Skylar both had the same shade of brown hair. Skylar is standing, looking down at Erin who is kneeling next to her, touching her barely-there baby bump. It's the kind of picture you would expect to see of a husband as he admires his pregnant wife. Yet it speaks volumes of their special friendship. I think Erin might have been right about the two of them being soul mates. This picture is a testament to that. Even being the professional I am, I couldn't have picked a better picture to display.

"I'm sorry," Skylar says, coming up behind me. "I know it must be hard for you seeing my things in here."

"It's fine." If she only knew. If I could only tell her that's not it at all. If I only had the balls to say my reaction is not because this room is no longer Erin's, but purely because I want nothing more than to take Skylar in my arms and have another incredible night with her. Only this time, I wouldn't run away. I would stay and worship every single inch of her over and over again. But I can't say it. Especially not with *him* just down the stairs.

"I had Mason move your belongings down the hall, and I boxed up Erin's clothes and moved them to the basement." I turn to look at her and she says in barely a whisper, "I didn't know what to do with them."

"I know. It's okay." I walk past her, taking one last glance back at the bed. On the way to the guest room, I pass the nursery. I pause in the doorway and see it hasn't been changed a bit since Erin decorated it. I make my way into the guest room to see my furniture. It overtakes the room, this huge, oak, four-poster bed Erin insisted we buy as our first piece of furniture in our new home.

When I see the nightstand on my side of the bed—*do I even have a side anymore?*—my breath catches as I spot the picture of Erin when she was young and going through chemo. Skylar set up this room exactly like it had been before. Right down to my cell phone that still sits plugged in and on top of a book I was reading.

I retrieve my phone and charger and I open the closet to grab a few of my favorite shirts. I walk out into the hallway to see Skylar leaning against the wall. "I'll come back another time for more."

She doesn't say a word, she just nods.

Going back down the stairs, I look over the family pictures that Erin had so tastefully displayed on our wall. Skylar hasn't removed any of them. The photo from our wedding is still in a prominent place in the center of the wall. There are new additions in the mix, however, that include pictures from Skylar's family. There's even a picture of Erin and me holding the ultrasound photo. It was one of the last pictures taken of her before she started looking really sick, right before she asked us not to take any more of her.

Walking through the living room, the silver urn on the mantle catches my eye, making me stop in my tracks. I go over to it and trace Erin's etched name with my finger.

"I didn't know what to do with that, either," Skylar's soft voice speaks behind me. "I couldn't bear to put it in storage with her clothes. It didn't seem right."

"No, it's the perfect place, until we can figure out a better one." I thought about it a lot the past few months, where to scatter her ashes. I have an idea. But it's not entirely my decision to make.

I glance out the back door to see John pretending to mind the steaks, which are probably overdone by now. He's shivering, having gone out without a coat. I debate telling him it's okay to come back inside, but then I think better of it. Let him freeze his balls off out there. Cold balls, tough steak, unwelcome visitor. Makes for one bad date if you ask me.

I head down to the basement. My studio is exactly as I left it, with a few exceptions. The couch from my bedroom has been switched with the couch that was once here. On the couch is a picture of me. One Skylar took of my dad and me at the picnic. Sitting next to it is my favorite camera. I know for a fact I didn't leave it there.

I pick up the camera and find a large duffle bag to put it and some of my others into. I stare at the wall full of pictures. Pictures of Erin. Pictures of Skylar. They all make me happy. They all make me sad. I look for my favorite one, but it's not there. Then I notice it on the floor.

That's right; I dropped it there when I started kissing Skylar that night. She left it there. For two months, she's left it sitting on the floor. Discarded like a piece of forgotten trash. Is that how she felt? How she feels? Like something I so carelessly discarded? I stare at it. She's so beautiful lying on the grass, her small hand pressed against the side of her barely-there belly. And the look on her face, I'm not sure I've ever captured a look like it in any photo I've ever taken. It makes me wonder if Aaron was moving inside her. She looks more at peace than I've ever seen anyone.

I pick it up and put it in my bag.

Not that I need a picture to remember Skylar. Her heart-shaped face. Her wavy hair that wants to be brown as much as it wants to be blonde. Her emerald eyes that put even the most priceless gems to shame. They are all burned into my memory.

Seeing the photos reminds me of what's in my pocket. I take the box out and run my fingers over it. I swing my bag over my shoulder and go back up the stairs.

"Maybe it would be best if I left, Skylar," John says, as I ascend the last few steps unnoticed.

Yes, John. Leave. I wonder if he feels the tension between Skylar and me. Surely it's thick enough to penetrate his rough exterior and clean-shaven pretty-boy face.

"No, don't leave. He'll only be another minute, I'm sure."

Damn. She didn't take the out. Maybe this is when I play the baby-daddy card. Get rid of him for good. I round the corner, ready to play my hand and damn the consequences. Then I see his hand on her arm, rubbing up and down as she looks into his eyes. They like each other. This isn't a first date. Maybe it isn't even a second date. All I can think of right now is punching Mason in the jaw for not warning me that she's found someone. Someone to replace me. Someone to raise Aaron. Because the way he's looking at her right now, it's the way I want to be looking at her. It's the way I want to be touching her.

She notices me and jerks her arm away from him, much to his dismay. His eyes look back and forth between us before falling on her belly. I wonder if he's just now putting it all together. He puts a possessive arm around her as her guilty eyes find mine. What are her eyes trying to tell me? That she's with him but doesn't want to be? That she's moved on but doesn't want to flaunt it?

Maybe he's the only one she could find willing to take on a pregnant single woman.

I shake my head at the ridiculous thought. Even twenty-eight weeks pregnant, she probably has guys lining up to date her. She's got this uncanny ability to draw men in and place them under her spell. She has no idea about all the men I had to drive away. No idea that eyes followed her everywhere. No idea of the intimidating stares, threats, and even punches I doled out to keep away the masses.

John stays in the kitchen while Skylar follows me to the front door. Before I walk through it, I place her gift on the entry table. "It's just something I found that reminded me of both the 'Erins' in our lives. I thought you might like it."

She eyes the box, wary of it. She nods her head. "Thank you."

I open the door and step through. "Call me when you're ready to talk, Sky."

I walk out without looking back. I don't want to know if my use of her nickname made her happy or mad. I don't want to know if she picked up the box to open it. I don't want to know if she walked back into the arms of another man.

chapter twenty-four

I walk through the door to Mason's condo, ready to lay him out for withholding such valuable information, when I hear the giggles of a small child. My lecture will have to wait. Mason's eighteen-month-old daughter toddles over to him when she sees me. I'm a stranger to her. I usually stay away on the weekends he has her. I suddenly feel like an idiot knowing he gave up part of his weekend with her to drag my ass back home.

She holds out her little arms and he swoops down to pick her up with one hand, swinging her up and onto his hip. "It's okay, sweet pea, this is my friend, Griffin."

"Hey there, Hailey." I tousle her platinum-blonde hair that is a replica of his, right down to the cowlick in the front that forces her short waves to fall on either side of her left eye.

Hailey hides her head in Mason's chest as he bellows out a laugh. Then I watch the two of them play. I watch this two-hundred-and-fifty-pound quarterback sit on the floor with his daughter and build a tower out of blocks. Then I watch him lie on his back and balance the tiny girl on his feet, whirling her through the air while he makes airplane noises. Then I watch him sing ridiculously embarrassing songs about patty cakes and pony rides as she giggles and tries to sing along with him, but mostly she just pats his face and tries to stick her fingers in his mouth, which he then kisses.

I watch them for hours, sitting on a barstool in the kitchen while nursing a beer. I don't move a muscle, not even when they fall asleep, her on his chest. I see her little lips quiver and make smacking noises as she sleeps. I see his hands instinctively wrap around her when she shifts her weight on him.

Then I see his heart break when Hailey's mom comes to gather her up before bedtime. I see the pain on his face, in his every movement. It's palpable and I can feel it from across the room. He's a broken man watching his little girl leave as she calls out for her daddy.

I will do anything and everything not to live through that myself.

He walks past me and I jokingly hand him a tissue. He bats my hand away. "Fuck off," he says, reaching in the fridge for a beer.

I hold up my hands in surrender. "That was painful to watch, man. Is it always like that when she leaves?"

He simply nods his head and then chugs half of his beer.

"Why didn't you tell me?" I ask.

"Tell you what, that I sometimes cry like a baby when Hailey leaves?" He means it as a joke, but I'm pretty sure there's some truth there and it guts me.

"No, tell me that Skylar is seeing someone." I close my eyes and shake my head thinking of how I felt when I walked up those stairs and saw his hands on her. "I walked right into the middle of a goddamn date."

He laughs.

"I'm glad to see you find this so funny."

"I don't think it's all that serious," he says. "Would it have changed anything if I had told you?"

I shake my head. "I guess not."

"Well then, that's why I didn't tell you," he says, as if that clears everything up.

"Who is he, Dix?"

"John something-or-other." He shrugs his shoulders.

"I know his name, douchebag. I met him tonight. Who the hell is he?"

"They work together, but he's not on staff at Mitchell's. I think he's a food or beverage supplier. I've never met the guy, so there's not much I can tell you."

"Never met him?" I give him my best *what-the-fuck* look. "How do you know he's not some deranged fucker who goes after pregnant women and then takes their babies?"

He laughs again. "Dude, you watched way too much television during your drunken hiatus. He's fine. Baylor says he's a good guy who has been working with her parents' restaurants for years."

I finish my beer and stare at the empty bottle after I set it on the counter. "Did I ruin my chance with her, man?"

He sighs. Then he puts another beer in front of me. "She still has feelings for you. I can tell by the way her face turns sad when we talk about you."

"You talk about me?"

"Of course we do. You're my best friend. You're her baby's father. She lost not only Erin, but you. She needed support. Plus, she needed my help to move your big-ass furniture around."

I laugh. "Yeah, that bed is huge. I don't know what Erin was thinking when she bought it. It took three guys to move it upstairs."

I'll never forget that first night in the townhouse. She jumped up and down on the mattress after the bed was delivered. We were twenty-two at the time and she looked like a little girl on a trampoline. She was so happy and carefree and alive.

"What is it?" Mason asks.

I realize that I'm smiling from ear-to-ear and it dawns on me that I just thought of Erin without feeling sad. I allowed myself to let the happy memories infiltrate the bad ones. "I don't know. I feel like I'm—"

"Ready to move on?" he interrupts.

I look guiltily into the neck of my beer bottle. "Does that make me a dick? That after two months, I want to be with someone else? Hell, if I'm being honest, it was a lot less than two months. What if it isn't enough time? What if I'm doing this for all the wrong reasons?"

"Answer me this, Griffin. If there wasn't any baby, would you still want Skylar? Or would you just be trying to use her to get through your grief?"

"What the hell, Dix?" I pick up my beer and walk into the living room so I don't take a swing at him.

He follows me, smiling. "See, I pissed you off by even suggesting it, didn't I? You want that woman with or without a baby. Two months, or two minutes, it doesn't matter. There's no set time to grieve someone. Especially not in your situation. I don't know what Erin wrote in that letter, but my guess is that she told you not to feel guilty about wanting Skylar. That she did everything in her power to push you together and that she wanted you to know it was okay to be with her." He points his beer bottle at me. "I'm close, aren't I?"

I nod.

"Then don't be a damn fool. Go after what you want, G. Skylar wants it too, you know, but you hurt her at a time when you both needed each other. She might not feel like she can trust you to be there for her if shit goes wrong again. And who can blame her?"

We drink a few more beers and talk football. Then I hit the couch, that was not built for a guy my size to crash on, and try to sleep when all I can really do is think of a way to get her to let me in.

I watch her walk down the street towards Mitchell's. I know her hours. I knew she'd be arriving soon. Yet, I still showed up here an hour early, at the coffee shop across the street, waiting for her to come to work.

I grab my camera and take some pictures of her. Her heel gets caught in a sidewalk grate and I hold my breath, watching her find her balance. She laughs at herself. *Snap.* I catch the moment on film. She doesn't look around to see if anyone saw her trip. She doesn't even care. My eyes move in both directions, searing into the men that turn their heads as she walks by.

Her growing belly is now evident under her winter coat. Yet even that doesn't detract from the stares she garners. As she gets closer and I zoom in tighter, I see it. The locket I gave her. I can see the sparkle of the diamond when the sun catches it. *Snap.*

I wondered if she would even open the gift, let alone wear it. I wonder if she thought to put a picture of Erin in it, like I had imagined.

I remember standing on a corner down in Miami Beach a few days before Christmas. I was watching happy couples walk down the street hand-in-hand, window shopping for what might go under the tree. Moms and Dads, going in and out of ice-cream shops and restaurants, swinging their young children between them. Trying to look like I fit in, and not a loser that abandoned his quasi-family, I started looking in windows myself.

The locket practically jumped off the blue velvet and bit me. Hanging from a stunning rope chain was a silver locket with a flower etched into it. I convinced myself it was a lily. The bud of the flower was a diamond—what would be Aaron's birthstone since he was due in April. There was no way I wasn't going to buy it. Even if all I ever did was keep it in the box. It was perfect. I knew instantly that Skylar would love it. I just didn't know if she would love it if it was a gift from me.

But there she is, wearing it only days after I gave it to her. Before reaching for the door, her hand comes up to touch the locket. *Snap.* Something stirs deep inside me. *Hope?*

I sit for a while longer, catching glimpses of Skylar as she makes rounds through the restaurant. I gather up my things to leave when I see John walk up and through the front door of her restaurant.

Jealously seeps from my every pore. Has she let him touch her stomach? Feel *my* baby move? Would he even want to, the sicko bastard? My eyes narrow and my fists ball so tightly, my fingernails break the skin of my palms. I can think of nothing else; *see* nothing else but visions of him rubbing his hands up and down her arms the other night.

It takes all my strength to remain glued to the chair instead of marching across the street to lay claim on what isn't even mine; what I gave up so that another man like John could come in and take my place.

The door to the restaurant opens and Skylar walks through, followed by John. She doesn't have her coat on, but he does. Good, he's leaving and she's not going with him. He makes a strange face and reaches out to touch the locket, questioning her. It's all I can do not to run over and rip his hand away from it.

She shakes her head at him, shrugging her shoulders while giving him a small smile. I've never wanted to be a fly on the wall so badly. He leans over to kiss her on the cheek and then she waves goodbye. The whole time, working the locket between the fingers of her right hand.

Suddenly, she turns to me and looks me straight in the eyes through the glass of the coffee shop window. Like she knew I was here. She briefly closes her eyes and tilts her head to the sky. She visibly takes a breath before looking both ways and crossing the street.

I quickly pay the check and meet her out in front of the coffee shop. She raises her eyebrows at me, in the same way she did the other night. She wants me to be the first to speak.

"Coffee?"

She raises her brows dubiously. "Haven't you had enough coffee, Griffin?"

She *did* know I was here. I put my proverbial tail between my legs and give her an innocent shrug.

"My wait staff all know who you are," she says. "Mindy noticed you hours ago. What are you doing here?" I see her warm breath meet with the cold air every time she speaks.

"You must be cold. Come inside."

She shakes her head. "I have to get back to the restaurant. I just wanted to thank you for the locket. It's beautiful. But I also wanted to tell you that I don't think this will work." She motions between the two of us and then nervously twists the ring on her pinky finger. "I understand you feel bad for leaving the way you did. That you feel guilty about not being there for Aaron. We slept together. It happened. It doesn't even matter that it was the best sex I've ever had. We did it out of grief, and that's no way to build a relationship. It's not enough. Aaron deserves more than that. And for the first time in my life, I think I do, too."

She looks over her shoulder at Mitchell's. "I have to get back now. Go home... er, wherever. Go back to work, Griffin. Do something with your life that Aaron will be proud of."

She starts to walk away, but I grab her arm and whirl her back around. She questions me with her eyes.

"What's your favorite flower?" I ask.

"Huh?" She eyes me skeptically.

"Flowers. Which are your favorite? It's an easy question, Skylar."

With a sad smile, she reaches up to touch the locket. "You already know." She checks the traffic before crossing the street. I could swear I see a genuine smile creep up her face in the reflection of a cab window, but it could just be my overactive imagination. The same imagination that has her dumping the food guy and giving me another chance.

I watch her walk away without so much as turning back once to look at me.

I should be upset. But I'm not.

I don't think I heard a word she said after *'best sex I've ever had.'*

chapter twenty-five

Gavin sets another beer down in front of me. He and Mason decided to take me out for drinks and get my ass off Mason's lumpy-as-hell couch.

I've given her some space. I haven't stalked her since the coffee shop earlier this week. Maybe once she gets used to the idea of having me back again, she'll come around.

Gavin shakes his head at me. "As the guy who had to win back one of the other Mitchell sisters, I can tell you they're all stubborn as hell. It took me months to get Baylor to let me back into her life and I didn't even screw up as badly as you did." He tips his beer at me. "You don't have months, Griffin. You need to do something now, before your kid is here. Take it from me, you do not want to miss the birth of your child. It's something you'll never get back."

I set down my beer, trying to perfectly match it onto the wet ring it left on the bar moments ago. "She hasn't lifted a finger to talk to me. What am I supposed to do?"

Mason and Gavin look at each other and back at me. "You're expecting *her* to pick up the phone?" Gavin asks. "Come begging you to go back to her? Don't be a fool. You let her blow you off and then you walked away, man. What is she supposed to think? I don't care what they say. Women want to be chased. They want some kind of grand gesture and shit like that."

Mason nods in agreement. "You need to show her, G. Not just tell her. Work your way back into her life. Do something unexpected. Claim what's yours. You never hesitated to do what you needed to take care of Erin. Why should it be any different with Skylar?"

I laugh at the absurdity. "Because Skylar is not a woman who needs to be taken care of."

"That's bullshit," he says. "All women want to feel like their men will take care of them no matter what. They want to feel like you would turn your world upside down for them."

I skeptically eye my twenty-two-year-old single friend. "How the hell is it that you don't have a girlfriend, Dix?"

"Hailey is the only girl I need in my life right now." He shrugs. "Anything else would just be a complication."

"So, what do I do then? You know, to claim her?" My eyes go between Gavin and Mason. "You two experts have any suggestions?"

"You could start by coming to brunch on Sunday," Gavin says. "It's at the new restaurant in Long Island."

My eyebrows touch my hairline. "Go in front of the firing squad? Are you fucking crazy?"

Gavin laughs. "Hey, I've had to eat crow with her family more than once. Believe me, they all understand what you've been through. Doesn't mean they're not upset that you up and left. But I don't think it would take much to win them over again. And I think it'd go a long way with getting back into her good graces."

I take a long swig of my beer. "Her dad scares the shit out of me."

Gavin gives me a pat on the back. "His bark is far worse than his bite, my friend. Take it from someone who's been there."

I nod. Then I notice the bartender as she writes something on a napkin and pushes it over toward the three of us. "I get off at two if any of you are interested." I spot her phone number scribbled on the white square of paper as she winks at us and saunters away.

The three of us share a laugh and then I put my beer bottle down on the napkin, smearing the numbers as they become completely unreadable.

I've never been a particularly anxious person. Even when the women in my life were slipping away. I was fortunate that I could take it all in stride and not be destroyed by it. In my business, I've seen more than a few people turn to lives of drugs, sex, and even crime to try and get rid of their demons. No, it took more than sickness, death, even emotional abandonment by my own father to break me. It took Skylar Mitchell getting knocked up with the kid I didn't even know I wanted to have. It took the guilt I harbored over wanting her so badly that it seemed she had become the very air I needed to breathe.

Taking the #7 from Midtown to Massapequa, I sit for the hour-long ride, entranced by how the tips of the white flowers shake, not from the movement of the train, but because my hands are shaking faster with every mile it takes me closer to her. Closer to her family. Closer to every person I need to make things right with.

When I get to my stop, I slowly make the half-mile walk to Mitchell's, needing the time to clear my head and prepare for what I'm sure I'll be walking into.

When I open the doors and step into the restaurant, the first pair of eyes I see boring into me are those same emerald-green ones that haunt my dreams. However, they do not belong to the girl that I dream of. They belong to her father. Bruce Mitchell is one intimidating son-of-a-bitch. But he's a walking contradiction. He's about as big as I am, and he makes sure everyone knows that his three daughters are his goddamn life and if you hurt them he'll break every bone in your pitiful body. Yet, he's one of the nicest people I've ever met.

I hand him the bottle of wine that I brought and he silently nods as he takes it from me.

It's moments like these that I question if I'm being confronted by the leg-breaker or the giant teddy-bear. I've never felt more like I might piss myself than right this very second, as he takes me by the elbow. "Come with me, son."

Son? He called me son. That has to mean he's not going to cut me up and put me in the meat locker. I try to breathe a small sigh of relief, but it's hard with his hand gripping me, pulling me behind him into the restaurant office. I don't see Skylar anywhere, but we pass by her mom and sister, who give me looks of sympathy that have me feeling like a lamb being led to the slaughter.

He shuts the door behind us, standing between it and me, eliminating any chance of escape. "How are you, Griffin?"

"Uh… I'm fine, sir. How are you?"

He scolds me with his stare. "Son, that's not what I'm asking." He walks across the room, shaking his head. He leans back, propping himself against the edge of the large desk as it creaks under his weight. "Your wife died and you're about to become a father. I'm asking how you're doing with everything."

I blow out a breath. He's not threatening me. He's not yelling at me. He seems genuinely concerned about my well-being. I guess it makes sense, I am the father of his grandbaby and all. I decide to be just as genuine in my answer. I figure I've got nothing to lose.

"I screwed up, sir."

He nods and motions to the chair behind me. I sit, putting the flowers on the floor next to me. My elbows meet my knees as I lean forward and try to maintain eye contact with him. "I'm sorry. I know I hurt Skylar by leaving so suddenly. I know I stayed away too long. I may have messed up my chances. I realize I have a lot of work to do to repair what I've broken. But, I fully intend to do just that."

He eyes me skeptically. "Why?"

I question him with the furrow in my brow.

He walks around behind the desk and takes a seat. "I'm not here to beat around the bush. What exactly are your intentions with my daughter? My grandson?"

"I... well, I want to be in their lives. I don't want my kid growing up without a father. I don't want Skylar to have to do this alone."

Disappointment bleeds from his deep sigh. He crosses his arms over his chest. "So, that's what this is all about?" He nods to the flowers lying next to me on the floor. "Doing the right thing?"

"Yes. Uh, no."

"Well, which is it, son?" He stares me down, awaiting my answer.

Shit, this guy is intimidating.

How can I explain myself to him without sounding like a complete idiot? "I'm not sure how to say this without sounding disrespectful to both Erin and Skylar. But, sir, I think I'm falling for your daughter."

"You *think?*" His eyes burn into mine, unwilling to accept anything less than the truth, no matter what the consequences.

My eyes close briefly as I envision Skylar's face. The soft waves of her silky hair. The smile that crinkles her nose and brings out tiny creases by her eyes when she's truly happy. The roundness of her belly that carries my son.

I shake my head. "I *know*, sir, but—"

"But your wife recently passed and you think it's too soon to move on."

I look at the floor and nod.

"Do you think you are trying to replace your wife?" he asks.

My eyes snap to his. "No, sir. I would never—"

"Do you think Skylar is trying to replace your wife?"

"No, of course not," I say in her defense.

He points to a picture on the wall behind him. It's the picture of a family. A mother, father and a young boy about ten years old. I see the resemblance immediately. The boy resembles Skylar. It must be a picture of him. I momentarily wonder if this is what our son might look like.

"This is my mother," he says proudly as he looks at the woman in the picture adoringly.

"She's beautiful," I say.

He points to another picture next to it. I have to do a double-take because although the family appears the same, upon further inspection, the woman is different. "This is also my mother," he says, viewing the picture with the same reverence as the first. "Well, biology says she's not, but I don't give a shit about that." He points to the first picture again. "A drunk driver took her from us when I was only nine."

Gesturing again to the second picture, he continues, "Three months later, my dad started dating Hannah, who was my fourth-grade teacher at the time. She helped me deal with my mother's death. They married only two months after their first date. They're still happily married today." He looks back at me. "Do you think he disrespected my mother by finding happiness so soon after her death?"

I shake my head. "No."

"Then why are you damning yourself for the very same thing? Especially, as I've come to understand, since your wife fully intended for you and my daughter to develop feelings for one another."

He stands up, walks around the desk and leans down to pick up the bouquet of flowers off the floor. "So, what are you waiting for, son? Either shit or get off the fucking pot." He shoves them into my hands and then opens the door and walks through, leaving me in stunned silence.

I stare at the pictures on the wall, looking between the two families. Both happy. Both real. Both looking filled with love. One woman did not replace the other. A person can never be replaced. But life goes on. I know that's what he's telling me. I know that's what Erin is telling me. I just wonder how long it's going to be before my head and my heart can both agree with them.

When I walk out into the main room again, my eyes immediately fall upon Skylar. She's holding Baylor's baby. The way her eyes illuminate and her face softens as she looks down at three-month-old Jordan makes my breath come quickly. I've never seen her react to a child like this. Skylar's always been standoffish when it comes to kids. Something has changed in the months I've been away.

When she glances up to catch me watching them, my heart thunders. She's absolutely fucking gorgeous. I take in the clingy white dress that shows off her growing belly. It falls to just above the knee, revealing toned legs that are evidence of her continued use of the bike. It's hard not to notice her generous cleavage accentuated by the locket that falls almost perfectly between her breasts. I want nothing more than to reach out and touch it, grazing my fingers along her every curve.

I take a moment to remind myself I'm in the presence of her family before my pants get any tighter.

"Griffin, so nice of you to join us."

I turn around to see Skylar's mom as I try to determine if the comment was genuine or sarcastic. Probably a little of both.

"Thanks, Mrs. Mitchell. I'm grateful to you for having me. Is there anything I can help you with?"

"Call me Jan." She points to my bag. "And if you've got a camera in there, I'd love it if you could take some pictures. Nothing formal, just a few shots."

"Sure. No problem." We talk for another minute, but my mind is somewhere else. Mainly on the hand of the asshole who has his arm draped around Skylar. The guy is tall and built like a goddamn Mack Truck. He's got spiky hair and two full sleeves of tattoos.

"Griffin?" Skylar's mom tries to get my attention.

"Sorry, ma'am," I say without looking at her.

She follows my gaze. "Oh, that's Scott Carlson, Gavin's partner from L.A. I think Skylar might have dated him a while ago."

My face snaps back to hers and she's wearing a huge smile. I'm familiar with this smile. It's Skylar's. They couldn't be more different in every other way. Her mom has light-blonde hair and blue eyes, and I'd be surprised if she was over five feet tall. But the gorgeous smile she shares with her daughter is unmistakable. This is amusing her, I can tell. What the hell did I walk into here? Am I being punished? Gavin invited me for Christ's sake. Invited me to a brunch where he knew Skylar's ex would be.

I return my attention to Skylar and watch her extract herself from Thor to make her way to the bathroom.

"Will you excuse me, Jan?" I say without breaking my stare of her daughter.

"Certainly." She laughs. "Good luck, Griffin." She walks away, leaving me to wonder—good luck with what?

On my way to the bathroom, I pull Gavin aside, not even caring that I'm probably bruising his arm with my angry grip. "What the fuck, Gav? Her family already thinks I'm a goddamn turd. But you brought me here knowing her ex was going to be here? That's just wrong, man."

He shakes my hand off his arm. "Yeah, sorry about that. I didn't know myself until a few hours ago that he was even in town. He wasn't supposed to be here until tomorrow for a project we're working on at the studio. Anyway, he's not really her ex."

"Not really her ex? What the hell does that mean?" I stare him down as it hits me. "Shit. You mean he hooked up with her. How many times?"

"I'm pretty sure it was just the one night. Last year when Baylor and I were in L.A. and she came to visit. It was no big deal, Griffin. He's a good guy. A player, but a good guy."

"If everyone can come take a seat, we're ready," Skylar's dad calls out.

I motion to the table. "Go on ahead. I'll be there in a minute."

Gavin walks away while I stand in the deserted hallway, leaning against the wall by the ladies' room as I wait for her to emerge.

The door swings open. She sees me and sighs. "Griffin, hi. I know my folks are glad you could make it."

I raise my eyebrows. "And you? Are *you* glad I could make it?"

Her hands come up to rub her belly. When my eyes follow the motion, she stops, putting them down by her sides. "Uh, sure." Her voice is tentative and very unconvincing.

"What about Scott Carlson. Are you glad that *he's* here, too?"

Her lips pucker and she chews on the inside of her cheek. "I'm not having this conversation with you, Griffin. You know what I was like before. I'm not that way anymore. Not that I have to explain it to you."

"Not like that anymore?" I ask. "Does that mean John-the-food-guy hasn't been invited into your bed?"

A stubborn burn shoots from her eyes. "He's a liquor distributor. And what I do with him is none of your business, Griffin." She turns to walk away.

I gently grab her arm as I come up behind her, pressing myself into her back and pushing her hair over to one side. "I plan on making it my business, Sky," I whisper into her ear. "I plan on making everything about your life my business. Everything about Aaron's life. Get used to having me around because I'm not going anywhere."

Goosebumps erupt on her neck where my breath flowed over her smooth skin. Even from behind, I can tell her fingers have come up to touch the locket that rests over her heart. I hear her let out a long sigh before her feet start moving again. I watch her walk away without looking back. Yet everything about her body tells me that she wants to.

I know what I have to do now. Before I join everyone at the table, I send a text to Mason telling him tonight will be the last night I crash on his couch.

chapter twenty-six

I don't have much. One suitcase full of clothes I bought in Miami. My duffle bag full of cameras. The few shirts I retrieved last week. Moving back into my townhouse should be easy. So, why does it feel like the hardest thing I've ever had to do?

When I came here last week, I wasn't thinking about Erin. Not with John-the-food-guy laying his hands all over Skylar. Today, however, there's nobody here but me. Me and Erin's ghost.

I stand in the entryway of the study, the room where Erin died. It's been transformed back to the way it used to be, but I'm not sure I'll ever be able to walk into it again. It was the place Erin would sit and grade papers for her second graders. She would work on lesson plans. She even did some in-home tutoring from time to time if a student was falling behind. Her teaching textbooks still line the shelves of the built-in bookcase. Pictures of five years' of second-grade classes along with some teaching awards she won flank the bookshelves.

Skylar hasn't changed a thing. The room is a shrine to Erin. I wonder if Skylar felt guilty about taking over the master suite so she decided to leave this room untouched. Maybe it would have been easier on everyone if she had boxed up all this stuff and put her own stamp on the study. Would I be able to cross the threshold then?

I carry my suitcase upstairs and unpack in the guest room, all the while wondering if I'll actually be able to sleep in the bed I once shared with Erin. I've never slept in it alone. When we moved Erin downstairs, I crashed on the couch. But there is no couch in here. The room isn't big enough. It's either sleep in the bed or sleep in my studio in the basement.

I focus my attention on the picture sitting on the nightstand. It's always been one of my favorites. Erin was only eighteen and had recently gone through chemo. Her hair was just beginning to grow back, but she had the face of an angel, and even in the absence of hair, was as beautiful as ever. I sit on the bed and hold the picture. *An angel.* Is that what she is now? Can she see me? Does she know what's happening and does she have any control over it?

I try to push the guilt down once again. The guilt over living in *her* house with the woman carrying *my* child. The woman I'm trying to get into my bed—well, maybe not *this* bed. And even though I keep telling myself it's what Erin wanted, I can't help but think about how fucked up this is. I want Skylar. I know I do. But I also know I'd take Erin back in a second if I had the opportunity. Is that fair? Is it fair to either of them?

I set the picture back on the nightstand and reach into my bag to retrieve my other favorite photo. I stand it up against Erin's picture and look at the two most beautiful women in my life as I wonder if it's possible to love two women at once?

Music blares from my earbuds while I watch the miles fly by on the digital screen of the treadmill. My eyes flicker over to the stationary bike that sits in the corner of the basement. I imagine her riding it. I can almost picture what she would look like with her hair pulled up into one of those messy buns women so effortlessly do, sweat trickling down between her full breasts.

I run faster to get my mind off her, but I almost trip over my own feet when I look up to see Skylar standing in the doorway. Her mouth is slightly open and her eyes are glued to my bare chest. She appraises me like a starving animal assessing a piece of meat. Shit, the way she's looking at me right now; it's how I see her in my dreams. It's how I picture her lying beneath me. It's the same look she had on her face the night of Erin's funeral when we made love. It's the look I want to put on her face every damn time she sees me.

She finally blinks herself out of whatever zone she's in and snaps her eyes to mine. The moment is over. Her stare changes from that of reverence to one of confusion. I can't pull my eyes away from her full lips as they move with words I cannot hear.

I slow my pace and pluck the earbuds from my ears. "What?"

She takes a defensive stance with her hands on her hips, her eyes searching the room for answers. "I said, what are you doing here?"

I power down the treadmill and grab a towel from the nearby hook on the wall, wiping my face with it before placing it around my neck. "Last I checked, I still own half this place."

She rolls her eyes and sighs. She knows she can't dispute it. She points to the treadmill. "So, you just decided to come work out?"

I guess she didn't bother looking upstairs in the guest room yet. I shake my head. "I live here, Skylar. I've lived here for five years. I love this place. Is this going to be a problem?"

I can practically see the cogs in her brain spinning. Maybe she's trying to figure out how to get me out of here. Maybe she's assessing her feelings for me. Maybe she's wondering what John-the-food-guy will think of her baby daddy moving back in. I raise my eyebrows at her, waiting for her to speak.

She chews on the edge of her lip before answering. "Are you going to ask me to move out now?"

"Do you want to move out?" I ask.

She shrugs and lowers her eyes to the ground. "I guess I could go back to my apartment."

I try to hold in my smile. I have reliable intel that Mindy already found another roommate. Skylar wants me to ask her to stay. She just doesn't want me to know it.

I walk over to her and stand close. So close I can smell her fruity shampoo. I want to reach out and pull her to me. I want to pick her up and carry her over to the couch in my studio where I'll peel that green dress right off her body. It's the same dress she wore when she gave me the cooking lesson. Even then, I couldn't tear my eyes from her. But then, I had a wife. A wife I loved. Skylar was forbidden. A fantasy I would never engage in.

My running shorts get tight as my eyes fall over her breasts that are so much fuller than the last time I saw this dress. Breasts that rise and fall with each heavy breath she takes. Breasts that surround the locket that still hangs from her supple neck. I reach out and take the locket between my fingers, causing her breath to catch. "Stay," I whisper.

She tenses up, but doesn't pull away. Her eyes close briefly and I'm almost positive she's inhaling my scent as much as I am hers. Suddenly she takes a step back and my hand falls away as the locket meets her chest once again. "I don't know, Griffin. It's all gotten so complicated. I'm not sure I should. And then there's John. And—"

I lunge forward and put my arms up against the wall, holding her captive within them. I ignore her reference to the food guy as I lean into her. Pressing the pad of my thumb against her bottom lip, I force it out from between her teeth as her expression twists with indecision.

I push her hair away from her ear. "Stay," I repeat. "It'll all work out, Sky. Have faith."

Before she can respond, I turn around and head for the stairs. As I reach them, I glance back to see her body sliding down the wall until her ass meets the floor. All the while, she's looking up at the ceiling, exhaling a slow, controlled breath. I bounce up the steps, two at a time, basking in my small victory on the way to the shower.

After my shower, I find Skylar dozing off on the couch in the living room. She's changed out of her work clothes and is wearing a casual light-blue dress that looks like it's just a really long t-shirt. The tight-fitting shift accentuates every curve of her body. It clings to her stomach like a second skin.

I walk over to the foyer where I left my duffle, taking quiet steps with my bare feet so I don't wake her. I retrieve a camera from the bag and zoom in on her beautiful face. I don't dare move any closer to her in fear of the click of the camera waking her. Without trying to think about how creepy it is, I snap pictures of every part of her body. I get close-ups of her full lips. The curve of her neck. Her legs that are propped up on a pillow. Her feet that reveal toenails painted to match the green of her eyes. Her breasts that frame the locket I gave her.

When I zoom in on her pregnant belly I almost drop the camera when I see it move. I slowly make my way over to her, hoping that I'm capturing on film what my eyes are taking in. Finally, I lower the camera and sit on the coffee table, mesmerized by the movements.

As I watch a tiny foot, elbow or knee trace a line from her hipbone to her belly button, I momentarily have flashbacks to a Sigourney Weaver movie where an alien breaks through her stomach. I quickly push the thought aside and embrace the fact that my kid is inside Skylar. And he's putting on a show just for me.

I want so badly to reach over and put my hand on her. Maybe poke my son and see if he pokes me back. I haven't touched her belly in over two months. And the only time I've ever felt Aaron move was the night Erin died. I remember feeling what could have been gas bubbles going through Skylar. It was nothing like this.

There's a fucking person in there.

I find myself having to fight back tears as I swallow a colossal-sized lump in my throat.

"You can feel him if you want."

I about jump out of my skin when Skylar speaks. I hadn't realized she was awake. I wonder how long she's been watching me watch her.

I lean closer to her and tentatively reach my hand out. She grabs it and places it on her. Immediately, I feel movement beneath it. My eyes go wide and I think I gasp in wonderment, but I'm so lost in the moment I don't even realize I've gotten up from the table and am on my knees in front of her with both my hands pressed firmly on her stomach. I can't move. I don't ever want to remove my hands from her. If I flinch, it could stop. And I want this to last forever.

I don't know how long I sit here, feeling my son kick and do somersaults under my hands. My knees hurt and my legs go numb but I don't dare move a muscle.

I look up to find Skylar smiling. "Pretty fucking great, huh?" she asks.

"Don't say fuck, Sky."

Redness overtakes her face as she recalls what her cursing does to me. "Don't call me Sky, Griffin," she quips.

She holds my stare as we enjoy feeling our son move. I wonder what's going through her mind. Can she tell what I'm feeling? Do my eyes show her how badly I want this?

The buzzing of her phone on the table breaks the perfect moment. She glances over at her phone and my eyes follow. I read the screen. *John McCormack.*

John-the-fucking-food-guy.

A look of sympathy flashes across her face. "Sorry," she says, grabbing the phone while pushing herself up off the couch with her other hand.

She walks into the kitchen and sits at a barstool. "Hey, John," she answers.

I follow behind her under the guise of getting a bottle of water from the refrigerator. She watches me as she listens to him. I make no attempt to give her any privacy.

She shifts uncomfortably on the barstool. "I'm not sure that's such a good idea anymore. How about I meet you there," she says. Her eyes briefly snap up to mine. "Can we talk about this later?... Okay fine. You win. I'll see you at seven… Bye."

I finish my water and place the empty bottle down so harshly that it crumples. "Going out with the food guy again?"

"Liquor distributor," she says.

I throw the disfigured plastic bottle into the recycle bin. "What?"

"He's not a food guy. He's a liquor distributor." She walks over to retrieve her own bottle of water from the fridge. "And yes. He's taking me out."

With her back to me, she takes a long drink while I come up behind her. I put my arms on either side of her, trapping her against the counter. I brush her hair aside and watch as goosebumps dot her skin. "Unless I can talk you out of it, that is," I whisper.

As I speak, my lips graze her ear, but not totally. My chest almost touches her back, but not quite. I can see from her reflection in the glass door of the microwave that her resolve almost crumbles—but not completely.

Her eyes close. Her lips part. She slowly exhales. She has no idea that I can see every nuance of her face. She thinks she's hiding these conflicting feelings from me.

When her eyes open, they are blazing with unspoken desire. She finds me holding her stare in the reflection. She tries to escape my arms, but I lower my hands to her waist and spin her around to face me before I cup her face with my hands. "Stay here with me tonight, Skylar. Talk to me. There's so much I don't know about you. I want to know you inside and out. I don't even know when your birthday is."

Every word has me inching closer to her until my breath falls over her lips. My groin meets her belly and I wonder if she can feel my growing erection as I press against her. Her eyes fall to my mouth. Her tongue comes out to wet her lips. Her breathing accelerates to match my own.

She wants this. She wants this as much as I do.

"Sky…" I close the gap that still separates our mouths. I can feel the softness of her full lips as mine lightly touch hers. My heart pounds so hard in my chest that I'm sure it's become audible and is echoing through this room where the only other noise is the faint hum of the refrigerator.

Suddenly, she pulls back and my pounding heart falls into my stomach. "No," she says, ducking under my arm and walking away. "You just don't get it."

I watch her walk slowly up the stairs as I speculate if the hesitation in her steps comes from Aaron's extra weight or from her indecisiveness. I think about her words and wonder just what it is that she thinks I don't get.

For the next few hours, I bury myself in work down in my studio. I blast music through my Bluetooth speaker so I don't hear the doorbell when the food guy comes to whisk the mother of my child away for a goddamn date. Then I lie awake in bed, waiting and counting the minutes until she comes home. What follows is a sleepless night knowing she's right down the hall, and long, painful hours wondering if she's thinking about me or *John-fucking-McCormack.*

chapter twenty-seven

I want to laugh at what I'm seeing through the lens. I wish I could tell the photo editor and the modeling agency that this is not what real pregnancy looks like. But I'm just the photographer. They don't want my opinion. They only want my photographs.

What I see before me is pitiful. Models on the verge of anorexia with false bellies strapped beneath their skin-tight dresses. Their surgically-enhanced tits spill over the edges of the so-called maternity wear clinging to their stick-thin bodies.

If this is how real pregnant women think they should look, I pity the children they are carrying as they'll probably die of starvation before ever being born.

"Hi, Griffin," a trio of models say in unison as they walk by me.

I lift my chin in greeting. "Ladies."

I hear one of them whisper something about my dead wife as they walk away giving me sad glances.

When we break for lunch, Katy Fields, one of this year's up-and-coming 'it' girls sits in the director's chair next to mine. She munches on baby carrots, grapes and a piece of fruit I can't identify, that in total barely fill her dessert-sized plate. "I'm so sorry to hear about your wife," she says.

I take a bite of my turkey sub, not even bothering to swallow before I respond with a muffled, "Thanks."

"I'm glad to see you back working. Some of those other photographers are simply awful."

"How's that?" I ask.

She purposefully touches my knee. "Well, they just aren't you, Griffin. That's how."

What a truly insightful answer. I take another bite so I don't have to engage in much conversation with her.

She reaches over to grab my hand. She pulls it toward her fake belly. "Do you want to touch my baby?" She giggles.

I rip my hand away before she can place it on the pillow beneath her clothing. She eyes me skeptically. I'll bet there aren't many men who would refuse the chance to touch a beautiful model. Maybe I'm the first. I shake my head. "That's okay, Katy. I've got the real thing at home."

Her perfectly-plucked eyebrows scrunch together. "Um… I thought your wife died."

"She did," I say. "But I'm still having a baby. Long story."

Katy gives me a confused look, but before I can explain, the models are called to make-up for re-touches. Katy hands me the small plate of food with the remnants of the lunch she barely touched. "That's me. Well, good luck, Griffin."

For the next three hours, all I can think about is getting home. The home I share with Skylar. The home I hope will be the place we both raise Aaron.

When I get there, however, I wish I had stayed at work.

Even before I walk into the kitchen I hear him. The food guy. It's been a week since her date with him. A week of shared glances, accidental touches, and optimistic conversations. A week without John. I thought maybe he was out of the picture even though I never came right out and asked.

He sees me walking toward them. I could swear he was on his way out, but after he catches my eye, he turns around and gives Skylar a kiss. On the mouth. Not a passionate kiss. Not a kiss with tongue. But a kiss designed purely to intimidate yours truly.

Then he rubs her belly and I almost run the motherfucker down. It takes every ounce of self-control I have to not lay him out, rip him open, and smear his internal organs all over my wall as abstract art. Skylar sees my reaction and quickly walks him towards the door as he follows behind her like a well-trained puppy.

"I have a few things to wrap up and I'll be back to pick you up around six." He's clearly talking to Skylar, but his eyes are burning into me. He's challenging me to a dual. A dual I have every intention of winning.

Skylar's phone rings back in the kitchen. She tells John he can let himself out as she goes to retrieve it.

"I'll walk him out," I say.

Her eyes widen and she shakes her head at me in warning while she answers her phone.

I pat John on the back as I walk him out. It's not a friendly pat. It's not even a cordial one. It's a *touch-my-baby-again-and-I'll-fucking-kill-you* pat.

I silently walk him to the door and open it for him, waving him through while glaring at him. I don't say a word, yet I'm one-hundred-percent sure I clearly convey my feelings man to man.

He steps through the doorway then turns around and says snidely, "She's a big girl, Griffin. She can make her own decisions.

You may live here now, but that doesn't give you the right to control her or the baby."

I lean close, getting up into his face. "If you like your pretty-boy face with those pearly-white teeth, don't ever fucking talk to me about my baby again." Then I slam the door. Through the sidelight, I watch him turn and walk away, shaking his head as he descends the stairs.

"What was that all about?" I turn around to see Skylar's hands on her hips, waiting for an explanation.

I raise my shoulders in an innocent shrug. "I was just seeing him out."

"What did you say to him about the baby?"

"I simply suggested he not talk to me about him."

She raises her eyebrows. "Suggested?"

"I may have added something about rearranging his face if he did."

"Griffin!" She gasps. "You can't go around threatening every man I date. It's not fair. It's not your place. You had your chance. You made your choice."

"No, I didn't." My hands come up to run over my three-day scruff. "Dammit, Skylar. I choose you. You and Aaron."

"I can't do this, Griffin. You can't just leave and then expect to walk back into my life like nothing ever happened."

"Are you begrudging me the time I spent grieving my wife?" I know it's a low blow, but I'm getting desperate to find a way in.

She looks horrified. "Of course not!" she yells, glancing over at the urn. "But you could have called. You could have texted or e-mailed. You could have not left that awful note." She paces around the living room. "Two months, Griffin. For two months I thought I was the biggest mistake of your life and now you just want me to forget that?"

"I'm sorry, Skylar. How many times do I have to say it? I was messed up. Leaving like I did was a mistake. *You* weren't the mistake. Maybe we should have waited to sleep together—but I don't regret it. I wanted it. You have no idea just how much."

She looks at me as if I've grown a second head. "Then why did you fucking leave?" she shouts.

I throw my arms up. "Jesus Christ, Sky. For once in your life, can you stop saying fuck?"

"Sure. Just as soon as you stop calling me Sky."

I know without a doubt I'll never stop calling her that. I also know that despite my apparent contradiction to the fact, I love her filthy mouth. There's nothing I want more this very minute than to shut her up by kissing it. I walk over to her and stop her from pacing. My hand lands at the small of her back, anchoring her against me. I lean in to kiss her, hoping she'll give in and let me. This is what we do, right? We fight and get all hot for each other. Maybe it's our thing.

She pulls away before my lips touch hers. "You just don't get it, do you?" she asks.

I shake my head. "Get what—the fact that you're a stubborn woman? That you want me but can't seem to let yourself accept it?" I run a frustrated hand through my hair. "What exactly is it that I don't get, Sky?"

"Ugh!" She stomps her foot and walks away. "No wonder I never wanted a boyfriend. Men are so goddamn obtuse."

"Obtuse?" I yell, following her. "I think I've been pretty fucking clear about how I want you. Want Aaron."

The front door opens and Baylor walks in. "I could hear you guys from the stoop," she admonishes us, looking back and forth between Skylar and me. "What's wrong with you two?" She drops her bag on the entry table and comes into the living room. "Erin didn't want this. She wanted you to get along. To love each other and be a family. It was written all over her. Literally."

Skylar and I both stop fuming at each other and look at Baylor. We speak simultaneously.

"What's that supposed to mean?" I ask.

"What are you talking about?" Skylar says.

Baylor's eyes narrow, putting a crinkle in her nose as she says, "The tattoo."

I look at Skylar in confusion to see she has the exact same expression on her face as I do. I turn back to her sister. "Uh, Erin didn't have any tattoos, Baylor."

Baylor's jaw falls open. Then her hand comes up to cover her gasp. "She never showed you?" Her eyes dart between me and Sky.

"What the hell are you talking about?" Skylar asks.

"The day of the ultrasound," Baylor explains. "The afternoon Erin spent with Mason and me. The day she gave us the letters. She made us find a tattoo artist willing to come to the townhouse. Then she swore us to secrecy. She said she was going to show you both when the time was right. I just assumed . . ." Her sad eyes fall on the urn. "Oh, God. I'm so sorry. She must have forgotten. I should have told you."

"What was it?" Skylar asks. "What kind of tattoo did she get?"

Baylor shakes her head. "I don't know. She wouldn't show us. She said it was private and only for you." She gestures to Skylar's belly. "The four of you."

"How did we not see it?" I ask. "Where was it?"

"I'm pretty sure she got it on her lower back," Baylor says.

My face is overcome with shock. "My wife got a tramp stamp?" I ask, incredulously, looking between the two women in the room. "*My wife.* The prim and proper elementary schoolteacher who wouldn't go outside without 100 SPF for fear of damaging her flawless skin."

All of a sudden, the three of us burst out in laughter. Skylar laughs so hard she crosses her legs, probably so she won't pee her pants. Baylor wipes under her eyes when they start watering. I feel like I'm having an out-of-body experience, watching the three of us as we bond over this completely out-of-character thing that my wife did.

"Well, it was on her bucket list," Baylor says, trying to catch her breath.

"Oh, shit." I immediately have another thought that has me sobering up and standing up straight. "She didn't get any piercings that we couldn't see, did she?"

"Uh…" Skylar draws her eyebrows. "Don't you think you would have noticed that? You know, when you—"

"Skylar!" Baylor interrupts, giving her an evil eye.

I shrug at them. "No. I wouldn't have noticed. We couldn't… she couldn't… not for a while."

"I'm so sorry," Skylar says. "That was insensitive of me." She walks over and touches the silver urn on the mantle. "God, I wish we could have seen her tattoo."

I look down at my own tattoos. I'm fully aware of the process. "Who was the tattoo artist?" I ask Baylor. "All the reputable ones keep records and drawings of their art. If we're lucky, they may have even taken a picture of it after they inked her."

Baylor writes down the name of the place where the artist works and hands it to me. I look at my watch to see that it's almost five o'clock.

I turn to Skylar. "You up for this?"

"Are you kidding? Hell yes!" She pulls out her phone and walks into the other room shouting back, "I just need to make a quick call first."

I can't help the smile that overtakes my face.

Griffin – 1

John-the-food-guy – 0

Okay, so technically, John has had a few more dates with her than I have. But as far as I'm concerned, the game starts now, and Griffin Pearce never fucking loses.

I can't tear my eyes away from the picture. It's definitely Erin's lower back. The photo shows the unmistakable mole that was right next to one of her sexy ass-dimples.

I trace my finger over the words and names that make up the infinity symbol.

Fate. Faith. Family.

She was always talking about those things. I take out my camera and snap a picture of the photo. I wish she would have shown it to us. The permanence of this is even more meaningful than the letter Erin wrote me. I wonder if we'd seen it back then, would things have played out differently? What was she waiting for and why didn't she show us right away?

Once again, I curse the cancer that, in the end, robbed her of her memory. Her personality. Her life.

I look over to find Skylar holding the tattoo stencil. "It's beautiful," she says, turning her attention to the artist. "Can I get a copy of this?"

Spike, the tattoo artist and shop owner, who I'm sure got his name by the way he wears his hair in blue four-inch spikes sticking out every-which-way from his head, takes the stencil from her. "I don't see why not. It was her design."

My jaw drops in surprise. "Really?" I examine the sketch that came from the woman who had trouble making stick figures. She used to complain that her second graders could draw better than she could. "She designed this?" I shake my head in amazement.

"She did." He nods, taking the stencil over to his copy machine. "It's a bit elementary, but when I offered to clean it up, she wouldn't let me change a thing."

Elementary. Skylar and I give each other a knowing smile as Spike makes her a copy.

He hands it to her. "Promise to come back here when you want to get yours?"

"Me?" Skylar's voice squeaks about an octave higher than normal. "No, I won't be getting one. I just want to remember it— put it in my scrapbook of her."

As we wait for a cab outside the building, she stares at the copy of the stencil, running her finger over the words just as I did. I look over her shoulder and admire it.

Without averting her eyes from it, she says. "I don't have a birthday this year."

A cab pulls up to the curb and I hold the door open for her. "Huh?" I ask, as she scoots across the seat to make room for me.

"Last week you said you didn't know when my birthday was. Well, I don't have one this year. I was born on February 29th. Technically, I won't have another birthday for three more years." As she talks, she stares out the window into the darkening streets of Midtown Manhattan.

I study the back of her head, taking in her long wavy hair. I reach out and take a lock of it, rubbing it between my fingers, contemplating if Aaron will have her unique blend of light and dark hair.

"And my favorite color is black," she adds quietly, as if divulging this information to me might somehow compromise her determination to evade me.

"Black isn't a color," I say. "In fact, it's the absence of color."

She glances at me long enough to roll her eyes before looking back out the window. "Whatever, Mr. Photographer."

I laugh. "Okay, black it is. And thanks for telling me."

She nods her head and goes back to tracing the tattoo as I turn my attention to my phone. I quickly text Mason, letting him know we have four weeks to pull off the best non-birthday party anyone has ever seen.

chapter twenty-eight

"Is there anything else you need to tell me, Dix?" Although he's been helping me plan the party for the last two weeks, this is the first time we've gotten together since we went out for drinks. The party has become more than just Skylar's non-birthday party. At Baylor's suggestion, it's also morphed into a baby shower.

"Tell you?" he asks, as we move the last of the boxes we packed down into the basement.

I neatly stack my box in the storage area. I pull the marker from my pocket and label it *'Erin's school stuff.'* Logically, I know there's no good reason to keep any of these things. It's mostly class pictures, correspondence and certificates. But I can't bring myself to just throw five years of her life into the garbage. It was hard enough to get myself to clean out the study.

"As in, are there any more secrets you've been keeping from me?" I replace the cap on the marker and stare him down. "First you didn't tell me about the letters Erin wrote. Then you withheld information about Skylar dating. And now, I find out my wife got a tattoo? What the hell else don't I know about? You seem to know more about my life than I do."

He holds up his hands in surrender. "Erin swore me to secrecy, man. What did you expect? She isn't someone you break a promise to."

Guilt permeates my every pore. I think about the promise I broke by running away. The one time I failed Erin. Failed Skylar and the baby. Failed all those who were most important to me. I have vowed to rectify my epic mistake. Maybe this party is the chance I need to do just that.

"How many letters are there?" I grunt, as we pick up the large desk we brought down, trying to fit it into the corner of the basement.

He shakes his head at me, shooting me a look of sympathy. "Sorry. I can't tell you that. You'll get them when and if the situation calls for it. Her explicit instructions. I gave her my word. Scout's honor."

I smack the back of his head as we walk towards the stairs. "You were never a damn Boy Scout."

He tries to duck away from my assault, laughing. "So, how are things with Skylar these days?"

I snort air through my nose. "The woman is a goddamn contradiction. I know she wants me. I can feel it. She's holding back, but I can't figure out why. And that asshole John keeps coming around. I wish she'd just dump him already. I don't get her, Dix."

We stand in the double-door entry of what was once the study, examining our handiwork. I put the finishing touch in the room—the flowers I had delivered earlier along with everything else.

Mason straightens a picture we hung. "Maybe she thinks you're just honoring Erin's dying wish. Have you ever told her differently?" He raises his eyebrows at me. "Could be it's time for that grand gesture, my friend."

"Isn't that what this party is all about?"

He laughs. "Anyone can plan a party, G. It's what you do *at* the party that counts."

I nod, thinking about his words when my phone vibrates in my pocket. I smile when I see the name on the screen. I slide my finger across the surface to answer it, putting her on speaker. "Piper. Thanks for calling me back, I know it must be late there."

"You wanted to talk to me about a party you're planning for Skylar? I'm not sure what I can do all the way from Istanbul."

I don't know Piper personally. But Skylar and Baylor talk about her enough that I feel I do. What I do know is that she rarely comes home. Skylar said the last time she was here was for Baylor's wedding and even then, she only stayed two days.

I know it's a longshot, but I ask anyway. "I would love to surprise Skylar by having you at the party."

There's a long pause before she says, "No-can-do, Griffin."

"I'd be more than happy to pay your round-trip airfare. Actually, I insist on it, Piper. It would be great to have you here."

"I don't think so," she says. "It's not the money. I just can't make it."

"Have you spoken with Baylor? Did she tell you that it's a birthday party *and* a baby shower? I know it would mean a lot to Skylar, and the rest of your family, if you could make an appearance."

"No, Griffin," she raises her voice. "Please just drop it. I'll send gifts. I'll call her. But I can't come. I'm sorry."

I look at Mason to see if he has any bright ideas. He shrugs.

"Please reconsider," I ask. "I'll do whatever it takes to get you here."

I hear her heavy sigh through the phone. "How many different ways can I say it? I'm not coming. I already told this to Baylor when *she* called to beg me. I have to go now. It's late."

Before I can say goodbye the line goes dead.

"What a bitch," Mason says, gathering his things to leave. "How is it possible that the other two Mitchell sisters are even related to that one? What the hell happened there?"

"I don't know. She didn't sound at all like the person they make her out to be." I walk him to the door. "Hey, thanks, man. I appreciate all the help. You're a good guy."

He leans in and gives me a hug that can only be shared by two confident heterosexual males. "Anything for you, G. You know that."

"Dad, would you please stop apologizing already?" I roll my eyes because my father can't see them through the phone. Every time we talk, which is about once a week lately, he tells me he's sorry for abandoning me and mom. I recline into the studio couch thinking of how I'd be a hypocrite not to forgive him now, after I basically did the same thing.

Okay, so maybe I only left for a few months while he checked out on us for years, but I'm trying to cut him some slack and repair our relationship as much as I can. I wouldn't go so far as to say we're planning family vacations together. But we're… amenable. Friendly even. Erin would be happy.

We start discussing Mason and the shit-sandwich served to him by Johnny Henley refusing to retire. My hand falls into the crack between the cushion and the arm of the couch. Something pokes me. I reach down and come out with a handful of pictures.

Pictures of me.

I scrutinize the stack of photos while making excuses to get off the phone. We plan to have lunch next week and then say goodbye.

I can't believe what I'm staring at. I remember seeing one picture of me there on the couch the night I came back for my things. But I didn't think much of it then; my studio is full of pictures. But this… this is a pile of pictures hidden by a woman with a serious crush. Not only are there several pictures of me that she took at Erin's picnic, but older ones, photos taken by Erin when we were in college. Pictures taken at birthdays, holidays, and awards ceremonies. Some of the pictures have Erin in them, but most are just me. Skylar must have found them when she went through Erin's things.

My smile widens as I think of her sitting here looking at them. She doesn't want me to know she thinks about me. I laugh to myself as I go over to a file cabinet and pull out a picture I'd filed away long ago. My senior picture. I was eighteen. My hair was even longer and more unruly than it is now and I'm pretty sure I didn't even own a straight razor. I take the picture to the couch and put it in the middle of the stack before I tuck them back where I found them. *I'm onto you, Mitchell.*

I hear the front door slam shut. When I reach the top of the stairs, I find Skylar staring wide-eyed into the old study. I'm not even sure she hears me come up behind her. I follow her gaze as her eyes take in everything Mason and I did while she was at work.

We transformed the room into a child's playroom. There's a play mat on the floor with one of those mobile things over it. A bassinet swing that will convert into a regular chair swing as Aaron grows older. Next to that is a play saucer with all sorts of beads and toys to keep him occupied. The bookshelves are lined with parenting manuals, Dr. Seuss books, and a bunch of other crap the baby superstore sent over. In the corner, I had them put another rocker so we won't always have to trek upstairs to use the one in his room. I finished the room out with a small pack-and-play crib that has a changing table attachment on the side.

She eyes the pictures on the wall. I'd blown up the photo from Skylar's night stand. The one with Erin touching her belly at the picnic. On the opposite wall, I enlarged the drawing of Erin's tattoo and had it matted and mounted in a wrought-iron frame outlined in the shape of flowers. Finally, her eyes settle on the vase of white lilies on the small table by the rocker.

Even from behind, I can see her hand come up to work the locket. I take a step closer and she must finally hear me because she startles. "Oh my God, Griffin. How did you... when did you?" She turns to face me, but her eyes don't meet mine quite yet. They fall beyond me, onto the new large play structure I had erected this afternoon in the back yard.

Her hand covers her mouth in surprise. "You did all this?" Her eyes lock with mine.

I give her a smile and a shrug.

She gestures to the swing set outside. "You know he won't be able to use that for years, right?"

I laugh and shake my head. "Just say thank you, Skylar."

"Thank you," she says, reaching out like she wants to touch my arm, but then pulling back before she makes contact. "Of course, thank you." She walks into the playroom and sits on the rocker. "It will be so nice not to have to go up and down the stairs for every little thing. And the pictures," —she waves her hand around the room— "they're perfect, Griffin. It's all perfect."

She plucks a single lily from the bouquet and places it across her belly. Then she closes her eyes and relaxes into the soft gliding motion of the chair. What I would give to have my camera in hand right now. What I would give to snap a picture of her belly while she's holding the flower against it. What I would then give to kiss the woman holding the flower and tell her every single feeling that is coursing through my body at this very second.

"Skylar." My voice is like sandpaper. I clear my throat and brace for her refusal. "I would really like to take a picture of you right now. Can I?"

She glances down at her outfit and tucks a strand of hair behind her ear. Then she nods.

Without giving her another second to think about it, I race down to my studio to grab my camera. In seconds, I'm back, snapping picture after picture of her. I must take dozens before I stop and take a breath. Then the photographer in me kicks in and I start spouting out directions. "I think it would be a really dramatic black-and-white if you'd lift your shirt a bit and hold the flower against your belly."

I look up from the viewfinder and catch her raised eyebrows. She wants to protest, but before her words come out, I say, "Skylar, I'm a professional. Believe me, you'll thank me later. It will be a beautiful photo."

She hesitates, but then acquiesces as the hand not holding the flower slowly raises her black shirt and tucks it under her breasts. The shirt bunches awkwardly so I ask her to stand up and turn sideways. I take dozens more pictures, having her move a hand this way or the flower that way. There isn't a doubt in my mind that one of these will be my new favorite picture.

She's fucking gorgeous. Absolutely flawless. How is it I never before saw the beauty in pregnancy? Through the lens of the camera, my eye traces every pronounced curve of her belly. Every faint line that is evidence of newly-stretched skin. Every quiver of her nervous hands.

I put down the camera, my heart pounding and my breath quickening. I walk over to her and press myself up against her bare belly. I hold her face in my hands as we stare into each other. I think of the pictures that are hidden away in the couch. She wants this. My eyes fall to her lips and I lean in, willing to take whatever she gives me. Willing to fight for whatever she doesn't.

I can see the hesitancy in her eyes; feel it in her body. My lips barely brush hers when I stiffen. I pull back and stare down at what separates us. Our son. The kid who just gave me a swift kick in the groin. My hand immediately goes to her belly to feel the squirms and movements I can now clearly see.

Her stomach moves even more, bouncing up and down when she giggles. "Someone doesn't think you should have done that," she says.

I fall to my knees and put both my hands on her still-bare belly. For the first time, I have words with my son. "Listen up, Aaron. You are not allowed to cock-block your own daddy. Dudes have to stick together."

"Dudes have to stick together?" Skylar repeats. "Those are your first words of advice for him?"

The doorbell rings. I silently curse it and whomever pressed it for ruining our family moment. Skylar looks down at me with guilty eyes. "Um… I should probably get that." She backs away from me and pulls her shirt down. She hands me the lily on her way by.

I don't even have to ask who's at the door. I already know. It's written all over her.

I put the flower back with the others and then casually lean against the doorframe, watching as she lets him in. John walks across the threshold, giving her a welcome kiss on the cheek before he sees me standing here, glaring at the two of them. He follows Skylar's eyes over to me. His brown eyes go cold as he nods his chin at me. "Pearce," he says. He doesn't wait for my response before turning back to Skylar, holding out a bouquet of red roses. "These are for you."

Skylar's eyes momentarily flicker over to the vase full of lilies in the playroom. It happened so fast, I'm sure John didn't even notice it. She plasters what I think is a fake smile on her face as she takes them from him. "Thank you, John. They're beautiful." She deposits them on the foyer table.

Skylar hates roses. How does he not know this about her after all the dates they've been on? Maybe he hasn't been paying attention. Maybe he doesn't know other important things about her either. Like how she twists the pinky ring on her right hand when she's lying, like she's doing right now. Or how her favorite color isn't actually a color at all.

Or how she has a stash of pictures of me in the basement.

I laugh, looking over at the asshole trying to steal my girl. "Roses. Nice touch, man."

"What's so funny, Pearce?" he says with a sinister smile and arrogant laugh. "After all, *I'm* the one taking her to dinner tonight."

"About that," Skylar says, rubbing her stomach. "I don't think I'm up for going out tonight. I've been having a lot of those Braxton-Hicks contractions and I just want to put my feet up and relax."

John watches her hands as they rub over her pregnant belly. Then he looks over at me while his lips form a thin line. He sighs. "That's okay, we can stay in. Want me to cook for you?"

Skylar shakes her head. "No. You don't need to stay and take care of me. I'll order out."

"It's no problem, really." He starts to remove his coat.

"John, I think I'm just going to turn in early. Can we reschedule?"

I find it hard to control the smile that struggles to break free. She's blowing him off. I watch the back-and-forth conversation like a Ping Pong tournament.

"Are you sure?" he asks. "I'd be happy to run and get you some food."

"I'm sure." Skylar reaches towards him and pulls his coat back onto his shoulders. I'm sure she didn't mean it to be an intimate act. In fact, I think she's doing it to get rid of him. But the mere thought of her touching him has my blood about to boil.

He turns around to open the door. "I'll call you tomorrow, then. Take it easy, okay?"

"Don't worry, McCormack, I'll take care of her," I say, still leaning in the doorway to the playroom.

He looks into the re-designed room, just now noticing how different it is. He stares at the picture on the wall before his eyes fall onto mine. If it were possible to shoot daggers from one's eyes, I'd be dead, pinned up and hanging bloody on the doorframe.

Skylar delivers me a scolding look before walking him out.

I go over and sit on the couch, knowing my plans for the evening include rubbing the feet of my kid's gorgeous mom.

Griffin – 2

John-the-food-guy – 0

chapter twenty-nine

A noise wakes me. I look around my dark bedroom and grab my phone to check the time. *2:00 a.m.* I pull on a pair of sweatpants and open the door to the hallway. In the dim light shining from the street into our hallway window, I can see Skylar's bedroom door open. I stop at the threshold. "Skylar?"

I walk through her room and check the bathroom. *Empty.* I make my way downstairs only to see the light over the stove illuminated like always. Skylar uses it as a night light. A habit from when she was a child and she would wake up for a glass of water. Her father got one too many stubbed toes walking her to the kitchen, so he started leaving the light over the stove on every night.

We don't need it. The light from the lamppost comes through the windows by the front door, spreading just enough light in the main level so you can see where you're walking. Still, she leaves it on every night. And if she forgets, I turn it on for her.

"Skylar?" I look at the couch to see if she fell asleep on it. I look in the playroom. I start to panic and decide to run back to my room and get my phone to call her. Passing by the basement stairway, I see a faint light. I descend the stairs and can't help smiling at what I find at the bottom. I quietly watch her sift through the stack of pictures from between the couch cushions that she doesn't know I know about.

My feet are cemented to the ground as I stare at her. Her hair is pulled up, long tendrils escaping the messy bun on the top of her head. She has on a short silky robe that falls slightly off one shoulder, revealing a matching spaghetti-strap nightgown. In the soft light of the lamp, I can't tell what color her nightgown is. I hope it's green. I know it would make her eyes look amazing.

She reclines back into the couch, pulling one of the pillows over her breasts. One of the pillows I used to sleep on when this couch was in my room. She brings it to her face, closes her eyes and takes in a deep breath through her nose.

Holy Shit. She's smelling me.

She's looking at her secret stash of pictures and smelling me.

I clear my throat and she jumps. She looks at the pictures in her hand and quickly shoves them down into the side of the couch, depositing the pillow right on top of them. Does she really think I didn't notice her looking at them?

She's quiet. She doesn't say anything about my senior picture that I put in the mix. Maybe she didn't see it yet. Maybe she just got down here right before I did.

She sits up and tucks her legs under her, eyeing my bare torso. Her obvious enchantment with my exposed skin makes me want to pound on my chest like King Kong.

I walk over as if I'm completely unfazed by her gawking. "Are you okay? Did you have more of those false contraction things?"

Relief washes over her face when I don't call her out on the pictures. She shakes her head. "No. Well, yes, I get them occasionally, but that's not why I'm down here."

I try not to smile. I know why she's down here. I know exactly why she's down here. She wanted to see me. Smell me. She wants me, but being the stubborn woman she is, she just can't admit it and let us get on with things. Things like kissing. And touching. And making love. And more kissing.

I eye her full lips and wonder if pregnancy has made them fuller, or if they've always been like that.

She puts her hands on her prominent belly and sighs. "I miss her."

I close the distance between us. I'm now able to confirm that her nighttime attire is in fact green. I long to reach out and touch it, knowing it's probably as silky as her skin. As soft as her wavy hair. I sit down next to her, leaving only a few inches of space between us.

"Me, too," I say. Maybe I was wrong. Maybe she was looking at pictures of Erin and not ogling me.

She nods. "She was my best friend," her small voice cracks out.

"Mine, too." I grab her hand in mine, letting them fall to the couch between us.

Her fingers tense, but she doesn't pull away. "I've never known someone so genuine and kind," she says. "Erin was like a sister to me. Sometimes I feel so selfish, being pissed off that she died and can no longer be my friend. Not that I don't have great friends. But it's just... I don't think I'll ever have another friend like her." She sniffs and wipes a tear. "I talk to her, you know. At night. I tell her about my job, about Bean, about life." She looks over at me. "Do you think she hears? Do you think she knows what's going on down here?"

I shake my head. "I don't know. Sometimes I wonder the same things."

"Do you think she would be disappointed in us?" she asks.

I shrug. I can't answer that. Not without guilt weighing down on me. Not without making Skylar feel guilty as well. I feel like a dick not reassuring her, but the fact is, I just don't know.

"She was the only one who never judged me," she says.

I watch as the tears roll down her face, some being stopped by her lips, only to be swiped away as her tongue comes out to catch them. It's all I can do not to reach out and wipe them. But we're talking about my wife. Seems an inappropriate time to touch her so intimately.

I give her hand a squeeze. "*I* never judged you, Skylar."

She pulls her hand away, tucking it under her leg to restrict my access to it. "Yes, you did."

"I did?"

She nods. "When we first met. I know you were only being diligent about the whole surrogacy process, but you made a snide comment about my promiscuous past."

I close my eyes. I did say that. But not for the reason she thinks. "I'm sorry. You're right that I said it, but it wasn't because I was judging your past."

Her head tilts to the side as her skeptical eyes question me.

"I said it because I was being a jackass. Because when I saw you, something inside me shifted." I shake my head, still harboring feelings of guilt over it. "I loved Erin. I always will. And I never would have cheated on her. But I couldn't deny my instant attraction to you. It scared me and I was trying to deflect my feelings."

Her eyes soften and she lets out an almost inaudible laugh. "I have a confession to make, too."

"Really?" I turn towards her, putting my arm on the back of the couch.

"This couch. I didn't move it out of the bedroom because it reminded me of Erin. I moved it down here because it smelled of you and it was... distracting having it up there." Her eyes fall to my chest once again. I wonder if she can see the way my heart beats faster every time she looks at me like this.

"Distracting, huh?" I find it hard to hide my smirk.

She ignores my expression, pushing herself up off the couch. She walks across the studio. She grabs a tissue from the desk and blots her eyes. The tissue box and the folder lying underneath it teeter off the desk, falling to the ground.

"Oh, sorry," she says, leaning down to gather the photos that scattered across the floor.

Before I realize what happened, she gasps. "What are these?"

I try to scoop them up, but she pushes me aside. She spreads them over the desk and turns on the overhead light to get a better look. Shock washes over her face as she takes in the pictures. They're the close-up photos I took of her weeks ago as she slept on the couch. Intimate photos of each body part. Then there are the ones I took while I waited at the coffee shop. Several of the pictures show the locket as it lies between her breasts.

Her hand comes up to touch the locket. "What the hell, Griffin? Why were you taking pictures of me when I didn't know it?" She turns around to face me, tightening her robe as if it will add a layer of armor to protect her vulnerability. "These pictures are fucking creepy."

I roll my eyes at her, but keep my comments about her word choice to myself. "Oh, right. I'm the creepy one." I walk over to the couch and pull her stash out, holding them up for her to see. I thumb through them and grab a few that she took at the picnic. "You did the same thing, Skylar. You took pictures of me."

"Ugh!" She stomps over and plucks the pictures from my hands, depositing them in the trash bin. "It's not the same thing."

"It's not? What is it then? Why do you look at those pictures?"

"Because I miss Erin, you ass."

I go over to the trashcan and pull one of the pictures out. "Because you miss Erin, huh?" I hold up the picture in front of her. "Look at this one—this close up of my face. Do you sit and look at it, fantasizing about my stubble rubbing between your legs?"

Her jaw drops. She grabs the picture from me, tearing it in two.

"Why are you so damn stubborn, woman? How come you keep stringing along John, knowing full well that I'm the man you want in your bed?"

"You?" She shakes her head. "If I recall, I *had* you in my bed. Then you ran away, Griffin. Why would I want to make that mistake again?"

"It wasn't a mistake. We're supposed to be together, Sky!" I yell at her.

"How come—because Erin said we should? And would you quit fucking calling me Sky!" she shouts.

"That does it," I say, pulling her to me and crashing my lips into hers.

Her whole body stiffens, but she doesn't push me away. She relaxes her lips and lets me kiss her. I take her full lips between mine, lightly sucking on them, playing with them, letting her get used to me. She lets me swipe my tongue across her bottom lip and then push it into her mouth. Our kisses start slow and reserved, but quickly become more demanding. Passionate even. I can't recall another time in my life when a simple kiss had my body on the brink of detonation. I pull her harder against me, squishing her belly between us. I grab the back of her head and angle her to deepen the kiss. She whimpers a soft, reluctant moan, but it's enough to make me crave even more of her. It's enough to let me know that she wants this.

Our tongues weave together as if they've done this a thousand times—not only a few. Our breathing becomes a choreographed dance, her exchanging each breath for mine in perfect synchronization. If our heartbeats were audible, I'm sure we'd find them to be precisely in time with each other. If I kissed a million women, I wouldn't find another kiss as perfect as this one.

Her hands grasp my shoulders and then run through my hair, gripping it as if it's her lifeline.

My hands wander every inch of her bare arms, from her fingertips to her neck. When my lungs scream for air, I pull back just enough to fill them, while trailing kisses along her jawline up to her ear. "Sky," I whisper breathlessly when I get there. "I want you so much."

As if my voice snapped her out of a dream, she puts a hand between us and pushes me away. "No. I can't do this." She turns and walks towards the stairs.

"Why not, Skylar?" I call out after her. "You can't tell me you don't feel it. There is no way in hell a kiss like that was one-sided. That kiss was the best goddamn kiss of my life. And I'm willing to bet it was the best kiss of yours."

Before reaching the stairs, she turns to me, her eyes burning into mine. Her head shakes infinitesimally. "You just don't get it, Griffin."

I watch her disappear up the stairs. I rack my brain to figure out what the hell she's talking about. I sit on the studio couch, replaying every conversation we've had in my head. I've said I'm sorry. I've said I want her and the baby. I've re-decorated for her. I've gone out of my fucking way to show her how I feel.

Haven't I?

Mason's words from the other day seep into my thoughts. Does Skylar think I'm only trying to be with her to honor Erin's wish? Surely that kiss proved differently. I momentarily flash back to something my mom said before she died, when she was trying to impart me with all her worldly wisdom.

'Women take everything literally, Griffin. Never assume girls know what you want. Always tell them. We're silly creatures and sometimes you have to just spell it out for us.'

I look up at the calendar on the wall. The party is two weeks away. I have fourteen days. Fourteen days to figure out how to get Skylar to be with me. Fourteen days to think of a way to spell it out for her. Fourteen days to plan out how I'm going to put my heart on the line for the woman I'm positive I'm in love with.

I look up at the ceiling. I look all the way through it to the night sky and what lies beyond. For the first time since she died, I talk to Erin. "If you're out there; if you do know what's going on; if you have any way to help me fulfill your dying wish—and my living one—now is the time to let me know."

I go to turn off the light but something on the floor catches my eye. It's Skylar's locket. It must have come undone when we were kissing. I lean over to pick it up. I run my fingers over the etched flower. I unwittingly hold in a breath as I spring the locket open.

A piece of paper falls out. It's folded over and over into a tiny square. I open it up. It's a small copy of Erin's tattoo. This is what she chose to keep by her heart. Not a picture of Erin like I thought. Not a picture of me, like I'd hoped. But a representation of the future she longs for. The future I desperately want to give her. And in fourteen days, I have to convince her I'm the one to do it.

chapter thirty

I'm not sure I'll ever completely understand the human capacity to love two women so unconditionally. I've never questioned my feelings for Erin. I was undoubtedly in love with her. I think I just loved her differently than I love Skylar, that's all.

I still feel guilty sometimes when I look at Skylar and want so badly to pull her into my arms and make love to her. I feel guilty when a stubborn green-eyed beauty infiltrates my dreams instead of the demure curly-haired blonde. I'm not certain the guilt will ever totally dissipate. I've just learned to accept it. Like I had to accept that Erin was going to die.

As I look around the restaurant, I know that Erin would be happy with what I have planned. She loved a good party and tonight I can only hope she'll finally get her wish. As I watch Erin's family help put the finishing touches on the tables, I can practically sense her here. White lilies sit amongst the pale-blue balloons that bob over every table as a centerpiece.

Everything has come together perfectly. As luck would have it, March 1st has fallen on Skylar's day off. All her family and friends are in on it. To throw her off, Baylor took her out for lunch yesterday and gave her a small gift. I played ignorant, not even mentioning her birthday. I had to hold in my smirk when she pouted around the house last night thinking everyone forgot her twenty-fifth birthday.

Mindy called her ten minutes ago with a restaurant emergency, telling her she had to come right away to avert a delivery disaster. As we wait in the relative darkness, Mitchell's having been closed early for the private party, I take one final walk around to make sure everything is ready.

A banquet table is piled high with gifts, some for the baby shower, some for Skylar's birthday. Another table is set up buffet-style with mountains of finger foods. The centerpiece on the food table is a framed copy of the picture I'd taken of Skylar's belly—the one where she was holding the white lily against her. My favorite picture. The picture to trump all others.

I look over at the temporary stage we've set up, both nervous and excited about what I've planned for the evening.

Skylar walks through the door, looking irritated. "Why are the lights off? And why the hell did someone put up the closed—"

"Surprise!" we say calmly and in unison, tactically agreed upon so we don't scare her into early labor.

She looks around at all her friends and family, a smile quickly overtaking her frown. "You guys!" she shrieks. Her jaw drops when her eyes fall on the table piled with gifts. She hugs everyone as she walks around, taking in the balloons, the flowers, the food. When she sees the picture, she spins around, searching for me.

As she makes her way over to me, Baylor whispers something in her ear.

Skylar stops in front of me and pokes me in the chest. "You did this? Really?"

I shrug. "I had some help."

"Thank you." She pulls me in for a hug. I get a whiff of her hair. It smells fresh, like she had just washed it before coming. I could stand here and smell it all day. I don't want to let her go. Before she pulls away, I run my hand down her arm, eliciting goosebumps and a shiver that I'm not sure she wants me to see.

She points to a huge balloon displaying her age. "I thought everyone forgot. I mean, we usually celebrate on the 28th since my birthday is technically in February. But I figured this year, with everything else going on..."

"No way," I say, shaking my head. "No way would anyone forget your birthday, Sky. You're unforgettable."

She blushes. It's fucking sexy. I have to look away and find something else to focus on so my blood will quit rushing south.

For the next hour we laugh, eat, and shower Skylar with gifts. It's a bit overwhelming seeing all the baby stuff. How can one tiny baby require so much crap?

The women play some sort of baby shower game while the men congregate and drink beer. I take a shot of tequila, knowing what's about to happen. Knowing I'm about to put it all on the line.

Five of us guys take leave and head back to the kitchen where we prepare for the baby shower surprise. I'm not even sure whose idea this was. Mason and I were out drinking one night and were tossing around party ideas when some drunk students did a hilarious karaoke version of Y.M.C.A. so we started joking about doing something like that at the party.

The music starts and I walk out on the stage with Gavin, Mason, Skylar's dad, and Chris—the manager of the Maple Creek restaurant. The five of us are wearing long blonde wigs and we each have fake baby-bumps strapped under our clothing as we sing and dance to our own rendition of '*Baby One More Time*,' by Britney Spears.

Laughter fills the restaurant and phones come out to take video that I'm sure will be posted on the Internet before the night is out. Every time we sing the line '*hit me baby one more time*,' we turn and bump our fake bellies into each other like athletes celebrating on a football field.

When I catch a glimpse of Skylar, wiping tears and doubling-over in a fit of giggles, as far as her real belly allows, I know this is what I want every day for the rest of my life. To make Skylar laugh. To see her so happy she can barely contain herself.

When the song comes to an end, we step off the platform, removing our wigs and 'bellies.' People clap and laugh before going back to eating and making conversation. Some approach us, wanting to try on the baby bumps. I look around the room nervously. It's one thing to get up on stage and make an ass out of myself with four other guys. It's entirely another to fly solo, especially with so much riding on this.

I rub my sweaty palms down my jeans. I take a number of deep breaths and hope I don't pass out from sheer anxiety. I've never done this before. I don't even sing in the shower for fear of offending music's very existence. I can barely carry the tune to '*Happy Birthday*,' let alone sound remotely like Jason Mraz.

Yet, that's exactly who I've picked to sing to her. A song with references to fate, and as luck would have it, the sky.

"You ready for this, G?" Mason says, coming up next to me, snapping me out of my stress-induced coma.

I nod tentatively.

I feel a pat on the back and turn to see Skylar's dad. "You've got this, son."

I climb the three steps to the stage and tap on the microphone to make sure it's still on. Jenna, who's working the karaoke machine, gives me the thumbs up and presses the button to start the music. I close my eyes and pray my legs don't collapse out from under me as I sing the first few bars of '*I'm Yours.*'

The restaurant falls silent except for the music and the sound of my shaky, untrained voice. Even all the wait-staff stop in their tracks. All eyes are on me as I make an incredible fool out of myself in the name of love and grand-fucking-gestures.

But after the first verse, everyone else fades into the background and all I see is her. Skylar's hand comes up to cover her mouth as I pour myself out to her through the lyrics of the song that tells her everything I couldn't. When my voice cracks as I sing the line about this being our fate, tears roll down her cheeks. I'm not sure either of us blinks the entire length of the song.

My left hand remains in my pocket, nervously fumbling with the small box as I belt out the last few lines. The music stops and you could hear a pin drop in the crowded room. Everyone is waiting to see what I do next. What *she* does next.

I clear my throat, trying to remember all the words I need her to hear. "Skylar, a wise woman once told me I had to spell it out to get a girl's attention. So this is me, spelling it out; hoping you'll listen to what I have to say and give me a chance." I run a hand through my hair. The hand that's not glued to the box in my pocket. Skylar nods and I continue. "The night I came back and you asked me what I wanted—I never had the chance to answer." I motion my free hand around the room. "I want this. All of it. Our friends, your family. Our baby. *You.* I want it all."

The door to the restaurant opens and in walks John-the-food-guy, sending my already racing pulse through the roof. What the hell is he doing here? Of all the times in all the days, he chooses to show up right-fucking-now. He eyes me up on the stage, then quickly goes to stand behind a group of people. But not before Skylar follows my gaze to see what's caught my attention. I contemplate walking off the stage and postponing the whole thing. I didn't think I'd have to do this in front of the guy she's dating. Maybe I didn't think this through. Maybe I should do this in private.

Her sympathetic eyes find their way back to mine. She raises a hand to grasp her locket and then she smiles. I swear it's the same smile from that photo I took at the picnic. The one of her lying on the grass, staring at the sky with her hand on her belly. That smile—it gives me the courage to do what I came here to do. I try not to give another thought to anyone else in the room and I focus my attention solely on her.

"You said I don't get it. And maybe I didn't. But I do now. Did you listen to the song?" I point my finger back and forth between us. "You and me. This is fate. We belong together. We were always supposed to be the bean's mom and dad. Erin knew it all along. It's why she threw us together. It's why she planted the seed. But it was up to us to do the rest." I brace myself with the microphone stand and take a deep breath. "I love you, Skylar Mitchell. And not because someone else told me I should. I love you because when you walk into a room, I stop breathing. I actually have to remind my lungs to inhale and my heart to continue beating, because everything in my world stops when I see you. I love you because I wake up every day thinking I don't want to be in this world if you aren't in it. I love you because I wasn't sure I would ever feel that way about anyone again. I love your beautiful green eyes and your undecided hair. I love the way you've taken care of our unborn child. I even love your stubborn, filthy mouth."

I look down at the tattoos that adorn my forearms. "I've been loved by some pretty incredible women in my life. Women who made me what I am today. Women who prepared me to be a good father to our son. Women who showed me how to be a better man for you."

I lock eyes with Skylar again. Her tears are overflowing, falling faster than she can wipe them away. My hand grips the box in my pocket, preparing to pull it out. "I want to be with you, Skylar. I *have* to be with you. I get it now."

I step down from the stage and make my way over to her, cutting the distance between us with purposeful strides. People quietly part like the Red Sea, clearing a path for me to get to her. I stand before her, my hand still firmly in my pocket, gripping the box that will change my life. I close my eyes, gathering the courage to lower myself onto a knee, when I feel soft arms around my neck.

My eyes fly open just in time to see her wet her lips before they reach mine. Our mouths crash together, but we smile more than we kiss. I hear cheers around us as she pulls just barely away from me, stretching up to speak into my ear. "Thank you. That was... wow. I didn't realize how much I needed to hear you say those things. I'd be honored to be your girlfriend, Griffin." She tilts her head and smiles up at me. "We'll take it slow, okay? One day at a time?"

Girlfriend.

I hope the shock I'm feeling is not registering on my face. My hand releases the death-grip I had on the box in my pocket as if it burned me. I wonder if she knew I was going to propose. Maybe her dad tipped her off. I search her emerald eyes for answers, looking for any trace of guilt that simply doesn't seem to be there.

I glance over at my best friend. Mason raises his eyebrows in question. I don't have any answers. I merely shake my head at him in disappointment. The moment is over. People have gone back to their conversations. The crowd is bustling around us. It's not going to happen tonight. Hell, now I'm wondering if it's going to happen before Aaron comes only a month from now.

Take it slow. Her words echo in my head.

"Everything okay?" she asks, still beaming at me.

No, she didn't know. I can read her like an open book. She had no idea I was about to fall to a knee and ask her to be my wife.

I pull her to me once again, kissing her softly on the lips before I whisper, "Everything is perfect."

"I love that song, you know," she says.

"Oh? I didn't know you were a big Britney Spears fan."

She giggles. "Not *that* song."

I laugh and kiss the tip of her nose. "I know. I hear it every time you blare it through your earbuds. I hope I didn't ruin it for you."

"Are you kidding? It was wonderful. I've never had a song with a guy before. I guess that one will be ours."

"Absolutely." I rub her belly, for the first time feeling comfortable doing it without asking permission. "A lot of things will be ours soon."

Someone clears their throat behind us.

I don't have to turn around. I know exactly who it is. The party-crashing food guy.

"Give me a minute?" she asks, her eyes begging me not to make a scene.

I bring her hand up to my lips, placing a kiss on the back of it. "Yeah, okay."

I make my way over to Gavin and Mason who give me sympathetic pats on the back. "It just wasn't the right time," I say.

Gavin hands me a beer. "It's the stubborn Mitchell trait. I think they're pre-programmed to make us sweat it out. Don't worry, it'll happen, brother."

I nod, never taking my eyes off Skylar and John over by the door. He tries to pull her to him but she resists. I'm focused so intently on him that I can see a muscle in his clenched jaw spasm. I'm sure he's trying to convince her why he's better for her than I am. She keeps shaking her head and I think I see '*I'm sorry*' fall from her lips more than once.

He puts a hand on her cheek and her eyes quickly flash to mine. Her head shakes ever-so-slightly in a warning for me to keep out of it. I swear if she was wearing my ring, I'd take the asshole down for laying a single finger on her. But she just became my girlfriend two minutes ago and I don't want to screw this up. Still, I stand here watching every move, ready to swoop in and wipe the floor with him if he does anything remotely inappropriate.

She hugs him and my blood starts to boil. My eyes are glued to his hand on her back while I pound the rest of my beer. But before I can reach for another, a defeated-looking John walks out the front door and Skylar smiles over at me.

Griffin – 3

John-the-food-guy – 0

I win.

In two seconds flat, I'm standing before her. "Everything okay?" I ask, tucking a strand of hair behind her ear.

"Everything's perfect," she says, throwing my own words back at me. "I told him I owe it to the baby to give us a chance."

My heart sinks into the pit of my stomach. Of all the things I imagined her telling him, that wasn't one of them. '*Screw you, asswipe, I'm in love with Griffin Pearce,*' or '*I can't deny my feelings for him any longer,*' were more along the lines of what I was thinking.

She reaches over and grabs my hand as we walk back to our friends. I lift our entwined hands, my right with her left, and look at her still-empty ring finger. I try to bask in the victory I should be feeling over her breakup with John. But all I can think about is how much I want her to be mine.

Mine. I've never wanted anything so badly in my life.

chapter thirty-one

Skylar plops down on the couch, tired from the party. I run upstairs to get my present for her. I didn't want her to open it in front of everyone. I wasn't sure what her reaction would be.

I put it on the coffee table and sit next to her on the couch, pulling her feet onto my lap, massaging her arches like I've done so many times before. But never as her boyfriend.

Maybe I was stupid to think I could go from roommate to fiancé in one night. She's right. We need to take this slowly. Neither of us is going anywhere. We're about to have a baby. We have all the time in the world.

With her eyes closed, she moans as I knead the tension from her feet. The noise does nothing to squelch my libido that hasn't been fed in far too long. I move her foot to the spot where she'll feel exactly what she's doing to me with her throaty sounds.

Her eyes snap to mine and for the second time tonight, she blushes. I shrug and nod my head to the gift on the table. "Open it."

"You've done so much for me already," she protests. "The party was wonderful. I can't believe you got my dad to dance on stage wearing a pregnancy belly." She laughs, her stomach bouncing up and down with every breathy giggle.

"It was my pleasure. I'm glad you had a good time." I reach for the gift and hand it to her. "It's not just for you. It's for Aaron, too. And me, if you'll let it be."

Her brows come together and that adorable wrinkle creases her nose. She takes the package from me. It's the size of a small shirt box. Her eyes keep flashing to mine as she rips the paper off. My heart rate increases exponentially, hoping she'll be okay with it.

She pulls out the contents of the box—brochures and vouchers. She examines them and then gasps. "Paris? You want to take me to Paris?"

I put my hand on her belly. "I want to take you both there. The vouchers can be cashed in for plane tickets at any time. When you're ready. When *we're* ready." I motion to the mantle across the room. "I thought maybe we could spread Erin's ashes there."

I've been thinking about it a lot lately; where to spread them. She always wanted to go to Paris. When we were at the Imax before she died, Skylar promised her she would go there someday and do everything that Erin dreamed of doing.

Skylar nods, trying unsuccessfully to keep the tears pooling in her eyes from spilling over. "It's the best birthday present I've ever gotten. It's the perfect place to spread her ashes. Thank you."

I reach over to catch one of her tears with my thumb. I wipe it away and lean over to kiss her. As I draw her face closer to mine, I realize this will be the first real kiss we share as a couple. I stop short of her lips. "Is it okay if I kiss my girlfriend?"

She smiles. Then she seductively bites her lip before saying, "Your girlfriend would like that very much."

I brush her hair back, holding it up with both my hands on either side of her head. We stare into each other's eyes for five seconds. Ten. There's no awkwardness. Just feeling. Emotion. Passion. Her eyes darken and become lidded right before our mouths touch.

When my lips reach hers, an electrified pulse courses through my entire body. My breath catches. My heart skips a thousand beats. My hands tremble. And I would bet my life the same exact things are happening to her.

She weaves her hands through my hair, deepening the kiss. We devour each other's tongues and lips until they're numb and we gasp for air. She climbs on top of my lap, straddling me, leaning her head into me, pressing the baby hard between us as she finds a spot on my neck to suck on.

I grow harder beneath her as she grinds down onto me. I reach out to touch her breasts, unable to contain my groan when I feel how full and supple they are through her thin shirt. I run my thumbs over her erect nipples, drawing sexy as hell noises from deep within her.

Her lips find mine again. Her tongue forcefully enters my mouth, taking control of our demanding kisses. She captures my tongue with her lips, sucking on it erotically. I pull the V of her shirt aside and push her bra down to give me better access to one of her breasts. She squirms hard on my lap when I pinch her nipple between my fingers.

"Oh, God… Griffin." Her words are laced with carnal need, driving my want for her even higher.

She throws her head back, moaning. I take the opportunity to pull her bare breast into my mouth. I support its weight with one hand while I lave her nipple with my tongue. Licking, sucking, nipping at it as she rides my crotch until she thrashes around, gyrating on my lap, shouting my name through her prolonged orgasm. I watch every twitch of her body. Every emotion that crosses her beautiful face as she rides wave after wave before finally settling down, her head falling to my shoulder.

She takes a sharp breath, pressing her hands on her belly.

I look up at her, concerned. "Are you okay?"

She smiles. "Pregnancy orgasms are the best. But they wake up the bean."

I put my hands on her stomach, mesmerized by how he's moving around inside her until I absorb the full weight of her words. I eye her skeptically, not entirely sure I want to know the answer to my question. "Just how many orgasms have you had while being pregnant, Skylar?"

"I don't know… hundreds?"

My jaw drops and my entire body stiffens.

She laughs at my shocked expression. "It's not what you think."

My eyebrows shoot up. "Exactly what am I thinking?"

"That I was sleeping with John."

"You weren't?" The corners of my mouth curl upwards in anticipation of her answer. Relief rockets through every blood vessel in my body as I realize what she's saying. My imagination goes wild. My smile gets huge.

She shakes her head. "No. You're the only man that's invaded this body in a long, long time."

I look at her in disbelief. "Hundreds. Really?"

"What do you think I was doing down on that couch with your pictures?" Embarrassed by her words, she buries her head into my shoulder.

I try to wrap my head around her admission. Hundreds. On the couch in my studio. Looking at pictures of me. I'm tempted to throw her off my lap and beat my hands on my chest. I'm goddamn Tarzan.

I pull her away from my shoulder and force her to look at me. "We are never getting rid of that fucking couch."

She giggles. "Don't say fuck."

I belt out a laugh. "That's my line." I bring her mouth closer to mine, breathing my words into her. "Does it make you horny, too, Sky?"

She climbs off my lap and starts to unbutton my pants. "What about you? How many orgasms have *you* had since that night?"

She takes my dick into her hands and I have to try really hard to remember the question because when her small hands encompass me, it feels like pure heaven. "About as many as you," I say. "And for the very same reason."

She smiles so big I can see tiny creases beside her beautiful eyes. "Do you want to have sex with me, Griffin?"

For a moment, I almost forget that her hand is stroking me. My jaw goes slack as I replay her words in my head. I'm tempted to scream out '*hell, yes*,' but instead I joke, "Is this us taking it slowly?"

She removes her hand from me and self-consciously looks down at her belly. "It's okay if you want to wait until I get my body back. I would totally understand."

I grab her hand and place it around my throbbing shaft. "Does it feel like I want to wait, Skylar?" I take her head into my hands and lock eyes with her. "I want to make love with you right now more than I ever want to hold another camera in my hands again."

Her yearning eyes tell me everything I need to know. I find the hem of her shirt and pull it up and over her head. Her wavy locks catch in her shirt and then fall back down around her breasts, one of which is still spilling out from the cup of her bra. I pull down the other cup, leaving her trussed up as I reach out to fondle her bare flesh, extracting throaty moans from somewhere deep inside her.

She tugs at my shirt and I quickly reach behind me and pull it off. Every inch of my chest is devoured; first by her eyes and then by her wandering hands.

I slip off the edge of the couch and position myself between her legs, leaning over her protruding belly to place kisses along the sides of her lips, down her neck, and all around her breasts. I slide off her skirt and panties, getting my first view of her very pregnant body.

In a thousand years, I never thought I'd be turned on by such a sight. She carries the baby so well you wouldn't even notice she's pregnant if you didn't actually see her stomach. Her thighs and calves are perfectly toned. Her arms are firm and strong. Her heart-shaped face doesn't hold even an ounce of extra weight. But, then again, I'm so blinded by my love and want for her, I'm positive she would look incredible to me no matter what her appearance.

I grab her hips and pull her to the edge of the couch. I lower my head, getting ready to place my tongue against her center and make her come even longer and harder than before.

She grabs my shoulders and I snap my eyes to hers to see that her heated eyes have been replaced with trepidatious ones. "No way, Griffin." She shakes her head vehemently. "I haven't been able to see my crotch for over a month now. I have no idea what's going on down there."

I glance down, barely able to see even a hint of soft curls peeking out from under her belly. I could care less if she's waxed or plucked or shaved—or whatever the hell girls do down there. For months, I've dreamed about tasting her again. About feeling her fall apart under my tongue. I run my finger up her leg, right up to the apex of her thighs. I feel how wet she is. Drenched with desire. I easily slip a finger inside her as my erection presses against her leg that is braced on the table behind me. "Skylar, you're beautiful. Every inch of you."

She pushes into my fingers, driving them deeper into her. "Please, Griffin. I want to feel you inside me. I need to feel you inside me."

I quickly push my jeans the rest of the way down and kick them off my body. I hold myself at her entrance, silently asking for permission before I push into her.

"Yes," she reaches down between us, guiding me inside her.

She's so tight. Tighter than I remember. Her walls grip me and it's everything I can do not to let myself go right now. "Sky," I breathe out, stilling within her; taking a second to calm myself.

When I start to move, I join her hands with mine, lacing our fingers together. In this position, with her reclining back against the couch, I can't get past her stomach to kiss her. But it only makes what we're doing more intimate as we stare at each other through every thrust.

She pushes against my hands, giving herself leverage to take me deeper. She gasps when I hit the end of her. "Oh, God," she moans. Her eyes darken and our gazes become intoxicating. Our eyes speak the words that our mouths are incapable of producing. The world falls away and nothing exists but us.

This woman has become my reason for living. My light in the darkness. In an unprecedented move on my part, I softly sing a few lines of the song from the party. Lines about this being our fate. Words that tell her once again that I'm hers.

Her eyes glaze over. She's close. I'm close. I extract one of my hands from hers and find her swollen clit. I rub tiny circles on it, watching her mouth open and her head fall back, thrashing around on the cushion behind her.

"Griffin!" she screams. "Oh, God, yes!"

Watching her fall apart, feeling her walls tightly squeeze me as she does, sends me over the edge right along with her. I still, emptying myself completely within her, my garbled words of ecstasy mixing with hers.

After we catch our breath, Skylar giggles, bringing her hands up to her stomach. "Every time," she says. She grabs my hand and puts it underneath hers. We lock eyes as our son somersaults beneath our hands even as I'm still inside her.

It's a moment I'll remember as long as I live.

I shake my head in wonderment. How could I have fallen in love with two such incredible women in one lifetime? How could I ever see myself living without this beautiful creature beneath me? Both of them. With a hand still on her belly, my other one cups her face. "I love you, Sky."

Her hand comes up to touch my jaw. Her thumb brushes across my lips. Her eyes soften and sparkle at the same time. "I love you, too."

I close my eyes and let her words sink in.

They fly open again when she declares, "I lied, you know."

"Lied?" My heart lodges in my throat for half-a-second before she explains.

"When I told you what I said to John," she clarifies. "I lied."

My eyebrows shoot up in question as I finally pull out of her and take a spot on the couch. "You didn't tell him you owe it to the baby to give us a chance?" I grab some tissues from the coffee table and gently clean her up while I await her answer.

"No." She shakes her head. "I told him I was in love with you."

A smile overtakes my face. I want to do a fist pump and high-five someone.

"I've loved you for a while, you know," she says. "Even before Erin died I was in love with you." She sits herself up, pulling the throw blanket over her middle in an attempt to hide her nakedness. "I'm sorry I made this so hard on you, Griffin. I think I just felt guilty falling in love with my best friend's husband. I was scared. Scared that we were betraying her. Scared that I would screw this up."

I touch her locket, working it between my fingers. "I was scared, too." I spring the locket open and unfold the small slip of paper, letting our eyes trace the words. "I'm not anymore."

"Me neither," she says, folding it up carefully and placing it back inside the locket.

I retrieve her clothes from the floor and help her dress before taking her hand and leading her upstairs. "Do you think it's too soon to ask you to move in with me?"

She giggles, pulling me towards the master bedroom where I fall asleep with her in my arms, spooning her from behind with my hand lying across her flawless belly.

chapter thirty-two

It's still pitch black when an elbow pokes into my ribs. I rub my eyes, trying to wake up when I hear Skylar say, "I need you."

Instantly I spring to life. I wrap my arms around her and chuckle into her hair. "Woman, you're insatiable."

Seconds later, a pillow lands on my face. Hard. "Not that, you animal." The light turns on and I shield my eyes while they get used to it. "I thought I was having false labor, but now . . . well, either I wet the bed or my water just broke."

The oxygen is sucked out of my lungs as anxiety overtakes my entire being. A million things run through my head. We aren't ready yet. It's not time. We haven't packed a bag for the hospital.

I'm gonna be a fucking dad.

"I'm scared, Griffin." Her hands tremble as she reaches for her cell phone on the nightstand.

Before she can make the call, I grab her hands. I try to put up a calm exterior even though I'm freaking out on the inside. "It's okay, Sky. We can do this. You can do this."

"But it's too soon," she cries.

I shake my head. "It's not. You're almost thirty-six weeks. Millions of babies are born healthy at this point." I rub her belly. "Aaron is going to be perfect, you'll see."

She tries to smile and then she makes the call to her doctor.

They exchange a few words about how long she's been in labor. Then Sky turns to me. "Look at the bed. Is there any blood on the sheets?"

I pull down the top sheet and hold my breath while I search her side of the bed. No blood. Relief rushes through me like a fucking tsunami. "Looks clear."

She relays that to the doctor and then, from what I gather, we're told to meet her obstetrician at the hospital. When Skylar hangs up, she doesn't look quite so pale. "She said what you did. He'll probably be perfectly fine."

I jump out of bed and pull on last night's jeans and shirt that lay in a pile by the bed. Skylar tells me to fetch a bag in her closet. I frown when I realize she was prepared all along, but that I wasn't a part of it. I vow not to miss another thing. Ever.

She tries to get dressed when a contraction hits her. She reaches for her phone and shoves it at me. "Time it!" she shouts. By the time I figure out where her stopwatch app is, the contraction is over and she's glaring at me.

I shrug. "I'd say it lasted about a minute or so."

"Maybe you should get *your* phone," she says, dryly, through clenched teeth. "At least write down the time so we know how far apart they are. Do you think you can handle *that?*"

I try not to laugh. I've heard about this. Women getting bitchy when they go into labor. I say in my nicest voice, "Sure, Sky. I'll write it down and then I'll go call a cab."

"Do *not* tell them I'm in labor. I've heard they won't come!" she yells from the bedroom.

I quickly throw some stuff in my own duffle, not knowing how long it will be before I can get back here. In record time, I race to the basement to get a camera. No way in hell am I missing out capturing this on film. When I go back up to get her, she's already coming down the stairs with her bags in hand. I run up, two at a time. "Are you crazy, Sky? What the hell are you doing trying to do this yourself?"

In hindsight, I realize calling a woman in labor crazy is not the appropriate thing to do.

"Well, if you weren't taking so goddamn long, you could have helped. What were you doing down there anyway? Eating breakfast? Folding laundry?"

I take her bags and walk her to the front door, not bothering to answer her stupid questions. "Who should I call? Baylor? Your mom?"

"No," she says.

She stops in her tracks and grabs my arm. Hard. I pull out my phone and check the time. I start my stopwatch.

A minute later, when she can talk again, she says, "I don't think I want a bunch of people coming in and out of the room like when Baylor was in labor. Plus, this could take a while. Why don't you wait and call them when it's almost time."

I nod. "Sounds like a plan." I see the cab rounding the corner and tell her to stay put while I take the bags down. The cabbie gets out, putting them in the trunk while I go help Skylar down the steps and into the back. "Mount Sinai Hospital."

He looks at Skylar, his eyes trained on her belly. "Oh, shit, really?" He shakes his head mumbling something about always getting the pregnant ones and how he's going to kill someone named 'Bubba' back at dispatch.

Despite Skylar's assurances to the cabbie that we have plenty of time, he makes it to the hospital in ten minutes flat. I guess it helps that it's the middle of the night. The bars have all closed and the only thing illuminating the streets of Midtown are the 'Open' signs in the all-night diners.

I swipe my debit card, leaving the poor guy an insanely huge tip before we head into the maternity ward.

Four hours later, Skylar's contractions are getting harder. We're waiting on an epidural and she's told by one of the nurses to use her Lamaze breathing. Skylar nods her head and points to her overnight bag. I put it on the bed next to her and when she's able, she pulls out a framed picture of her and Erin. The one from her nightstand. "My focus point," she says. "Can you put it over there on the table?"

Focus point? Lamaze breathing? "How do you know all this stuff?" I say, placing the picture where she directed.

"From Lamaze class."

"You went to Lamaze class? When?"

"Back in December. Baylor went with me."

I sigh, berating myself for missing yet another part of this monumental thing.

Thirty minutes later, I'm trying to find something on the television to take her mind off things while the epidural kicks in. However, the only programs on are the morning news shows and they're downright depressing.

"Turn it off," she requests. "Tell me a story." She shifts around to try and get comfortable. "Tell me about the first time you met Erin."

I sit beside her bed, letting her squeeze my hand through every contraction as I tell her about my first love. I tell her about how we ran in different circles. I was more of a loner, having lost my mom. I didn't belong to any group. Erin was a popular cheerleader who I'd had a crush on for years, but never had the courage to approach. Then one day I saw her pulled over on the side of the road, in our little rural town in Ohio, flagging me down for help. She'd gotten a flat tire and didn't have a spare. I offered her a ride home. Then as luck would have it, or as I now know... *fate*, my own car failed to start and we sat there on that dirt road for hours, talking, waiting for another car to pass.

Skylar tries to smile, but pain riddles her face instead as she crushes my fingers once again. I've decided being in labor is like being bi-polar to the extreme. One minute, I half expect her head to spin around like that girl from '*The Exorcist*'—the next, she's completely back to normal, talking about her sisters or the restaurant.

A large nurse comes in the room. Her scrub top, adorned with storks carrying pink and blue bundles, tightly stretches across her rolls of flesh. Skylar asks her, "Exactly how long does it take for this epidural to work?"

The nurse looks surprised. With a smile plastered across her face, she says, "Sweetie, it should have kicked in by now. I'll have the doctor come check you out, but there's a possibility it just didn't work for you."

Skylar's eyes widen in horror. "Didn't work? Are you kidding?" she yells at the nurse, who's now checking the baby monitor printout.

"It happens in a small percentage of women." She flashes Skylar a sympathetic-yet-practiced smile. "Don't worry, sweetie, women have been doing this since the beginning of time without any epidurals. It's the way God intended. You'll be just fine."

Skylar's eyes follow Nurse Happy as she exits the room. If looks could kill, that nurse would be flat-lining on the bleach-mopped floor of the maternity ward. "The way God intended?" Skylar yells. "Screw that!" She grabs my arm. "Griffin, get me some drugs. This hurts. Like really, really hurts. Not like stubbing your toe hurt, or like breaking your arm hurt, it really hurts—like body being ripped in half hurt. Like hot lava running through me hurt. Ahhhhhh...!" She grips my arm like a vice as another contraction takes control of her.

With my free arm, I rub her back and speak words of encouragement. I look at the door, hoping someone will come through it to provide whatever relief they can. It's tearing me apart seeing the woman I love in pain like this.

She relaxes back into the bed, sweat dotting her hairline. I wipe it with a cool cloth.

"I feel sick." She rubs the sides of her belly. "Do you have a piece of gum or hard candy? I know they won't let me eat, but maybe gum would be okay." She looks at me with hopeful eyes.

I stick my hands in my pockets, searching for the pack of gum I can usually find there. My hand hits something hard and I realize that in throwing on my jeans from last night, I still have the engagement ring with me. As I retrieve a piece of gum from my other pocket and give it to her, I contemplate my choices. But there really is no choice, because it occurs to me right here, right now, that I don't want Aaron coming into this world without knowing how committed I am to his mother. Surely this was fate, me having the ring with me at this moment. I grip the box. "Skylar, you believe in fate now—I mean, we both do, right?"

She gives me a hard stare. "You think it's fate that I have to have this kid without any drugs?"

I bite the inside of my mouth so I don't laugh. "Just answer the question, Sky. Do you believe in fate or not?"

Her hand comes up to touch her locket. She nods. As another contraction grips her, she looks at her focus point, giving me a chance to pull the ring from the box and lower to a knee. Her contractions are only a few minutes apart, so I don't have a lot of time and I need to make every second count.

When the contraction is over, her head falls back on the pillow and her eyes close. I reach over to pull her left hand into mine. "Skylar."

She opens her eyes and looks around the room quickly as if she's woken up in a dream. She takes in my stance, as I balance on one knee. Then her eyes fall to the ring and she gasps. She stares at the ring I had made for her. The engagement ring like no other. It's a platinum infinity symbol, boasting a diamond within each circle. I had it designed with the tattoo in mind.

I clear my throat, praying my words come quickly and before pain overtakes her again. "We're about to have this incredible little boy. I don't want him coming into this world wondering if his daddy loves his mommy. Fate brought us together. Fate had me put on these pants so I could give you this ring at this very moment." My voice cracks and my vision becomes blurry with tears. "And fate will have me loving you and Aaron until the end of time." I eye the monitor and see the line starting to go up again, indicating another contraction is coming. I quickly blurt out, "Skylar Mitchell, will you marry me?"

Tears flow from her eyes as her smile changes into a wince, her face scrunching up as she pulls her hand away and tightly grips the sides of her bed. Through her gritted teeth she grunts, "Are you seriously asking me to marry you when I'm in fucking labor?"

Trying not to laugh, I say, "Don't say fuck, Sky."

Instead of focusing on the picture, her eyes bore into me for the entire contraction. We silently stare into each other and I swear we become one, and through her eyes, I can almost feel the pain ripping through her body.

When the pain retreats, she nods to the ring in my hand. "How long have you had this?"

"I had it made weeks ago. I was going to propose last night at the party, but it wasn't meant to be."

Her hand comes up to wipe a tear. "Oh, God, Griffin. When you walked off the stage and came over to me. You were going to propose right then, weren't you?" Her eyes go sad. "I ruined it. I'm so sorry."

"You ruined nothing, Sky. It wasn't supposed to happen then." I turn the ring over, pointing to the inscription. "Anyway, it was too dark last night to read the inscription."

She smiles, taking it from me, squinting to read what I had inscribed on the inside.

Fate ~ Faith ~ Family

I reach out to catch more of her tears. She starts to tense up and I glance at the monitor, confirming another contraction. "So are you going to fucking marry me, or what?"

Her answering grin flashes white teeth before her face falls into a grimace from the oncoming contraction. "Yes," she grunts. "I'll fucking marry you, Griffin Pearce. Ahhhh…!" She squeezes my hand so hard, I'm sure I will suffer some sort of paralysis.

"It's a good thing I didn't video this moment. We'd never be able to show it to our kids," I joke.

"*Kids?*" she shouts out in pain. "You've got to be fucking kidding."

I laugh, slipping the ring on her finger when the contraction subsides. I rise up and lean over the bed, placing a kiss on her salty lips as I hear people enter the room behind me. "Come on," I kiss the tip of her nose. "Let's do this."

After twelve hours of labor, my fiancée is getting some much-needed sleep. My tiny-but-healthy son lies still in my arms, his mouth puckered and making little sucking noises as he sleeps. He is the perfect little version of Skylar. He has a heart-shaped face and a full head of hair that can't decide on a color. I can only hope his baby-blue eyes will one day turn green.

Family and friends have come and gone, leaving a room full of blue balloons, teddy bears and, of course, white lilies. Along with the decorations, sits a letter from Erin. One that Baylor raced home to get once hearing of our engagement. While the nurses cleaned up Aaron, Skylar and I read the letter together, both rejoicing that Erin got to somehow be a small part of this joyous occasion. Both crying that she couldn't be here in the flesh.

"He's perfect," Skylar whispers, looking at Aaron and me through sleepy eyes.

"Just like his mom." I reach over to touch her arm.

She fiddles with the new ring on her finger and something dawns on me. "Sky, will you go on a date with me?"

She laughs quietly through her beaming smile. "Wow, we really do things backwards, don't we? First we get knocked up, then we get engaged, then we go on a date."

I raise my eyebrow at her. "Well, if you want to make it even more interesting, we could just go ahead and get married now, before we go on that date. I'm sure they have a chaplain here in the hospital."

Her hand comes to her chest. "My parents would kill me, Griffin. Plus, Piper promised to not only come home, but plan my entire wedding if I ever got hitched. I wouldn't give that up for anything. Imagine, a whole three months or more with my little sister." Her eyes light up.

"I have to wait three months to marry you?" I joke.

"Or more," she adds, laughing. "I only plan on doing this once, Griffin, so if it's okay with you, I'd like to do it right."

"It's more than okay." I look down at our sleeping son. "It's perfect."

"I wish I could take a picture of you right now," Skylar says, beaming at me. "You look so happy."

"I am happy. Happier than I've ever been." I lean down to kiss his little forehead over the blue-striped hat he's wearing. "I don't need a photo to remember this, Skylar. Everything I want for the rest of my life is right here in this room." I look at the tattoo on my right arm and realize that for the first time, I said those words without feeling guilty. I said them knowing it's what Erin would have wanted. I said them knowing she loved me enough to give me away. I said them knowing this little boy and the amazing emerald-eyed woman that gave him to me are everything Erin said they would be.

My fate.

epilogue

Dear Aaron,

My name is Erin Pearce. I guess I'm your namesake, but please don't take it personally that I'm a girl. We both have cool names. But you can call me Saint Erin. Because as far as I'm concerned, I performed a miracle.

The greatest gift I could ever give you is the love of two incredible parents. You may have started out as a dream of mine, but it was their fate to raise you. To love you. To always be there for you.

Be patient with your mom. She's the most stubborn woman I've ever met. She also has the kindest heart and the sweetest soul. If you grow up to be like her, you should consider yourself a lucky man.

I'm sure by now you know that your dad was once married to me. He saw me and your grandma through some very tough times. You can rely on him when things in your life seem out of control. He will be your rock. He will never waver in his undying love and support of you.

I want you to remember if life gets tough, you need to have faith that everything will work out the way it should. Trust in your family to be there for you and help guide you through life. Always follow your heart. Believe in fate. Fate is what brought you to this earth. It's what brought your parents together. It will make you the man you are intended to be.

Most of all, I want you to trust in the fact that you will always have a guardian angel watching over you.

If I only have one piece of advice to give you, it is this—let your parents love you. Let them love you hard. Let them love you forever.

Your friend in heaven,

Erin

acknowledgements

Upon the completion of any book, I have to first and foremost thank my family for putting up with chaos around the house. This one was particularly difficult to juggle while moving kids to college, attending countless travel baseball practices and games for my ten-year-old son, and coordinating rehearsals and performances for my twelve-year-old daughter's musical. You guys only complained once or twice about having pizza or sandwiches (again) for dinner. I promise to cook all your favorite meals during my week or two hiatus.

Thanks to my editors, Jeannie Hinkle and Ann Peters, without whom none of this would even be possible. Ann, I appreciate your creative skills in helping me design Erin's tattoo. Like Erin, I'm not capable of drawing much more than stick figures.

To my attentive beta readers, Janice Boyd, Debbie Weigel and Tammy Dixon, I'm grateful to you all for being honest and meticulous. I hope you continue to enjoy this wonderful ride with me.

White Lilies is my fifth book and upon release, I had published all five books in less than eighteen months. There may come a time when I slow down, but it will be after all these pesky characters quit waking me up at night, demanding to be heard.

about the author

Samantha Christy's passion for writing started long before her first novel was published. Graduating from the University of Nebraska with a degree in Criminal Justice, she held the title of Computer Systems Analyst for The Supreme Court of Wisconsin and several major universities around the United States. Raised mainly in Indianapolis, she holds the Midwest and its homegrown values dear to her heart and upon the birth of her third child devoted herself to raising her family full time. While it took time to get from there to here, writing has remained her utmost passion and being a stay-at-home mom facilitated her ability to follow that dream. When she is not writing, she keeps busy cruising to every Caribbean island where ships sail. Samantha Christy currently resides in St. Augustine, Florida with her husband and four children.

SAMANTHA CHRISTY

You can reach Samantha Christy at any of these fine places:

Website: www.samanthachristy.com
Facebook: https://www.facebook.com/SamanthaChristyAuthor
Instagram: @authorsamanthachristy
E-mail: samanthachristy@comcast.net